MW00461345

BAD REPUTATION

S.L. SCOTT

BAD REPUTATION

Copyright © S. L. Scott 2018

The right of S.L. Scott to be identified as the author of this work has been asserted by her under the *Copyright Amendment (Moral Rights) Act 2000*

This work is copyright. Apart from any use as permitted under the Copyright Act 1968, no part may be reproduced, copied, scanned, stored in a retrieval system, recorded or transmitted, in any form or by any means, without the prior written permission of the publisher.

This book is a work of fiction. Names, characters, places and incidents are either a product of the author's imagination or are used fictitiously. Any resemblance to actual people living or dead, events or locales is entirely coincidental.

ISBN: 978-1-940071-77-0

Cover Design: RBA Designs

Marion Archer of Making Manuscripts

Marla Esposito of Proofing Style

Jenny Sims of Editing4Indies

Proofreader: Kristen Johnson

Team Readers: Lynsey Johnson and Andrea Johnston

Photographer: Wander Aguilar

Cover Model: Andrew Biernat

ALSO BY S.L. SCOTT

To keep up to date with her writing and more, her website is
www.slscottauthor.com
To receive the Scott Scoop about all of her publishing
adventures, free books, giveaways, steals and more, sign up
here: http://bit.ly/2TheScoop

Join S.L.'s Facebook group here: S.L. Scott Books

Audiobooks on major sites.

The Crow Brothers
Spark
Tulsa
Rivers
Ridge

Hard to Resist Series
The Resistance
The Reckoning

For You

BAD REPUTATION

PROLOGUE

Hutton

"I'M GOING to talk to her."

"Damn, dude," my friend Gear says. "You have balls of confidence."

"Why do you say that?" I ask, unable to tear my eyes away from the most beautiful woman in the bar. Despite wearing the frumpiest costume I've ever seen, she stands out among the crowd. Beauty like hers doesn't blend in.

"She's the hottest chick in the place, even if she is dressed like that," Gear says.

"Exactly."

She brushes a strand of chestnut-colored hair off her perfectly poised shoulders as she takes a sip of her drink. Her skin is smooth and without the tanning bed glow most women my age have. It's refreshing. And compelling. And a complete turn-on.

"Lemme ask you something. I know the Everest brothers tend to get what they want, but have you *ever* been shot down, Hutton?"

"No."

Gear rolls his eyes. "Well, I have and it sucks."

A group of college-aged kids huddle at the end of the bar. There's no doubt they're trying to summon the courage to talk to her.

"Do you have a point?" I ask. "Because, if not, I'm heading over there."

Two fingers come out from around his pint glass and point her way. "There's a reason no guy is approaching her. She's gorgeous, but for fuck's sake, I bet she's a cold-as-ice princess, man. And you didn't even dress up for Halloween."

I glance at my attire. The same gray dress pants and white button-down shirt I left Houston in this morning cover my body. I didn't have time to plan for Halloween.

"Check out the devil in the corner."

Three women dressed to be noticed stand in the corner with empty glasses. Their coy act—looking around innocently while batting their eyelashes—stand in stark contrast to the costumes they chose this Halloween. And Gear falls right in line with what they are going for. He nods his approval.

I check out the woman he's eyeing, but there's nothing there that draws me. She's sexy—hot, even—but when I shoot a glance back at the other one in the corner, there's no comparison.

"She's all yours," I say. "And probably anyone else's who wants her tonight. I like to fuck, but it's not about quantity. It's about quality."

"So you're saying the frumpy princess is quality? How do you figure?" Gear asks, then takes a sip of his beer.

"Because she doesn't have to show off that sexy little body she's hiding under that dress. Pay attention. See how the top hugs her chest?"

"Yeah."

"I can tell how her breasts are shaped—full teardrops that are more than a handful. And I have big hands. Also, they're real, or they'd ride high."

"What's wrong with fake tits?"

I laugh. "Nothing. Just telling you how I break it down."

"Okay. Go on," he says, setting his glass down and then crossing his arms. "What else, oh wise one?"

"Is that sarcasm I detect?" I joke. "Just for that, I'm not giving you anything else. You can figure out life on your own."

Gear pops back with some ridiculous retort, but his words fall on deaf ears. My eyes return to the beauty just in time to catch her eyes on me. I nod out of habit and instantly kick myself for it. *Fuck.* That's not going to impress her.

She smiles but turns away to talk with her friend who's dressed in what appears to be a deflated ball gown. Then I get it. And as soon as I realize what they're dressed up as, I start laughing.

"I get the frump," I state.

"Huh?" Gear motions for another beer. "You get what frump?"

"I know what she's supposed to be." The bartender draws my attention when he tosses a bottle in the air, much to the amusement of the small crowd watching. I'm amused, too, but not with him. A single plastic slipper sits unattended at the end of the bar. It appears to be a discarded costume prop.

Perfect.

"This is all I need," I tell Gear, grabbing the shoe.

He laughs. "A shoe can't save you from blue balls. Save your balls the trouble." I tuck the shoe into my belt at my back.

I take a deep breath. "I'll be back . . . unless I get lucky, and then I'll see you tomorrow before I leave."

He takes the filled glass from the bartender and tips it my way. "I'll bet you the next round you're back here before I can order another one."

"You're on," I say, already walking away.

The pretty woman tracks me as I make my way over, a small smile playing on those delicate lips I hope to be kissing later.

Her gaze heats my blood. The slight lift of her chin making it hard not to walk too fast or start talking too quickly.

Play it cool, Hutton.

The bandana on her head only hides the top. The rest of her brown hair flows down over her back in soft waves. She clasps her hands in front of her and stands, angled my way, as if she's waited her whole life for me.

I get the evil eye from her friend, but I don't let her derail me from my mission. "Hello," I say, holding out my hand.

She sets her hand gracefully on mine. I bring it to my mouth and kiss the top. But before she pulls away, I gently turn her hand over and kiss the underside of her wrist, letting my lips linger and my eyelids dip as our connection overwhelms me. I release her hand and look up, noticing that her breathing has picked up like mine. I'm about to ask something stupid like, "You felt that, right?" but stop myself. I would sound like a lunatic.

Then the beauty whispers, "Do it again," and I realize I'm not insane. She feels it too.

I kiss her wrist again, feeling her pulse race beneath my lips. Blood rushes through my veins, causing my heart to pick up its pace even more. Her smile tells me everything. If destiny had a name, she'd be called . . . *wait.*

"What's your name?" I ask.

"Ally."

Ally. "That's a beautiful name."

"Thank you. What's yours?"

"I'm Hutton. Hutton Everest."

A smile plays on her lips. "Like the mountain?"

"Just like it." Noticing her empty hands, I ask, "Can I buy you and your friend a drink?"

"We'd like that."

A grin splits her cheeks, the tops of which are perfectly pinked. I need to say something to get the drinks I promised, but all I can do is look at her.

Her friend takes a step forward. "Before we go any further with this—"

Ally taps her friend's arm. "Don't be rude, Margie."

"I just want to test him," Margie says as though it's an inside joke . . . at my expense.

"It's okay," I say. "I can handle it. I don't mind being put to the test. Nothing great was ever gained without effort."

"Emerson?" Margie asks.

Detecting animosity in her tone, I try to maintain my grin and attempt to keep things light. "Everest. My dad. It's his motto. Work hard. Work harder."

Ally giggles. "I think he forgot the *play* part."

"Nah. That's just his sense of humor. It's another Everest gem."

Margie rolls her eyes. "Sounds like a bundle of fun."

"Maybe not fun, but he's a good man."

Ally ignores Margie and squares her shoulders toward me. "His strong work ethic is admirable."

Unpretentious. Confident. Gorgeous. *She's* easy to admire.

"What do you do for a living, Hutton?" she asks.

"I'm a financial analyst for Everest Equity."

"Is that your company?"

"My dad started the company twenty years ago, and when I graduated from UT, I joined him."

Ally's eyes sparkle. "I go to the university. I'm getting my master's in business communications and international relations." She tugs at the waist of her dress, drawing my eyes to her breasts when they jiggle.

"Impressive," I say, focusing on her degrees and not her great tits. "What made you choose that path, Ally?"

"Like you, just following in my family's footpath."

"Footsteps?"

"Yes, sorry, that's what I meant." A tinge of embarrassment colors her cheeks. "I can earn all As in school, but I always mix up idioms."

Could she be any more endearing?

Quality.

Margie sighs as if we're boring her to death. "I didn't think I'd be listening to talk of idioms on Halloween night."

"Me neither, but here we are," I tell her.

She looks me up and down. "Were the stores having a sale on your costume?" Rolling her eyes, she adds, "Perfectly Styled dark hair and cognac eyes. I bet you drive the ladies wild dressed like that."

"Actually, I drove from Houston to see a band play. I didn't have time to change after work."

"Oh." She furrows her brows. "I thought you were Prince Charming."

"I guess it comes down to the eye of the beholder," Ally says, eyes focusing on me.

"Seeing is believing," I add.

"Well, do you know what we are?" Margie asks.

"I do." Reaching around, I pull the plastic slipper from where I had it tucked into my belt and kneel before Ally. "Cinderella . . . and a wicked stepsister."

Ally's hands fly to cover her mouth when it drops open. A smile to rival the sun beams on her face. "What are the chances that we'd meet?"

"Some might call it destiny." I'm not really expecting her to put on the fake shoe, but her flat shoe is dropped from her foot, and she points her toes.

Guess we're doing this . . . acting out a fairy tale as if it's real . . . in the middle of a bar.

"If the shoe fits," I mutter in astonishment.

"Destiny. Indeed." She rests her hand on my shoulder and slides her shoe back on. Her eyes stay on mine when I stand again. "I think I'll take that drink now if the offer is still there."

"It is, but under one condition."

"What is that?"

"That I can see you again."

That pretty smile returns. "How do you already know you want to see me again?"

"I don't *know* it. I *feel* it. There's just something about you."

Destiny.

1

Hutton Everest

TEN MONTHS LATER . . .

A few beauties are perched on stools nearby.

Two friends. One blonde—pretty—but the brunette is stunning with her amber eyes and long legs. I can tell by the way they're eyeing me that I could probably chat up either or both and score. But that's not what, *or who*, I want tonight.

I used to elbow my brother, Ethan, but since he's newly married, I aim for Gear instead. His gaze pivots to my side. "Looks like you have your pick."

"I'm not wasting the night on a group of women who would be happy with any guy who buys them a drink."

"Wise choice," Ethan replies. "It's not about easy. It's about—"

"Quality. I've heard this story before." Gear rolls his eyes. "Anyway, we get it, man. You're happy. You've met your match. Blah. Blah. Blah."

I haven't seen my middle brother since he moved to New York City. Until recently, it was because he was embroiled in a bitter *fight* with his ex-girlfriend and ex-best friend. Now it's because he's entangled with a different woman who fills his life with light and love—his words, not mine. He's become a sap thanks to his newlywed life, and wife, Singer.

After the year he's had, he deserves the good life.

Despite Ethan and Gear being on the other side of buzzed, I've only had one beer since we arrived an hour ago. And I'm anxious; something I'm not familiar with. I have an idea why.

Coming to Austin has another appeal for me, and I'm eager to get this night started as soon as a certain someone shows her pretty head. I haven't stopped thinking about her. I need to touch her, kiss her, hold her. It's not just my body that aches for her anymore. It's my sou—*I'm not going there.*

And then she walks in.

"There's just something about her," I say. My core calms. My heartbeat increases, tapping out an accelerated rhythm only she manages to do to me.

Tight jeans. Tight top accentuating her sensational tits. Leather jacket and black boots that ride high above her knees, hugging her toned legs.

She's here.

Finally.

Want. Lust. Need.

Ally.

"Damn." Gear beats me to the punch.

I let my smugness shine by smirking. "There she is."

"I'd forgotten how . . . *God* . . . fucking gorgeous she is." It's my friend, so I won't kick his ass. *This time.*

"I haven't." When I see her, though, it's as if I'm seeing her for the first time again. Breathtaking. Appreciating the view as she crosses the room, I hit the back of my hand against his chest. "Now, eyes off."

Ethan laughs. My brother's visits to Texas are rare these days. I'd like to say he came down to hang out with Gear and me, but as he's continuing to grow his new business venture, he was in meetings all day.

Gear chuckles. "I was wondering why you dragged us downtown tonight."

"I wanted you to see The Crow Brothers," I insist. "The fact that Ally's here is a nice bonus."

"So even though your brother's in town, you're dumping us for a lay?" Gear asks.

"She's not just a lay, man. You know that."

Gear and Ethan don't blink. It's amazing how I can still hear their silence as they stare at me in this loud bar.

"What?" I ask.

"What?" Ethan asks, calling me out. "You never talk about women like that."

"It's not like I ever disrespected a woman who didn't ask me to. We'll just leave it at that." They love to give me shit about my dating life. I can't help I've been blessed with a few . . . or a lot of qualities that the ladies dig. Anyway, they apparently haven't been paying attention. "I haven't kept her a secret." Though I feel like she might have kept me a secret from everyone except her friend who hates me.

Ethan pats me on the back, but I can see the mocking grin on his face. "Ah, Hut's growing up."

"You act like I chase any woman who looks my way."

"We all know you don't have to chase anybody," Gear says, "but you seemed to enjoy"—he coughs, letting his sarcasm out—"less commitment."

"That's one way to put it," my brother chimes in.

"You two can both fuck off." I shake my head. "It's not like you think."

Surprise pops into Gear's eyes. He looks briefly at Ethan and then back at me. "Holy shit, dude. Are you in love?"

Lust? Definitely.

Love? *Gulps.*

Both?

The stress I left at work tenses me again, but I have a feeling it's not because of the files on my desk. "I need another beer."

Although his attention turns to the stage, I can see Ethan's thoughts are somewhere else. He glances my way. "I'll go with you."

"Something on your mind?"

"Yeah." He nods. "I've been meaning to talk to you about something for a while now."

"Let me guess. Business?"

He cracks a grin. "How'd you know?"

"Wild guess."

"I can't help it. It's always on my mind."

Laughing at his unapologetic shrug, I point a finger his way. "That's why you're a billionaire at twenty-eight."

He ignores my amusement. Already in business mode, he crosses his arms over his chest. "How do you feel about a shot at millions?"

"Billion sounds better," I say, trying to hold my poker face.

"Yeah, I bet, but considering this opportunity is falling into your lap, let's start with millions and work our way up from there."

I'm not sure if he pauses to be a dick or to drum up the anticipation. Either way, I start to walk toward the bar.

"Come to New York," he says. "I'll even let you fly on my dime."

I stop midstride. "On the jet?"

"Dime. Not jet."

Slumping my shoulders dramatically, I sigh. "Fine. First class?"

"All the way."

"I knew there were perks to having a sibling strike it rich."

He swallows half his beer. "I earned every dollar, my friend. Anyway, I have a job waiting for you when you're ready to move up north."

"The pay sounds good if we're talking the big bucks."

"Better than you're making working for Dad, and it comes with more perks than me being rich."

The band takes the stage, and the crowd's cheer temporarily drowns out our conversation, so I say, "We'll talk before you leave."

Gear elbows me. "The Crow Brothers are awesome. They're going to be huge one day."

"I ..." Lose all train of thought.

Ally walks by again, letting her eyes linger on mine before she's tugged away by her friend. We usually don't last this long apart, but pushing each other's limits is something we're getting good at.

As I'm warring with myself on whether I should go after her, Ethan's hand clamps down on my shoulder.

"Just because I flew a thousand miles to hang out doesn't mean you're stuck with me all night," Ethan says.

Rubbing my thumb over my lower lip, I watch as she walks away, that ass round and enticing my mind to remember how fucking great it looks naked. I'm not doing a good job at sticking to the role I'm supposed to be playing—a stranger who picks her up at a bar and has my wicked way with her later. That role was once real, but now I've tasted her too many times to pretend I'm not intimately acquainted with every inch of her body. My fingertips burn in anticipation, craving the feel of her skin again.

Living in two different cities is not convenient when the only woman you want to get off with is three hours away. Tonight we'll have that conversation. It's been a long time coming.

I'm about to do what he said and get out of here, but he nudges me first. "Stop wasting your time, or someone else is going to want to keep her company."

"What about you?" I ask, conflicted about leaving him after he came all this way to see me.

"I'll hang out with Gear."

"Too bad Singer's not here," I say.

Gear whacks my chest. "Hey. He doesn't need his girl here to have a good time, right, Ethan?"

"Sure, man," Ethan replies, "whatever." A deep chuckle follows.

Setting his glass down, Gear adds, "The Everest brothers used to bring the ladies. I need some of that luck again."

There was a competitive streak running through everything we did growing up through college, except when it came to women. That was one area we gave each other the respect deserved.

The crowd settles as The Crow Brothers get situated on stage. Ethan pulls at the collar of his shirt as if the mere mention of his wife has him hot and bothered.

"You always did make a solid wingman, Hut," Gear says.

"What can I say? I got my mom's good looks and my dad's charm."

Ethan rolls his eyes. "You know what I got from you?"

"A hard time."

"Yep," Ethan says, laughing. "And for the record, it wasn't luck, Gear. It was skill and the Everest good looks."

"Oh, yeah?" Gear brags, countering, "Well, I used to see a Dallas Cowboys cheerleader on the regular. She had her pick of guys and always chose to go home with me. I also used to have a regular hookup with a flight attendant based out of Houston. I got more than first class service on those flights. It was a real bummer when she got engaged to a pilot on her route."

I ask, "You know what Ethan would do in that situation?"

"What?"

"He'd buy his own damn plane."

"Did," Ethan corrects. "I bought a jet, and now I fly private."

Shaking my head, I can't help but laugh. It's cut short when Ethan crooks a brow at me as though I'm crazy.

"You're still here." His voice straddles interest and distraction. "What is this? A game you play?"

"Something like that." I look back at her. Ally Edwards moved well past a one-night stand just over a year ago when I came back to Austin the following weekend to see her again. We didn't typically spend much time on dates per se, but there were a few walks along the river, lazy breakfasts, and fairly frequent check-in texts. It didn't take long for her to mean more to me, especially since she told me she's not seeing anyone else. *But* we still play our games from time to time, circling, pretending.

I order a vodka and tonic with a twist of lime for her. I'm done circling; I want to spend time with her, given it never seems to be on our side. Carrying her drink and my beer, I work my way through the crowd to the back of the bar as the band kicks into their chorus.

Ally keeps her gaze ahead, watching the entertainment on stage. The number of guys who have their eyes on her is not lost on me. Her angular jaw leads to the tip of her chin, the bottom point of her heart-shaped face. Her lips are red and full with a sweet little bow at the top. Soft waves of cappuccino-colored hair caress her shoulders and lower. She has the body of a tennis player—strong with lean arms, defined thighs, and full breasts that shadow a toned stomach.

Her signature scent has hints of seduction layered beneath floral tones despite trying to leave her smelling of the subtle claims I try to stake when I'm with her. From behind, I lean down and whisper, "I wasn't sure you'd show."

Without turning back, she replies, "I couldn't stay away."

I'm tempted to say a few things regarding her staying away, but I want to enjoy this night, so I let it slide. "You're looking more beautiful than ever, Ms. Edwards."

She spins into my arms, which naturally open for her. The games are done. Now it's just the two of us. Her hand slips under my shirt, her fingertips dipping into the top of my jeans. Closing the distance between us, she radiates heat. "You aren't alone tonight."

"Neither are you."

"Tell me you're still single, or are you seeing someone in Houston?"

This is a shift in our dynamic, voicing for the first time our formerly unspoken understanding. I don't see jealousy in her eyes, though I would pay good money to know she felt that strongly for me. "Not in Houston, but there's a woman in Austin I can't stop thinking about. Drink?"

Taking the glass from me, she takes a sip, and then says, "Thank you. Now about this woman—"

"Stunning. She's breathtakingly beautiful with eyes that eat my soul alive when we're in the most compromising of positions. Our time is too short, flying by too fast or freezing like nothing and no one else exists. I wish I could turn back the clock just to relive the seconds, minutes, hours I've shared with her."

A sly smile appears, and she teases her fingers around one of my belt loops. "She sounds amazing, and you, sir, sound smitten."

"She is, and I might be."

Whispering into her ear, I add, "My time isn't the only thing of mine she consumes. She also takes what she wants but gives better than she gets."

"It sounds as if she's a woman who knows what she likes in bed and in men." My insides tighten over her use of men, instead of man. Has she been lying to me? When her middle presses to mine, I slide my arm around her waist and hold her closer, not wanting to let her go again. She says, "Tell me more about this woman who gives so good."

"She's got these eyes that see through my lines, so I don't lie or waste my best moves. She's too smart for that. I stick to the basics and open myself up for rejection."

"If you're so open, she'll see your sincerity."

"And if she doesn't?"

"Then come find me."

"Found you."

2

Hutton

TILTING MY HEAD, I lean forward and rest my temple against hers. "I've missed you, or are we not allowed to say that?"

Ally's silence is loud over the energized crowd, her heavy thoughts palpable. When I lean back enough to draw her gaze from the stage to me, she whispers, "We shouldn't," before she looks at the drink in her hand.

"Okay. We'll keep it light with no strings." I mentally pack away the string I'd planned to attach to her in some form of commitment this weekend.

The warmth is gone when her hand joins her other by wrapping around her sweating glass. "We used to be a lot simpler."

"Yes, it used to be. But now? Since my lips have tasted yours? It's no longer simple."

"You can't say things like that, Hutton."

"I just did, sweetheart."

I see the smile she tries so hard to hide before she takes a sip. The crowd is loud as The Crow Brothers finish another song. "They sound amazing."

Nice try, Ms. Edwards, on the distraction. I'll give her a little space on the issue. *For now.* "Yeah, they do." I take her by the wrist, wanting to kiss the delicate pale skin of it and selfishly vying for all her attention. "Hey?"

Her gaze slides from where I'm touching her to my eyes. "You hurt me, Hutton."

My eyebrows shoot up in surprise. *What the hell?* "How'd I hurt you?"

"The last time we talked."

Oh . . . I remember a different version of that conversation last month, but we can start with hers first. It's too noisy in here to have *this* conversation. "Come on. Let's talk out back."

Holding her hand, I lead her to the bar's patio where picnic benches and tables full of people are hanging out drinking. We find a spot less crowded near a short fence dividing this place from the neighboring bar.

"You were hurt because I told you I wouldn't wait around for you any longer?"

"My life is already complicated, and you don't understand. I still don't think you do."

"I want to, though. That should matter."

She lets out a heavy breath, and then says, "You came along and made things messy."

Meet up and fuck. The lines have blurred between what we were and what I want us to be. "Relationships are messy." We've been lying to ourselves and each other. We're more than what we said. We're what we felt inside but never shared. Taking her hand, I hold it, running my thumb over her knuckles. "I wouldn't know how complicated your life is because you never share it with me."

"I share my body and soul with you, which is more than I can normally give."

"Four weeks ago, you didn't show up. That was when I was ready to share more. So tell me something, Ally. What's so fucking complicated in your life that you stood me up?"

Even though another song starts, we can still talk and be heard out here. She laughs to herself. "You once told me you didn't do more. Now you're saying you would have?"

"Yes, if you'd have let me."

"Why then? What changed your mind?"

"You. That's the truth." I wish I wasn't holding this beer so I could hold her tighter, feel the curve of her waist to her hip, and then slip my fingers under her shirt to feel the skin of her lower back. Images of that lower back before me as I fucked her and then turning her over so I could see her face . . . "I still want to see you." The song comes to an end, and I don't waste a second of the quiet. "I waited. For you, I've waited. I'm always fucking waiting."

Turning around, she presses her back to my chest. "You shouldn't."

"I know every inch of your body, probably better than you. Let me get to know the rest of you."

"Complicated—"

"I know. I know. *Messy*. I don't care, though." The left side of my mouth slides up. "I like messy."

She laughs, and there's a genuine sincerity this time. "You like getting messy between the sheets."

"True. When it comes to you, I do. As for complicated, we can simplify things in time. What do you think about going from having an occasional meetup to dating exclusively?" It's an offer I've thought about often but didn't know it'd come out tonight. She makes me crazy and scrambles my thoughts.

Her head whips to the side, her mouth falling open . . . God, I love that mouth. "Hutton?"

"Ally."

"You want to date exclusively, and I haven't even been introduced to your friend."

"You've met Gear."

"Who's the other one?" Her gaze goes from them back to me, and she says, "You look like you could be brothers."

"We are. That's Ethan. I want to introduce you to him." I'm not sure what one thing has to do with the other, but I pick up the crumbs she's setting down, trying to follow her train of thought. "But not meeting my family before we start dating can't be the reason you're holding back."

"I'd like to meet him." After taking another sip of her drink, some of the tension leaves her body, and she turns completely to face me, her arms maneuvering around my neck. I like when she gets possessive in public. With that sexy, sweet smile on her face, the one that attracted me to her the first time I saw her, she asks, "How long are you in town?"

"Tonight."

"Then let's make the most of it." The pressure of her lips on mine is a quick reminder of the heat we've always shared.

I give in to her like I always do and kiss her back. I care about her. I can't stop thinking about her and what she does when we're not together, which is ninety percent of our lives.

I like the way she feels against me. I like the feelings she stirs inside. I like that hope seems to find its way through the dark nights we've spent together, letting me believe, if only for a short time, that we might be together come dawn.

When the audience starts clapping, Margie eyes me, and then asks her, "I'm heading home in a few songs. Are you staying?"

Ally smiles at me. "I am."

"Are you sure?" she follows up, seeming to understand more about where Ally stands with me than I do.

Confident in her answer, she tightens her smile, and replies, "Absolutely."

"Okay then." I'm tapped on the shoulder, Margie's ash-gray eyes home in on me. "Take care of her."

"I will." I stand firm in my stance and response. I like that Margie cares about her, but I'm not the enemy she's made me out to be.

She then raises her eyebrow at me as if to say, *really*?

"Scout's honor." *Even though I was never a boy scout.* My retort earns me a smirk before she turns to Ally. "I'll see you in the morning."

They give each other a hug and say their goodbyes. When Ally turns to me, I say, "Margie doesn't like me."

"She doesn't have anything against you. She just doesn't like some of my choices."

Chuckling, I shake my head. "Like me."

"Stop it." Playfully patting my chest, she still smiles, amused by the conversation, or maybe I make her happy. "It's me, not you. That sounds like a cliché, but it's true."

"She knows about us?" *Is that a good thing?*

"I've told her how I feel." I just wish I knew exactly what that meant. Does Margie think I'm truly a menace to Ally? I want to know what this girl thinks. I want Ally to believe we could actually be more.

"You know, I'd love for you to clue me in, sweetheart. After all, I'm smitten, remember?"

There's that sigh mixed with a smile again as she rolls her head to the side. "Hut—"

"Shhh. Not now, beautiful." Time for a redirect. "Let's go brave my brother. He's had a few beers, so I take no responsibility for what comes out of his mouth."

"Meeting your brother, hey? That feels pretty big."

"I know firsthand that you can handle big." I wink.

Her laughter fills the air, the building depth of conversation having been put off a little longer. The mood lightens between us. "I meant a big *step*."

"Why take any if they're not big and moving in the right direction?" As I lead her by the hand, we cut through the audience watching the band. When we reach my brother and Gear, I pull Ally from behind so she's front and center.

When the song ends, the band announces an equipment check, so I take advantage of the quick break. "This is Ally Edwards. Ally, this is my brother, Ethan, and my friend, Gear."

She shakes their hands and then glances back and forth between Ethan and me. "You and your brother look a lot alike."

"Strong genes," I reply.

"Genes of Everest proportions." She laughs with a little snort, punctuating the bad but completely adorable joke. "You have another brother, too, right? Mount?"

I'm not sure how much she's had to drink, but the alcohol has apparently kicked in. The guys are amused. It's not the first time we've heard mount or climb in reference to us. Ally, a little loose from alcohol, is a bit of a spitfire. Carefree. Fewer inhibitions. And for the most part, we've always kept things fairly fun and easy, never getting too deep, as if the risk was too high. *So why am I so intent on risking that now?*

"Yes. Bennett."

Peeking up at me, she says, "I can only imagine the trouble the three of you were in high school."

"And college," I reply, laughing. "But we don't need to talk about that."

Orrrr we can . . . To Ethan, she says, "I bet you have some good stories about Hutton."

Ethan chuckles but is smart enough not to get into that. "Too many to tell."

"I can imagine," she replies as if she's in on the joke. Her independence was something else that caught my attention the first night we met. She doesn't need a warm-up. She's comfortable talking to anyone, and it's as if she's known them her whole life. Welcoming. Kind. Funny. She continues to talk to him. "Let me ask you something. Was he always such a ladies' man?"

Glancing back and forth between us, he takes a swig of beer. "I'm pretty sure that anything I say will be used against him, so we'll go with, he was very popular in school with the ladies. Their boyfriends, though? Not so much."

It's only a light punch to the shoulder, but I was tempted to do more, like when we were growing up. I'm pretty certain I owe my brothers a few real punches from all the years of annoying sibling fights I endured.

Ally's eyes go wide. "They had boyfriends?"

I'd love to avoid this conversation because clearly, I've matured since then. I almost laugh at my thought. I answer instead, "Only a few—the head cheerleader, the home-coming queen, that cute girl who worked at Subway, and . . . okay, more than a few had boyfriends, but I can't help that they stepped out on their relationships."

Fisting my shirt, she pulls me close. "God, you're just the kind of trouble I used to look for." She practically purrs as she sinks against me. "You are so not innocent. I find that so hot."

What the? Who is this girl? This possessive, touchy—greedy—girl. I like this side of her. *A lot.*

3

Hutton

THE MUSIC KICKS IN AGAIN, and Ethan and Gear finish off another pitcher while Ally sips her drink. By the end of the set, I tell my brother, "We'll be right back."

Holding tight to Ally's hand, I make it clear I want her with me. Hopefully, she wants the same. By how tight she holds on to me, I'm thinking she does. I really like this change, both of us showing how we feel instead of the usual guessing game.

People start clearing out, so it's easier to reach the stage. "Hey, Jet," I call out. I met Jet Crow in college. I was a senior, but this freshman punk ass was hitting on a girl I dated briefly back then. We settled the score in a parking lot, but I gave him props for holding his own. We never had classes together, but I dug going to his shows. We've been friends ever since.

Since I moved to Houston, I don't get to see him much. When he looks up with an amp cord in his hands, he says,

"Well, look who came back to our old stomping grounds."
Walking closer, he hops down. "Good to see you, fucker."

The band is still struggling to break out. They've had
some local success, enough to pay the bills, but nothing to
retire on. It hurts my financial soul.

Jet's always been cool, but his youngest brother reminds
me of Bennett and is a pain in the ass. If there's a good kind
of pains in the asses. He's funny, no doubt. Tulsa eyes up
Ally. His dirty thoughts about my girl are written all over his
face. He lowers his voice and holds out his hand. "Tulsa
Crow, guitarist and vocals. And whom might you be?"

"Fuck off," I tease, feeling possessive and stepping closer
to Ally. She's with me. I don't have to say that to him, but the
thought crosses my mind. Jet outgrew his angst, though he's
still not settled down. Rivers is still recovering from some bad
breakup, but Tulsa wears a smile no matter what life throws
at him. The three of them don't date, but don't have any
trouble hooking up either.

They honor the bro code, though, so the only logical
deduction I can make of my reaction is because of who
they're meeting. "This is Ally Edwards." Bothered by feeling
this way, I flex my fingers before wrapping them around her
waist again.

She used to be softer, her face a little fuller, her hipbone
less obvious. It's been almost two months since we've seen
each other. Something's going on with her. We don't confess
our feelings, not the real ones, but maybe, like our behavior
this time, she'll open up to me and talk about what's gone
wrong since we last saw each other.

When she didn't come to Houston like we planned, I
tried to move on. *Tried.* Figured since she was a no-show and
then never returned my calls or texts, she wanted nothing to
do with me.

But here I am, in Austin after one of our coded text conversations.

Her: *I'm sorry.*

Me: *Me too.*

Her: *You have nothing to be sorry for.*

Me: *I'm sorry you stood me up.*

Her: *Yes. I regret it every day.*

I liked her . . . I still do.

Me: *Saturday*

It took her two hours to reply, but when she did, I started breathing a little easier.

Her: *4th Street?*

She knew to look up where the band was playing. I'd seen my friend's band play a thousand times but still supported them when I could. If I'm in town, I go out.

More details weren't shared. She liked the mystery, the intrigue, and finding me. She liked pretending we didn't know each other, at first anyway. She loved to flirt but never with another man.

My chest tightens just holding her, and I swallow harder. My throat thickens with all the questions I want to ask her, more than just to be mine.

We've gotten by with courtesies and compliments, surface conversations that never strayed too far into deeper waters, but tonight is different. A hurricane of truths is brewing. I can sense it. I can feel it. I can see it in her eyes.

"Good to meet ya, Ally Edwards. So you're with this guy?"

"Save it, Crow," I say, laughing.

Her head leans against my arm, her hand flattening across my stomach, and she nods. "I am."

"That's cool. He's a good guy."

"He is," she adds.

To me, Tulsa asks, "You guys hanging out a while or heading out?"

"We'll hang out for a drink or two. Can I get you a beer?"

"Grab a pitcher at the bar for my brothers and me. Tell the bartender to put it on our tab and add a round for you guys." He goes back to clearing the equipment off stage.

Ally's hand slides down my arm and into mine. Our fingers fall together, entwining. Tonight is definitely different. Everything's not about getting out of here to have sex. There's an intimacy we've never shared in public before. "You doing okay?"

"I'm good." I detect sadness in her tone, matching something in her eyes. She's missing the light that used to shine from within. Is that the tradeoff? The shine, her happiness, in exchange for this closeness? How does that work when this closeness is what makes me happy?

It's a lot of heavy. I need a drink. Leading her to the bar, I ask, "Do you want another?"

"No."

I'm about to order something for me, but my gut tells me I should stay sober. I grab two pitchers for the guys, though. We sit at a table Gear and Ethan nabbed once the place cleared out.

When the guys from the band come over, we shuffle our chairs to fit the extras for Jet, Rivers, and Tulsa. I've met them plenty of times, but the others haven't, so I do the introductions and pour the drinks. "Great show."

Jet's not moody, but he carries the weight of responsibility that older brothers seem to have. I relate. Jet says, "Thanks. We've been working out a few songs." Looking at Rivers, he adds, "I think the crowd liked them."

"Yeah, it was a good audience," Rivers says. "They didn't even notice when Tulsa screwed up the chorus."

Tulsa chimes in quick, "Hey. Hey. I can't help it when there's a little honey in hot pink distracting me from the front row."

Jet rolls his eyes. "Try harder next time."

Ethan says, "Hutton's tried to get me out to a show for a few years now. Glad I caught your concert tonight."

Rivers leans back. "It's good to finally meet you. Hutton's not all bad," he says, chuckling. "Where are you living? Houston?"

"New York. I started a new company last year after settling up north. I don't get back to Texas much anymore."

They keep talking, but I notice Ally looking down at her phone. Leaning over, I ask, "Everything all right?"

"Fine. I just . . ." She looks at me as her hand slides onto my thigh. "I'm glad you're here."

"Me too, but why do I get the feeling I'm missing something?"

She lifts and kisses my neck. With her lips on me, she whispers, "I want to be alone with you, Hut."

Rubbing her thigh, I turn and kiss her mouth. That craving she stirs deep inside me is aroused. "We can leave." I stand. "We're cruising out." I shake their hands and then Gear's. "I'll see you tomorrow."

"Yeah, just text me. Not before noon, dude, or I'll hurt you something fierce. We'll leave for Houston around two."

Ethan says, "I leave at noon. Text me when you're up, and we can grab something to eat before I fly out." I want to crack a joke about him having a flight schedule when he owns the damn jet, but I don't. He's outgoing in many ways, but when it comes to his money, he likes to keep things low-key.

"I'll text you."

As soon as Ally and I are out the door, she shivers and

leans against me while the wind whips around us. "Where are you staying?" she asks, huddling closer.

"Omni. You don't want to go to your place?"

"No." I notice that she looks away when she answers.

We always go to hers. She has a downtown condo overlooking Lady Bird Lake. "What's going on?"

"I'm cold, Hutton. Can we go?" I try to catch her eyes, but she walks toward the corner before I have a chance. As if she wills herself not to look back at me, she says, "We can walk if you want."

Hurricane . . . "Okay." I pick up my pace until we're side by side walking north. Shoving my hands in my pockets, I keep it light. Weather is always a good non-confrontational topic. "It's gotten cold. You sure?"

"Yeah, walk faster." She crosses her arms over her chest.

The winds of her emotions are picking up as well. We cover two blocks before I get tired of the silence. Quiet is not usually an issue between us like it has been tonight. "What's going on with you?"

"What do you mean? I'm just walking."

"I mean all night. You're quiet, more reserved. Then hot, cold, handsy. Not that I'm complaining about the handsy part, princess."

"Princess?" she snaps. "Why do you call me that?"

Shrugging, I reply, "I don't know. Like sweetheart. It just came to me, but as for the emotions, you're all over tonight. Almost like you're ready to get tonight over and done with."

Stopping, she appears wounded as if I hit a raw nerve. "I don't mean to. I like my time with you. I wish we had more of it."

"We can," I reply, moving to her. "Surely, you can tell I want more with you." Her long hair blows across her face, so I reach forward and slide it behind her ear.

"What do you want, Hutton?"

You.

What am I doing? Am I being impulsive? A year is a long time to be faithful to a person I'm not sure is committed to me. We don't have rules of dating to abide by. We haven't ever defined what *this* is between us. I just like it. Maybe I'm a fool for exposing my heart, but this feels like a last chance, so I'm taking it. "I meant what I said earlier. I want you in my life. Every day. I want you to think about us being together. Waking up. Going to bed. Eating dinner." Smiling, I slip my hands around her waist. "Fucking. Making love. Spending our lives together."

"No." The word comes fast like a spear to my chest, and she realizes the wound she's inflicted just as quickly. Wrapping her arms around me, she leans her head on my chest. "Don't do this, Hutton. Let's just have a good time like we always do and—"

"And part ways like we always do around four a.m.?"

"That's not fair."

"This isn't fair." I remove her arms from me and walk ahead. I only make it about ten feet before I turn around. I don't want this night to go badly. *How do I fix this?* When I look back and find her where I left her, the pounding muscle in my chest tightens. *Come on, man. Get it together.* "Let's just go, beautiful." She looks down, and I can see her hesitating. *What is going on?* "Fuck. Is there someone else?"

"No." Another quick answer. "There's not been anyone since I met you."

"Then what do you want from *me*, Ally?"

"Nothing."

"Then why are you acting like this is a meaningless fuck?"

"I'm not. We're not meaningless. That's the problem." Standing near the curb, she looks around as if the whole world has become her cage and she's trapped. "I should go."

"What are you doing, Ally?"

"What I have to."

"Why?"

"Don't you see, Hutton? This is all I have left to give. Tonight. Me. That's it."

I don't want to lose her. I finally found someone who makes me want to make commitments like coffee in the morning and pizza in bed. Cuddles. Fuck, she made me want to fucking snuggle the last time we saw each other like I'm a fucking wuss. But damn if I didn't love cuddling with her. "Why? Why is this the end when we never even got a real start?"

She's looking at her shoes like she'll find the answer there. "Please," she starts, her voice so soft that I automatically move closer to hear her speak. When I take her hand and bring it to my lips to kiss, she looks up and has tears in her eyes. "I'm sorry, Hutton."

"Don't be sorry. Just be honest."

"We only have tonight."

With that last swath of words from the sword of her tongue, she's won, mentally bringing me to my knees. I stare at her. When I normally see a beautiful and sexy woman, I now see one who pleads to leave as if someone's after her. "One night and that's it?"

Tugging me in the direction of the hotel, she says, "That's all I can give you."

"What do *you* want? Because I'll give it to you if it means we have a tomorrow."

"I want tonight to be like our other nights—fun, free of outside worries, and peaceful."

Peaceful? What the fuck is going on?

She stands in front of me, strength found in her shoulders. "I can't tell you anything more, Hutton. You just have to trust me."

"But you haven't told me anything."

"I'm sorry. I shouldn't have come out tonight. I never meant to hurt you. It was selfish for me to continue as though nothing is wrong, as though my whole life hasn't changed since that first time we met on Halloween."

"It was fate." We went for the band and probably, if I was honest, to get laid. I didn't expect to find my dream girl in a drab brown dress waiting on her Prince Charming to arrive. I didn't have a white horse, but I did find a discarded slipper.

It was a perfect fit, like us. As soon as she smiled, I was a goner.

I didn't realize how far I'd fallen until now. The winds die down, and she licks her lips, then tugs her bottom one under her teeth. "Ally—"

"Look. I can catch a cab home, but I'd rather spend a few more hours with you. I know what I'm asking is selfish, but I'm asking you anyway. Will you be with me one more time?"

I'm not going to say no to her. I'm not even going to pretend I can. I want more than one night, but I'll take just as selfishly as she is this last time. I have tonight to make this right; one night to make her see how good we are together, how good we can be.

Taking her hand, we start walking again, but I sing, "One more time around again."

4

Hutton

We ride up in the glass elevators with our eyes on each other instead of the view of the expansive hotel lobby. Ally's beauty takes my breath away. Her hair is windblown and in disarray, the shiny brown strands tangled together. Her face is more bare than at the bar earlier, her makeup fading away with the hours. She doesn't need all that stuff anyway.

She still takes the time to reapply her lipstick.

The elevator doors slide open, and she walks into the hallway ahead of me. We haven't spoken since we walked into the hotel. This night holds more meaning than our other nights ever did, along with a whole slew of what-ifs. The possibility of us coming to an end has added weight where there once was none.

Just shy of the door, I stop and stand in her way. "Hey."

"Hey," she replies with an easier smile sliding into place.

"No matter what happens in there—"

"What's going to happen in there?" She arches an eyebrow.

"I'm going to show you how much I care about you. It's going to be rough emotionally. It's going to be raw and real, and this time you won't walk away unscathed. When you walk away, walk down this hall, and take that elevator to leave, you're going to know exactly what you're leaving inside that room. This time, I'm not leaving anything to chance because we may have been fate, but it's up to us to create our destiny."

"Hutton," she says, her chest expanding as tears fill her eyes, "kiss me."

I cup her face and run the pads of my thumbs across her cheeks, wiping away her tears. Leaning my head against hers, I look deep into her eyes. "Why are you crying, princess?"

"Because you're too perfect to be real."

"I'm real. I'm right here, so real." When I kiss her, I give her everything I have because this is it. My last shot to make sure she never forgets. Her body hits the wall behind her, mine pressing against hers.

My needs begin to overtake reasoning as her little moans elicit an intense reaction within me. Every time we're together, it's better than the time before. I'm always turned on by her, muscle memory kicking in. I know her likes, her desires, and her fetishes, and she knows mine. Her hand dips into the top of my jeans, her warmth embracing my hardness.

My tongue finds a home with hers, and I can't stop my middle from pushing against her. "It drives me wild when you wear clothes this tight. It's as if you're wearing them for the whole fucking world to see."

"I love to drive you wild."

Leaning back, I look into her eyes, the eyes that hold so much more power over me than she'll ever know. "Why do you torture me?"

"I like to know that I'm not the only one who gets jealous."

"Jealous? You're never jealous."

Her grip tightens around my cock, causing me to suck in a sharp breath. "You think I don't see how women look at you, how they vie for your attention? My jealousy boils inside every time another woman talks to you or touches you or brushes against you." My breath is harsh but regulates with each stroke of her hand around me. "As long as I'm here, this is mine."

"It's yours long after. *I'm* yours long after."

Her hand stops when she pushes up on her toes to kiss me. And as much as I like her hand wrapped around me, I like her mouth on me more.

A hint of lime from her drink lingers, and I stroke her lower lip as I kiss my way to her ear. "I'm going to make you feel so good, baby."

"You always do." Her fingers pull at the hair at the back of my head, and she whispers, "You always make me feel so good."

Reaching into my pocket, I pull my key card out and open the door. There could be this frenzied sex session. That's how most of our nights begin—taking down a lamp or a plant, a stool along the way, a couch tipped over or a lounge chair broken. It's happened at her place. But those times were when we knew we had more nights ahead of us.

We don't have that luxury tonight, so maybe we're both willing to take it slow to absorb every minute.

The door closes behind me. The drapes are still open, which gives enough light for me to see her in the dark. Her jacket slips from her shoulders and is tossed on the chair. When she starts on the zipper of her tall boots, I kick off my shoes and socks and work off my belt.

I can hear her swallow and wonder if she can hear my heart pounding. "Why are we nervous?" she asks.

Easy. "Because we matter to each other."

She pulls her shirt over her head and tosses it to the pile of other discarded clothes. "That should put us at ease, not the opposite."

When we're standing in our underwear, I go to her. Running my hands over her soft skin and the curve of her back, I whisper, "It doesn't make it the opposite. It makes it better."

When I kiss her, a fire ignites between us. My boxer briefs are taken down when she slides to her knees in front of me. The pale pink straps of her bra almost blend in with her alabaster skin.

So delicate.

So perfect.

So right.

Reaching down, I take her hair in my hand and move it to the side so I can watch those pretty red lips part and take me. She looks up at me as she covers the head, but then closes her eyes and slides down my length, taking me deep. "Fuck," I mutter, my eyes briefly closing. My hand fists her hair, and a full breath covers my dick in response.

She likes when I take control as much as she likes to take turns being in charge. She's a giver and a taker, submissive and dominant.

I cup her face, wanting to fuck her mouth. We only share a look, but in that exchange, she reads my needs.

When she relaxes her jaw, I begin to pump in and out, her mouth hugging my hardness, sliding almost the full distance and then back to the tip again.

Giver.

I want to slam into her, come down her throat, and own

her in ways that some might consider depraved. I want to fill every opening and fuck until her muscles only remember me.

My stomach clenches, and I pull back. This is not how I want to come. Lifting her to her feet, I admire how the ruby color that covered her lips is smeared—some on me, some on her. Ally's a fucking fantasy come to life, but she doesn't care about that shit. It's part of what makes being together even more erotic. I've never had a lover like her.

I still run my thumb over her lip, appreciating how swollen it is from the sexual act. "I want you naked."

There's no hesitation.

Giver.

"How do you want me, Hutton?"

Such a fucking loaded question. "I want to be buried inside that tight pussy when I come. How do *you* want me?"

"I want to come on your mouth."

Fuck me.

Taker.

The sexy little vixen.

"Get on the bed." I love watching her ass move. It's not just toned, but she's still got some curves to her backside despite the weight she's lost.

Stretching out on the bed, she watches me as I climb onto the mattress and hover over her. I kiss her once on the mouth and then work slowly down her body, kissing between her breasts and past her belly button. She's already squirming beneath me, so I anchor those hips after kissing each one. Her smooth legs spread open, and I finally kiss where she wants me most. Her sweet lower lips are a soft pink and bare.

Taking her clit gently between my teeth, I don't waste time. I flick it a few times with my tongue before sucking until she's bucking. She's already so wet for me that I slip a finger, and then another, inside her and return that blissful torture she doled out to me, bringing her closer to that edge of ecstasy.

My hair is tugged, my head squeezed between her thighs, but I don't retreat. This is a war I don't intend to lose. I fuck her harder with my mouth and hand until I win. "Hutton. God. Yes. Yes."

Her orgasm strikes hard as her back arches and her body gives in. Another wave hits and rolls through her until she melts to the mattress. Her arms go wide and her eyes close, relishing in the heavenly aftermath.

It's in the aftermath that I see her soul. She can't hide that look in her eyes—the one where she looks replete, as if I'm the only man for her. In my mind, she sees me as everything she needs. *At least, that's what I want to see.*

She doesn't make demands but gentle requests while lying there, vulnerable and exposed. The tips of her fingers encourage me to come higher, to kiss her, to savor the emotions we've stirred. She never allows herself to indulge for long, but in those few minutes, after she falls apart, I see the truth.

She's a free spirit with a kind heart. Playful. Clever. Vivacious. Gentle. Quiet. Introspective. She's every color of the rainbow and a myriad of emotions in the span of a few hours, tenderhearted before me now. She carries the weight of the world in her irises but lives like there's no tomorrow.

I start to get up to grab a condom because I stupidly forgot to get one out before. But Ally holds me in place, staring into my eyes. "It's not fair to ask of you—"

"You can ask me anything."

"Will you make love to me?"

Not fuck.

Love.

I nod and kiss her collarbone because it doesn't matter

what I thought we were going to do. It only matters that we're together doing it.

She adds, "I want to feel you, Hutton."

Okay.

"All of you."

Oh. That's not what I was expecting.

"Wait . . ." It's stupid to question. I know she's on the pill. I've known since the first time, but we still always use condoms. Just so I'm clear, I ask, "You're still on—"

"The pill." She nods.

This changes things. We've not done this before. I haven't *ever* done it. I'm always safe, even when I've been drinking.

But Ally is different. She's the only one I've been with since we started having sex together, and she said there's been no one but me since we met. So the offer is tempting, and I don't even have alcohol to blame for some careless decision.

This choice has been taken under consideration. *She's thought this through.* And if I'm honest, I have too. I've lain awake at night imagining what it would be like to go bare, to give Ally all of me. Now it's as though I'm craving that connection, something I've wanted with someone special. *Maybe that's always been her.*

I maneuver over her again and position myself between her legs. "You're sure?"

With her hands on my shoulders, she looks so relaxed, exactly how she should be when she's with me. "So sure."

Pushing in, I take it slow, but as her warmth envelops me, I'm tempted to thrust hard. So fucking hard. *Sloooow,* I remind myself.

My head drops to her shoulder. *Fuck.* "You feel incredible."

Arms wrap around me as I gather up the pieces of my soul and put it back together under her embrace. And then I start moving again. Slow at first, but when I lift up on my elbows, I pick up speed.

Love.

Love.

Thrust.

Love.

I promised to give her everything I had. We move together as if we were born to please one another. She meets me thrust for thrust as we kiss and caress, knead and need.

I'm about to lose more than my mind. I can't last all night. She feels too good. Just as I start to pull out, she says, "Stay. Come inside me."

Fuck me.

My thoughts are blurry as my body moves. Sweat glistens across her body like diamonds catching the light. I grunt and come, my arms holding her tightly to me as I pour everything I am into her until there's nothing left of me.

Physically and emotionally. I'm yours, Ally.

The feel of her nails scraping lightly across my scalp brings me back to this heaven on earth, and I kiss her cheek. Sliding to the side, I drape my arm across my forehead and close my eyes. I could sleep for days, weeks, or even months in this sated state as long as I knew she would be here when I wake.

She won't be, though, so I force my lids to reopen and look at her, to take in her beauty once again. *Something's holding her back.* In the glimpse of her sated expression, I wonder if it's not *what* I'm asking that she's withdrawing from, but something different. But then all I can see is her beautiful eyes, soft skin, and lips I love, and everything else flees my mind.

When we catch our breath, we take turns in the bathroom before returning to bed. Lying next to each other just after two in the morning, I broach the topic I've let slide for too long. "Why'd you cancel your visit to see me? I don't get it as I thought the game . . . well, I thought we were past that."

"I didn't cancel because of a game, Hut. I was confused . . ."

"But why—"

"You were never a game to me, even when we were pretending. Life was throwing me curveballs, and I needed to think . . . I needed time."

"Okay." I kiss her shoulder and stay there, finally allowing my eyes to close before confessing, "Each time we've been together, I haven't pretended. I haven't been playing with you."

I hear the intake of her breath, and with my arm resting across her stomach, I feel the depth of her inhale. "Neither have I."

I'm tempted to keep her talking, to keep her awake until she decides to leave. I can tell how tired she is, so I pull her against me and hold her because it doesn't matter what I say or do. She'll be gone before the sun rises.

5

Hutton

I WAKE UP, but before my eyes open, my arm spreads wide to confirm an empty space beside me.

I don't find an empty bed.

I find Ally.

And smile.

When I open my eyes, sunshine floods the room, and I find cloudless skies staring at me. "You're here?"

I don't know what I'm really asking, but she replies, "Not *you're awake*?" A giggle comes. "Just diving straight into the shock of *you're here*?" The tips of her fingers run along the scruff of my jaw, her smile dipping into a straight line before her lips part. "So now that you've seen me in the morning, what do you think?"

"I think the makeup that was left when we arrived here is smudged under your eyes and there's no lipstick left—"

"It's on you." She rubs lightly over the corner of my mouth.

"Your hair is messier than we are."

"Why does sex hair only look good on men?"

I gently bite the tip of her thumb and then kiss it while catching her wrist. "You have signs of being ravaged by an animal in the sack with hickeys on your neck.

"I was." She laughs. "I look that good, huh?"

I don't laugh. "You're breathtaking. The most beautiful I've ever seen you." I kiss her palm and lower to her wrist. "Tell me what to say to keep you here. I'll say anything you want if I can wake up to you looking this gorgeous every morning."

Silence fills in her answer. Just when I look up, ready to plead my case, she says, "Every morning? You'll be sick of me."

"Never."

"Don't you know never to say never?" She sighs as though she doesn't have the energy for this kind of banter. "There's nothing you can say, Hutton. It doesn't matter what I want. I have obligations—"

"It changed from complications to obligations?"

She sits up, so I lean against the headboard. Holding her knees to her chest, she rests her cheek on her knee while keeping her eyes on me. "You're very good-looking. You know that. Maybe even more so in the morning."

"What do you see when you look at me?"

"I've paid good money to have that perfect shade of dark brown before. Tall. Dark. And handsome."

I laugh. "What else?"

"Your eyes are intense; the brown is inviting, warm instead of dangerous. Welcoming, though I know you like to think you're more cocky than comforting. I like how tall you are, and when we were watching the band, your body curved around me. I feel safe and protected when you feel possessive or just horny."

This time I chuckle. "I do feel possessive of you. I feel

protective, and I want you to always feel safe with me. But how can I protect you when I don't know what I'm protecting you from?"

"You're the fairy-tale ending I wish I could have."

"I don't understand why you can't."

Resting back on her elbows, she says, "I want to tell you everything, but once I do, we'll never be the same. So I have a favor to ask, though I know I have no right to ask it."

I tuck a section of her hair behind her ear. "You have more rights with me than you know, but once you're gone, will I ever hear from you again?"

"Can we not talk about the world outside this hotel room?"

Her head hits the pillow, and she turns on her side to face me, the palm of her hand covering my heart. Just as she's about to answer, I press two fingers to her lips. I don't know why I even asked when I know the answer already. "Don't answer that. Surprise me."

I don't get the smile I wanted, which says more than her lips ever could. When I pull my hand back, she closes her eyes and moves closer. "Hold me, Hutton."

This woman is fascinating. We've always had the best conversations, and boredom has never entered our time together. That's why the mere idea of letting her go is unfathomable.

I do. I hold her cheeks in my palms and do my best to kiss the sadness away, hoping to keep the world at bay for the night. Moving to her neck, I kiss over her pulse and then move to claim her mouth again. I trace her body with my tongue and then enter her on a moan. I move inside her while all is quiet except for our panting breaths. And then I hold her . . . until we fall asleep again.

The bright light of the day rouses me awake. Again. I don't want to open my eyes this time because I know she's gone. While I slept, the air has become stale—her scent fading too fast—the warmth she brought gone, leaving the room cold.

I pull the covers down and finally face reality.

Ally Edwards is gone, and I stupidly never even knew what Ally was short for. Staring at the ceiling, I rattle off a few potential names—Alison, Alexandra, Alyssa, but maybe it's just Ally.

Thinking back on the many good times we've had, I wish last night could have changed our fate.

I want a redo so I can ask her the questions we avoided the first time around. I want a redo to prove I can be something good in her life, something that helps her untangle the mess we made.

My phone buzzes on the nightstand, and I reach over and grab it. Maybe she's coming back . . .

Ethan: *Get your ass out of bed and down to La Casa del Fuego.*

I shouldn't feel disappointed to see my brother's text, but Ally's absence is beginning to sink in. I'm not ready to accept her leaving, so I text her. Unfortunately, I get no reply. I text my brother: *Be there in thirty.*

My brother might be short on time, but I need a shower, so I cram in a quick one before hurrying to meet him at the food stand. This place is a tradition. He's already ordered my food when I arrive, knowing I order the same thing every time. We lean on a railing and eat our tacos. I'm in no mood to talk, but in pure Ethan style, he won't let me be. "What happened?"

Tossing the remains of my taco into the basket, I watch a car drive by, squinting from the bright sun. "She left."

"For good?"

I drag a chip through the salsa, my appetite waning. "Seems that way."

"Sorry to hear that."

"I knew it was coming." I did too. I just didn't want to deal with the facts. Two months ago, she made it clear where we no longer stood. Last night, she wanted one last go of things, but she didn't lie.

Ethan nods. "We talk about girls, but we've never really talked about the women in our lives, the ones we spend more time with. I like Ally. She was more your match than your past girlfriends."

"True."

"So there's no changing the outcome?"

I chuckle. "She's a woman, not a business deal."

"Bennett might argue otherwise."

"And you?" I ask.

"I'm still trying to get used to you being grown-up enough to talk about love. That's what we're talking about, right?"

I answer a little quieter, the topic feeling as foreign as the emotions defining it. "I think so."

"If you love her, Hut, you should tell her. If you told her and she still left, then maybe it's not meant to be."

Sirens wail, making it impossible to hear the rest of what he's saying. I look back over my shoulder as a cavalcade of black SUVs with a police escort stops at the corner. "What the hell?"

Ethan stands, alarmed.

One of the Suburbans brakes so fast it rocks on its tires. Both doors open and a man in a suit with one hand on his earpiece is stating calmly. "On the move. She's on the move."

But my attention quickly goes to Ally when she hops out from the back seat. "Hutton?"

My mind is still trying to connect the dots that Ally just

ran from a parade of vehicles that looks like the president is in town. But the flags flying on the front aren't American. I don't recognize the flag or what country it represents. I only know the woman running toward me with secret service-looking dudes on her tail looks very different from the one I've spent many nights with.

Her hair is straight except for a wave in the front and around the bottom edges. It's pulled back on one side by something sparkly, and even though she's moving quickly, not a hair is out of place.

I can't stop myself from staring at her. She's a woman I know on the most intimate of levels, yet I hardly recognize who's in front of me.

Ally's lips are a softer shade in the morning light, the palest of pinks, and those incredible blue eyes are made up subtler than I'm used to seeing. I've never seen her look so prim or proper. My mind goes wild with thoughts of the dirty role play we can reenact . . . *until I remember last night was our end.*

When she reaches me, she grabs my arms in a panic. "Hutton, I'm so sorry. Just please remember that I love you."

"You love me?"

She nods enthusiastically. "I do. I love you."

"I love you too." I take her by the face, ready to kiss her, but she stops me, and my mind has time to catch up with her words. "Wait. Why do I have to remember that? We love each other. That means something. That means we should be together."

Backing away, she slips out of my reach. "I have to go, but I had to tell you. You are the best person I've ever known. Thank you for treating me like you did. I'll always remember you and the times we've shared."

She's already starting to back away. I reach for her, the railing dividing us. "Stay, Ally."

"Goodbye, Hutton."

When she turns to leave, I notice two men in suits standing nearby. They move apart to let her walk between them as they head back to the waiting SUV. "Stop."

She turns back and looks at me with questioning eyes.

I pause, but my brother shoves me from behind. "Last chance, Hut."

He's right. I jump the railing because there's no way I'm letting her go without a fight. I just didn't count on these two guys stopping me. Their hands land hard against my chest, each taking one of my arms and tugging it back. "What the fuck?"

Ally gasps, her hands covering her mouth.

The one on my right tells me to stand down as he twists my arm back.

I'm not in pain, but one wrong move and I'm starting to think they wouldn't mind snapping my arms back until I am. Ethan pushes the guy on the left off me, and says, "Get the fuck off him."

Under a thick accent, the guy warns, "He needs to stand down, and you need to step back, sir."

Ally comes back, and demands, "Release him."

His hands are gone in an instant. My gaze darts to those little flags again, memorizing the lion and hawk on the orange and red diagonal-striped background, before I look at her for answers. I rush forward again, this time grabbing her arms so she can't run away. "What's going on, Ally? Why are you leaving? I need to know."

"I need—"

"It's time to go." The asshole leers at us and then has the balls to reach for her. "Princess All—"

Knocking his hand away, I say, "Don't fucking touch her." He crosses his arms over his chest, annoyed as he stares at us. Turning back to her, I repeat the one word taking front and center from everything else. "Princess?"

"Look at me. Please." She holds my face in her hands. "Only me, Hutton."

Though I'm bothered by the asshole, she doesn't seem to feel threatened, so I look at her.

Blue skies.

Long walks.

Soft kisses.

I see all those things when I see her, and the tension in my shoulders dissipates. She lifts up and kisses me. "I don't have the right words to say goodbye to you, Hut. I'm struggling with the reality that I have to, but know I love you."

When I start to speak, she places her fingers over my lips. "I want you to be happy. Please, Hutton. Please be happy." She doesn't wait for a response or even allow me another kiss to remember her by. This time, she turns and dashes into the SUV. The door shuts behind her, and the assholes get in the other SUV before it pulls away, the procession of vehicles continuing on their way.

What the fuck just happened? My brother comes up behind me, his shoulder bumping into mine. "Did they call her princess?"

Princess Arabelle Allyson Edwards Sutcliffe, also known as Ally Edwards. It didn't take long to discover Ally wasn't hiding her real identity from just me but from everybody. She managed to get her master's degree right under the noses of everyone in the world.

She was right about leaving. The last time I saw her was the last time she stood on American soil. The next time was some wedding in France she was attending.

I only knew because of the media frenzy that surrounded it and because my sister-in-law was watching it the following Saturday before college football came on. "Her mother, Queen Aemilia, has to abdicate," Singer says. "Then Arabelle will wear the crown."

"Why would she do that?"

"I don't know. I'm just telling you how it works."

"What about her father?"

"The crowned prince, Werner, is technically beneath the Queen."

Suddenly a lot more interested in this nutty monarch stuff, I ask, "The crowned prince versus what? The uncrowned prince?"

She nods. "I looked it up because they have a different tradition than other European countries. The crowned prince is the one who sits on the throne."

"Interesting."

"Royals are fascinating. I can't believe you dated her."

What happened between us? I can't seem to wrap my head around the beautiful but down-to-earth woman who could wear cutoffs or tight jeans, a T-shirt, or something sexy for me to rip off is the same woman I was seeing on TV— hair too stiff, pleasant smile but not genuinely happy. Conservative clothes.

"Me either."

Ally now resembles every other woman in the lineup of royals standing atop that red carpet leading to the palace doors.

Singer says, "She's beautiful."

Okay, maybe not every other woman. "She is."

Palace.

Red carpet.

Crown.

Pomp and circumstance.

None of it makes sense. I can't riddle my way into figuring out how Ally Edwards is Princess Arabelle Allyson Edwards Sutcliffe. To me, they are two different people.

Shutting my laptop, I sit back and stare out the window of my downtown office. A fog hangs low at this floor of the high-rise, keeping me in the clouds while my thoughts focus on the developing situation.

I've never stalked a woman before—online or in person. But Ally's different. We shared those three words that I've never told any another woman. Has she said them before?

How can she tell me she loves me and then leave so easily? Do her words matter at all? Did she say it to placate me? "I love you, but stay." Is that what she meant?

No. I know her. We may not have spent every day together, but the time we did spend together mattered. It was real and not just an act.

I know her well enough to know she wouldn't say them if she didn't mean them. She didn't have to stop at all, much less say those three words. She meant them, just as I did.

None of it matters now, though.

She's gone.

For good.

I push off my desk and grab my jacket. I want to loosen my tie, but that can't happen until I do what needs to be done. Packing my heart and these messy feelings away, I try to forget the time I spent with a woman named Ally. I need to embrace the future I've been given instead of thinking about the one I'll never have.

The day she kissed me goodbye, my brother told me to look at my relationship with Ally for what it was—just a moment in time, a blip on my dating radar.

He's right. I miss her. I miss what we had, but I'm also glad she came and said goodbye. I can't be angry with her for that.

I also can't waste my life pining over a woman I can never have. There are plenty of pretties looking to hook up with me, so if that is all I'm capable of for now, it's time to . . . well, move on. It might take me a while. Pesky fucking emotions. But there's no doubt that I'm a red-blooded man who loves sex too much to give it up, so there is that . . . Picking up the phone, I call Ethan. When he answers, I ask, "You still have that job for me?"

"When can you be in New York?"

Nothing's keeping me in Texas. No one's holding me here anymore. "Next week. I'm heading into a meeting with Dad now."

"This is good, Hut. He may hate it, but it's better for you to get out of there. Come to New York for a fresh start."

"I think a fresh start is just what I need."

6

Hutton

The view has changed, but I'm still kicking it high in the sky among the clouds. Manhattan seems a world away from Houston. Although I've been here many times before I moved, I don't think it will ever feel like home.

I'm more anxious here, the pace faster. My patience thin. *Unsettled.*

Although I've settled in the same building as my brother, my office is down the hall from Ethan. My paycheck went from a healthy to wealthy, from working for my dad to working alongside my brothers. Considering the crazy real estate market should eat so much of it up, it doesn't because Ethan kept his promise. I became an owner of Everest Enterprises.

My two brothers have always been my best friends. We're

friends. Allies. So seeing them most days is not such a bad thing.

Since I've started my newly created position as chief contracts and negotiations officer over the media division, my hours are better than I expected. But with nothing at home but a fifty-five-inch TV and slim pickings in the fridge, I don't rush home at five o'clock.

The money is good—nothing like what Ethan earns—but enough to keep me happy. My share may only be a quarter of the pie, but it's enough to retire on too young . . . *if* I want to.

I've been focused on my career and aspirations since I graduated. I'm doing more than I dreamed, but now it seems my dreams have changed. My routine has become mundane: wake up, workout, work, workout, watch TV, sleep. I never needed fame or pats on the back. I know I'm good at what I do. I've always done well when I put my mind, or heart, into something.

I should feel like a king, but things have shifted. One part of my life is fulfilling and the other is empty. Has that been affected by Ethan's relationship with Singer? *Possibly.* But I'm ready to strive for more of what money can't buy.

I don't give the thought a voice, ever. But I know what's changed, and I know why.

Ally.

She changed my orderly world, throwing it upside down.

And now a life that should be satisfying has lost its shine. Because of *her.*

My office door opens on this warm summer night, and Ethan comes in. "Why are you still here?" He checks his watch. "I'm heading out. Singer's going to be pissed. I promised to be home earlier."

I chuckle, keeping it light. "You should get going then.

I'm going to work on this proposal. I want to get it wrapped up by Thursday."

"You will. In the morning. Come on. Let me give you a ride home."

I think about the offer. Since I have the ability to work from home, I stand. "Yeah, I'll look at it at home."

Ethan has a magic touch—a belief that anything is possible—and he inspires others to believe the same. Although it's after seven and getting dark outside, enough employees are still working to convince someone not in the know that it's noon.

When we walk out of my office, Ethan says, "Go home, people. The work will be here tomorrow."

That earns a few laughs, but not one person gets up. Their dedication is admirable. Or maybe like me, they don't have anything or someone worth rushing home to.

Unlike Ethan.

I'm happy he's found someone. After all the bad in his life, he deserves every ounce of good.

So do I.

I can't seem to shake the feeling that something is out of alignment or that a piece of this new life is missing. I could fill in the blank if this were a test, but it's not, so I try not to think about the woman making headlines as she settles into the life she hid from me.

"Want to come over?" Ethan asks, holding the phone screen toward me. There's a text from Singer, his wife, that reads to ask me to come to dinner.

I check the time as if I have something else going on. I don't. I don't even remember if I have food at my place. "Sure."

Singer sits next to me on the couch, curling her legs under her. I don't have to look her way to know she's staring at me. With my eyes on the football game, I ask, "What is it?"

Although my tone is steady, a little annoyance sneaks in. It's not her I'm annoyed at. It's me. Even a game can't hold my attention tonight.

Singer is actually one of my favorite people to hang out with. Besides being a little quirky, she's funny, and she's a great match for my brother. With her, he's the guy he used to be before he became a target of the media and the scum who wanted to either use him or steal from him.

We may be in a penthouse in the middle of New York City, but by how casual Ethan and Singer are, you'd never know it.

When she doesn't say anything, I roll my neck to the side. "What, Singer?"

She untucks her legs, and her heels push against my thigh. "Why are you so down all the time? Is it the princess?"

Princess. *"Why are you crying, princess?"*

So much more makes sense these days that made none back then. "Sure. It's woman troubles," I reply sarcastically, sliding down and resting my head on the cushion behind me.

"I see through you just like I see through your brother." She rests her head to the side, continuing to stare at me. "You could go see her. Maybe if she sees you—"

"You read too many romances. This story doesn't have a happy ending."

"That's disappointing."

I can't help but chuckle. Tapping her foot twice, I say, "Sorry about that. I know you'd love to see me living the princely life, but that's not the life for me."

Ethan cuts through the living room from the hall to the kitchen. "Princely life?"

"Your wife is trying to get me to go after the girl." I laugh again at the thought. There are so many things in Ally's and my way that I wouldn't even know where to begin to get to her. *And if there were any possible ways of us being together, wouldn't she have sought them out?*

Sitting on the arm of the couch behind her, he says, "I'm sure you've thought about it."

"I have, but she's not just any woman. She's a princess and next in line to rule an *entire* country."

Ethan adds, "A bit dramatic."

My eyebrows shoot up. "Me? Maybe you don't understand. She will literally inherit a country. To rule."

Shaking his head, he laughs. "See? Dramatic."

I introduce him to my middle finger and turn back to Singer. "I always liked you better than him anyway," I tease. "How do I get her out of my head?"

"You don't," she says. Her eyes round like coffee cup saucers. She sits up and clasps her hands in front of her. "You don't because she's in your heart. Am I right? Is she in your heart, Hut?"

Rolling my eyes, I sit up. "Yes, she's in my heart. Happy?"

"No. Not until you are."

"Don't worry about me. You have enough to worry about right there." I signal toward Ethan.

He kisses her head, and then says, "He's right. I'm happy to have all your attention on me."

"You already get all my time." Pretending to pout, she crosses her arms over her chest, looking back at me. "I want to meet a princess. Oooh, and go to a ball. Do you think they have balls in Brudenbourg?"

"I have no idea what they do there."

"Maybe we should look it up." She moves to get up, but I grab her ankle before she can escape. As she hops on one foot, she says, "Please let me look it up."

"The country or Ally?"

Standing steady on her right foot, her hands go to her hips. "Hutton, you can't give up. Your heart is not ready to."

I release her, hoping she doesn't start stalking Ally online, and lie back. "What about the rest of me?"

"You're going to be okay. I promise. Things will work out exactly how they're supposed to."

"Famous last words."

Sitting in a private room of an Italian restaurant, I'm bouncing my knee under the table as I finish off the bourbon, no ice to clink around the glass when I set it down.

"When are we going to eat, Huddy?"

Huddy . . . grrrr. Hearing the *d*'s instead of *t*'s raises my blood pressure. Add the *y* and I need another stiff drink. I shift my gaze to my left. The wrapping is so pretty, but the present is empty when it comes to Starla. It's the second time I've taken her out, but by how she's acting, you'd think we were a thing. *We're not.*

It may be rude, but I'm ready to go, and we haven't even ordered. "When is Bennett getting here?"

Ethan shakes his head. "He said in ten like thirty minutes ago."

Our youngest brother joined the company two months ago after moving from California. Since I started a new division off the parent company, Everest Enterprises has diversified into media. Bennett is leading the sales team to become a global provider of media entertainment.

He's got the Everest charismatic genes to seal the deal, and after spending time in Hollywood, he's using his knowledge and connections to our advantage. But the fucker is always late.

The door opens. I'm expecting the waiter, ready for a fresh drink, but my brother finally shows. "Thanks for gracing us with your presence, Benjamin." It's not his name, but Ethan and I use that name when we want to fuck with him.

A file hits the middle of the table, sending a breadbasket to topple over. "Read it and weep, fuckers."

When Ethan takes the folder, Starla points at the bread that's rolled onto the table. "Thank God he's here. I almost resorted to eating the carbs."

"You could. It would be okay."

"One piece of bread and I wouldn't fit in this dress. Don't you like me in this dress?"

I hate when grown women talk in a baby voice. I reach for my drink because I hadn't really noticed the dress if I'm honest. But then I see it's still empty. I'm definitely not good company for her. Rhett Matthews, the CFO, set me up with her. I never asked how he knew her, but I guess she had been asking him about me, and on a drunken night in Brooklyn, I asked her out.

The problem is, I need to be drunk to tolerate her company, and I only have myself to blame for the second date. Sure, she was texting me all the time, but I could have said no, like I did to having sex with her. Ever since . . . I'm careful to dance around the princess's name, the bar has been raised way higher than Starla can reach in her six-inch platforms.

We can't be more opposite. "It's a nice dress."

"See?" she preens proudly. "That's why I don't eat carbs."

Surprised by this tidbit, I ask, "What are you going to eat at an Italian restaurant?"

"Salad."

Ethan stands. "You did good, Bennett. This exclusive could put us on the map." His eyes dart to me, but then he hands the file back to Bennett. "You need to talk to him about this. It's his division."

Bennett has the same percentage of shares in the company as I do, but he gets the perks of not having to be the boss. I need to learn to negotiate better. All those times I argued with my dad like we were in court didn't pay off. I saw dollar signs and signed on the line.

My brother sits in the empty seat across from Starla. "Hey, how are you?"

Acting coy, which is something she's never been with me, she replies, "Great. How are you?"

I get it—nice packaging—but I want his attention on the news, not my date. I snap my fingers to get his attention. "What exclusive?"

Bennett replies, "We made the cut."

"For?"

"Exclusive and full coverage of the crowning."

It's like pulling teeth. "What crowning?"

With his eyes on Starla, he replies, "The Brudenbourg ceremony."

My vision sharpens, and I tilt my head to the side. *Did I just hear that right?* "What?"

Bennett finally turns to me. "When the princess becomes queen. The coronation."

None of this makes sense; a lot like it didn't the last time I was dealing with something involving Ally. *Damn it.* Her name slips off my tongue as if it's been lying in wait to fuck with me again. I hate the way my heart beats against my ribcage, and my throat feels thick when I think of her. It's fucked up that my palms sweat and my body heats thinking about her.

Why the fuck am I even bothering to pretend with Starla? This is not who I am. I take the file and stand to leave. "When is the coronation?"

"Not sure. There's no date set yet. The public relations firm who represents the family—"

"The family?"

"The royal family. They've requested the bids be submitted in two weeks."

"Two weeks?" I bark before I even know what I'm upset about. *I know.* I just refuse to acknowledge it in a room full of people.

Bennett adds, "In person." He shifts when the waiter comes in to top off the glasses and fill his wine glass. He takes a drink while Ethan smirks.

Fuckers.

Holding the file, I push through the door and leave.

7

Hutton

THIS FILE FEELS like the key I've been searching for, the key I need to unlock time and turn back the clock. *One more night.* Ally gave me one final night, but it will never be enough.

Other women don't come close to the life I'm living in my memories with her.

Shit. I almost forgot about Starla in the dining room . . . *What the fuck am I thinking bringing her here?* She practically mauled me the last time we went out, using that little girl voice that's a total turn off to try to turn me on.

After escaping by twisting and wriggling out of her hold, I made a fast exit. I need to get laid, but I'm not so desperate to overwrite Ally's and my last night together.

"Hut?"

I turn back to the sound of that voice. *Singer.* I know she's going to try to talk sense into a situation that makes none. I'm already shaking my head, not wanting to negotiate. "Singer, I just want to go home."

"I know you do," she says, putting herself between me and the door. "Talk to me."

"About the sky. It's blue." *Like Ally's eyes.* "My favorite coffee?" *Cappuccino, like her hair and something I started drinking since she left.* "Taco stands?" That's the last place I saw her, touched her, though not the way I wanted. "Work? I've been buried." I bury myself in the day for hours, so I'm too exhausted to think about Ally at night when I'm lying in bed alone.

She touches my shoulder. "You're one of the best men I know. I see so much of your brother in you. Admirable characteristics like your work ethic and drive, the kindness you've always shown not just me, but everyone you meet, and you have that whole bad boy thing going on like Ethan." She shrugs. "Bad boys sure are hard to resist, but you know that already."

"Ha. Ethan is more like a Boy Scout."

"To you, but he has a side to him with a sharp edge. I'd hate to cross it, but I sure do appreciate it."

"Did you come to talk to me about my brother?"

"No. Ally."

"I don't want to talk about her."

"That record's getting old. How about we try to change your tune?"

Moving off to the side behind the hostess stand, I say, "I appreciate everything you're saying and doing, Singer, but you can't fix this just because you want me happy. Life doesn't always work out the way we want; it works out how it's supposed to."

"It makes me sad that you're giving up."

"Giving up? I gave her everything I had to give. She doesn't want me, or can't be with me, and I finally recognize it. She's a fucking princess." My head is still blown over that. "She has responsibilities and obligations to her country.

Maybe that's why she's not calling me or contacting me in any way. So what do you want me to do?"

"Contact her."

"You have a heart of gold, Singer, but I tried to no avail. The phone has been disconnected. She's not returning my calls or texts. I can't force her to because I want her to."

Her excitement evaporates, and she sighs. "I know. I just thought that maybe . . . I saw a difference in you. This girl affected you."

"She did, but she's also gone." Tapping the folder against my palm, I add, "I'll look at this opportunity with objectivity, so don't worry about the company, or this deal." I know what she's about to say, so I beat her to the punch. "Or me."

She smiles and then shoves my shoulder. "You know me well."

"I do."

Taking a step back, she says, "Stay and have dinner."

"I won't be good company."

"Don't stay for you, stay for us. Save us, Hut. Starla asked where we're spending Christmas. You can't just leave her here."

Chuckling, I wrap my arm around her shoulders. "C'mon, I'll save you, but you better save me too."

"Deal."

When we enter the room, Starla has a piece of lettuce on her fork poised to devour. Her hand lowers, and she says, "You're back?" as if I'm not welcome.

My gaze shifts to Bennett who shakes his head enough for me to notice, but not her. I say, "Yes, I just needed fresh air." I set the file down as I sit back in my chair. "Have we ordered?"

I drop the file on Ethan's desk the minute he sits behind it Friday morning. "This says we have to submit our bid in person."

"I know. I read the details last night. It's a pitch."

Resting the tips of my fingers on his desk, I lower myself to his level. "In. Person. Ethan."

His eyes narrow on mine. "I'm. Aware. Hutton."

Standing, I walk to the windows that span the wall and cross my arms over my chest. My voice may be calmer, but it's still firm when I say, "We need to withdraw our application."

"We're bidding."

"No." I turn back. "We're not. Not only is this crossing lines that are well beyond a personal conflict, but—"

"But that's all it's about when it comes to your argument." He comes around his desk and stands toe to toe with me. "This will be one of the biggest events of the year, and we have a young media company. This could bring the media division into the limelight and make us a fortune in licensee rights. As a financial analyst, you know I'm right."

If I take my personal feelings out of the situation, I can admit he's right. But I'm too stubborn for that. "We'll have more opportunities for big events. That studio we're building in Brooklyn will pay for itself."

The phone on his desk buzzes, but he ignores it. He does, however, move back around and sits again. "This is a global event, Hutton. I get that we're wading through tricky waters, but you can't let personal feelings get in the way of business."

"You did." *Shit.* I shouldn't have said that and regret it the moment it leaves my mouth. "I didn't mean—"

"Don't drag what happened to me into this." His hand goes up. "I lost my company, but I rebuilt my empire. This is about you avoiding anything to do with Ally. I get it. I spent time away from Singer and then wondered what the fuck I was doing. But you know what I did?"

"Took your private jet to win the girl back?"

That makes him laugh. "Yes, and you can use it too."

"I don't need it since I'm not going to Brudenbourg. Bennett will take the jet. He's the lead and will pitch the bid."

"Actually, I want to talk to you about that . . ."

I hate my brothers so fucking much. "How did I get talked into this?" I grumble.

"Lighten up, man. You're making me anxious from all the anxiety rolling off you."

Whipping my gaze away from the window and trying to set Bennett on fire with my glare, I ask, "Tell me why I have to go again?"

"You need to relax. I hear Brudenbourg is beautiful this time of year."

"Heard from who? I'd barely heard of the country before."

"Ethan."

"Great source," I reply sarcastically.

"Treat it like a vacation."

I run my hand through my hair, not relaxed at all. My knee is bouncing, and I drag my sweaty palms down the top of my jeans. "I can't."

"Ethan told me about the girl." The pause comes dramatically. I almost expect to hear dun dun dunnnn . . . but it doesn't come. "A princess, huh?"

"Yeah, so it seems."

"Any chance—"

"Nope. No chance of anything." The number of times I

have thought about her words. Had she hated only giving me some of the information? "*I have obligations . . . You're the fairy-tale ending I wish I could have . . . I want to tell you everything, but once I do, we'll never be the same . . . I love you and want you to be happy.*" She hadn't been free to offer anything, and I get that now.

I look out the window again, my mind running through all the memories I have with Ally as well as what it will be like to see her again. What will she say? What will she do? How will she react to seeing me again? Will she be happy or mad or . . . act like we were never together in the first place? "How much longer until we land?"

"We've only been in the air for thirty minutes. Buckle up, buttercup. We're in for the long haul."

"I was afraid you'd say that." I don't know what the future holds, so I recline and close my eyes, trying hard to hold on to my memories.

Seven hours later, I stretch my neck to one side and then the other. The luxury of a reclining seat on a private jet still isn't the same thing as the comfort of my bed. With my suit-case parked behind me, I look around until I spot him. I say to Bennett, "The driver is over there."

We head toward the man holding the sign for Everest Media Corp and follow him to the black SUV. The Cadillac Escalade is solid black with a matte black grill and rims. Getting a closer look when we approach, it's the sexiest SUV I've ever seen. The windows are tinted so dark I can't even see the driver, and the country's flags wave at the front. Bennett says, "That is a sweet ride."

"Custom Caddy. Damn. All money." It's even nicer inside. Maybe this trip won't be so bad. A quick in-and-out meeting and we'll never even have to see the woman who stole my heart.

I've wanted to pin my hurt on her shoulders, thinking

that I'm the only one suffering, but what if she's been as lonely and miserable as I have? *Is she happy?*

The ride to the hotel is smooth, and the scenery is incredible. The architecture is a cross between a Bavarian village and English manors. It's like time has stood still in Brudenbourg. Snowcapped mountains stand like guards along the distant border, and green pastures blanket the hillsides to the valleys below the winding roads of the lowlands as the vehicle climbs higher above sea level. Passing through small idyllic villages reminds me of the Christmas village my mom sets up at the holidays.

"Holy—" Bennett says, the word dragging.

"What? What is it?" I peer out his window, ducking until I see where he's already looking. "Is that a castle?" It's the stupidest question I think I've ever asked. On the highest peak of the tallest hill stands a grand gray stone castle watching over its country. Tall spires and turrets anchor the corners and a drawbridge is open like a mouth ready to feed. "It looks like it's straight out of the history books or a fairy tale."

The driver replies, "Brudenbourg Castle. Built in 1476. A fortress that stands as a symbol of our long history, sir."

"Is that where the royal family lives?" Bennett asks.

"No," the driver replies. "The Sutcliffes live there." He points to the other side of the SUV. Bennett and I turn to look out my window.

"Holy shit." My eyes dart to the rearview mirror, meeting the driver's wide with surprise eyes. "Sorry."

He chuckles. "No apology necessary, sir. It's quite impressive."

Bennett says, "More than quite. It's fucking huge."

Now the driver laughs. "That would be the Sutcliffe Palace. Construction started in 1755. Built in honor of the new Queen Sutcliffe born five years prior. It took twenty years to build and was ready the year she was crowned after the assassination of her mother."

"Vicious," Bennett says, sitting back.

"Barbaric, even for those times," the driver adds.

I watch as we get closer to the palace. "What's the name of the hotel, Ben?"

"I don't know. I wasn't given a final email with details. Just that we'd be picked up at the airport and taken to our quarters."

"Quarters?" My gaze darts back to the palace as we approach the long tree-lined gravel road leading toward the front of it. "Are we staying here?"

The driver responds, "I was told to drive you to the palace."

Ally. My heart starts beating hard in my chest. "Does the entire royal family live here?"

"Oh no. Some of them live elsewhere—other palaces and some even in the villages, depending on the title. They are all granted property."

I release a heavy sigh of relief, relaxing back into the soft leather. He adds, "Only the queen and her husband, the prince, and their children who are not yet married can live here."

Staring at him in the rearview mirror, I feel my heart begin to race again as all relief is wiped from my body. I'm not sure if I'm panicking because I might see Ally again or find out she's already married. I don't think she is, but I ask just in case. "Are any of their children married?"

"No, sir. Hutton," he tacks on my name with a friendly grin.

"Shit." There goes the quick in and out without seeing her. "All of them?"

"Prince Jakob stays in the Sutcliffe Village some nights, but Princess Marielle stays at the palace. And now that

Princess Arabelle has returned from her studies abroad, she resides at the palace full time."

Princess Arabelle . . . *Ally.*

Bennett taps my arm. "Don't worry. We'll close the deal, and then we're out."

I nod and turn back to the blue, white, and gold palace looming in front of us when the SUV comes to a stop.

In.

Close the deal.

Out.

Simple.

But it's not simple at all. There's no way I can come all this way and not see Ally. An armed guard in a blue and black suit opens the door. Right then, I realize I'm going to do everything in my power to see her again.

When we reach the top of the palace steps, a man in a suit with tails says, "Welcome to Brudenbourg."

8

Princess Arabelle Allyson Edwards Sutcliffe

"You're in such a mood, Belle. Why are you being so difficult?" My sister, dressed in a crinoline slip, flops with distaste onto my four-poster bed, messing up the pristinely neat covers and pillows.

Sitting at my vanity, I push the stem of a diamond earring into the hole of my ear. "I'm not being difficult. I just don't think we should have to humor a bunch of businessmen by sitting like dolls at a banquet where our opinions hold no weight. It's not like anyone's going to ask what we think. Let them make the decision as they usually do."

"Maybe they want our opinions now."

"If they did, we wouldn't be wearing evening gowns and told to look pretty for dinner. We'd be wearing business attire and sitting in an office."

She sits up, her light brown curls losing some of the bounce they had when she walked into my room. I never liked the ringlet look anyway. Reminds me of the gilded paintings hanging in the great room of our ancestors—old and dusty. *Archaic . . . like some of our traditions.* My younger sister is beautiful, but she needs to get with the times and stop listening to our mother so much. I'd do anything to see her in a pair of jeans. Her riding breeches are the closest I'll get her to casual unless I can get her out from under the watchful eye of our parents and the Brudenbourg press.

The press tried to ruin my reputation with the help of an unscrupulous ex-boyfriend. But I served my time overseas to let things settle as a favor to my parents and for my own sanity. But now I'm back, and with all that I had to give up to be here, no one will come between me and my right to the throne.

It's all I've been raised to believe—my right to be queen. I may have stepped out of line a few times, but beneath my rebellious streak, I intend to fulfill my destiny. From the economy to our tourism, I will elevate Brudenbourg's standing. I'll help those in need and abolish stupid laws that hold little bearing on today's society. Women won't be held down by restrictions put in place in the sixteenth century. I have so many plans and changes I want to make.

Hiding my struggles to be perfect as much as I can, I put on a smile, and say, "Yes, my grace," in an effort to follow my dreams.

I've watched the way my mother ruled, letting my father speak for her, but I won't be like that. They aren't equals in a partnership. She wears the crown, but he pulls the strings.

When I'm queen, I will decide everything, and when my Prince Charming comes along, he'll sit equal to me, and together, we will rule the queendom.

Of course, I still have to restrain that pesky wild side, because sometimes that side is more persuasive. *That* side that wants the freedom being a Sutcliffe will never afford. I must not let that side win. If that means dressing like we lived during the Renaissance, then I'll play my role. Look pretty.

Be quiet. Wait my turn to rule. *And then, I will make some changes.*

Angling to face her, I lower my voice. "What do you think about taking the train and skipping over to Luxum tomorrow to party?"

"Sneak out?"

I guess the bad girl in me isn't gone yet. "Yes, but we can catch the last train back to Sutcliffe."

As she pushes off the mattress, her slip falls back into place, covering her knees. She tugs at a twisted bra strap, and says, "I thought when you came back, you'd be more, I don't know, all grown-up. More adult-like. Acting your age."

"I'm not a grown-up because I want a night away from the palace, a night without the worries of who I'm supposed to be marrying, a night to be me instead of a princess who is supposed to reside in a tall tower waiting for her knight in shining armor to rescue her? Is that what you mean by adult? If it is," I say, sighing, "I'll never fit the mold of that expectation."

"It's not your past that's holding you back. It's your future. Your decisions affect how you're perceived, and more importantly, how you're treated."

I spin back around but eye her in the reflection of the mirror. "For a twenty-three-year-old, you sure do act like a granny." I swipe setting powder over my face and wait to hear the door close, wanting to be alone.

But I also know her well enough to know that she may be prim and definitely overly proper, but she has a bite when pushed. "Screw you."

I laugh. "Vicious, sis."

Huffing, she sets her hands on her hips, digging her fingertips into the skin. "I can be young and fun."

With my lipstick in hand, I lift my gaze to meet the irritation clear in her eyes. "Prove it." Giving my attention to my lips, I slowly glide the creamy red over my bottom lip, waiting to push her just hard enough to rebel.

As I start on my top lip, she says, "I don't have to prove anything to you. You've been bad news since the day you were born. You're just trying to drag me down with you." *Bite.* I still wait . . . knowing she'll give in if for no other reason than to win. She hates that I'm the firstborn, ruining her chance to reign. But most of all, she hates losing. "What time?"

I don't bother looking back. There's no point in making nice when the fish is hanging from your line. This is not a cut bait situation. This is a whale I'm reeling in, so I continue to play it cool. "I was thinking we'd catch the eight twenty."

Setting my lipstick in the tray, I reach for my perfume and spritz my neck, chest, and wrists. Not a day goes by that I don't do this simple act and think of Hutton. But it's not this act that makes me think of him. I wake up hoping to be in his arms. I close my eyes at night, missing the sound of his slumber. I touch myself, hoping to recapture the same high he gave me.

I can't.

So my frustration grows. The wild nature I was supposed to get out of my system in America is budding deep inside. I feel it. The ache is scratching my insides, growing impatient and needy. A casual affair won't satisfy it; the thought of being with anyone else the way I was only ever with him hurts my soul. I miss him.

So much so that my throat tightens and I reach up, wrapping my hand around my neck. I suck in a harsh breath and then another before trying to soothe my yearning heart.

"Why do you do that?"

My sister's voice brings me back to the reality I'm stuck in the middle of, the nightmare that I'll never love as I once did. "What?" I play it off like nothing is out of the ordinary.

It's not for me, but I see the concern from others when I let my sadness get the better of me. I brush the curls, not wanting them so big, but to fall softly like they used to in Texas.

"You don't have to talk to me, Belle, but if you ever want to, I won't tell anyone. I promise."

That's the sister I know, the bond strong. "I'm fine, but I'll let you know if I ever do."

She nods, well aware I'm not going to share today. "I should get dressed. We have to be downstairs in less than an hour."

"I'll see you down there."

"Pretty and quiet as a mouse," she says, repeating what we were raised hearing every day of our lives.

All wrong.

All wrong for queens in training.

I'll never tell my daughter to be anything less than extraordinary. She'll voice her opinions loudly to make sure everyone hears her loud and clear, and I'll teach her that looks may be an asset for some she encounters, but intelligence is valued by all.

Standing up, I run my hands over the curves of my waist. I work out hard to look good, but I won't be silenced when it comes to standing on equal ground in business or my personal life.

In the closet, I know what I'm supposed to wear. The black dress is long, just past my ankles when on, and fitted with dainty straps of diamonds. I inspect it closer, wondering if they're real. My mother never wears fake anything, and she did give me the dress. Even though it's pretty, I just don't feel like wearing black tonight.

I pull a red dress from the formal dress section of my closet. I've only worn it once, and I loved how it made me feel—powerful—with all eyes on me. Although I didn't crave the attention, it was a great introduction to the world at twenty-one when everyone else was wearing white.

Of course, this dress is part of the reason I got bad press. It was too scandalous for high society, especially of the royal kind, when tradition dictates the future queen is to wear white when she reaches the age of reign. In Brudenbourg, that age is twenty-one. If anything happens to my mother, God forbid, my reign will begin.

I'm about to slip on the red dress, but I stop. This is a business dinner. I want to be taken seriously and don't need the scandal of pissing off my parents tonight or the lecture later. I return the red dress to the closet and put on the black dress, step into sparkling heels that match the straps, and check my appearance from head to toe one last time before heading downstairs.

Taking the back stairs, I wind through the hall on the second floor and then slip through a door to one more hidden staircase used by the staff that leads directly to the kitchen prep area. Everyone stops, but I quickly wave them off. It's only me. I don't want to interrupt. Pushing through the swinging door, the kitchen is warm, so I can't stay long, but I want to say hello to Birgit and Gerhart.

I find them busy in front of the stove. Flames flicker as curse words in German pepper the air. They weren't born in Brudenbourg, but the couple accepted chef positions here after attending Cordon Bleu in France and working their way through Michelin-starred restaurants. I'm not sure who the Chef de Cuisine and the Sous Chef is between them, but they are true partners, even if they do annoy each other some nights. This kitchen gets heated from their arguments as often as it does from the food.

It's an amazing place to spend time, and I have wiled away many hours learning how to cook as well as how to love. I blame them for my wilder ways. They are the best and the worst of influences.

Keeping the prep table between us, I never get in their way when they're creating their delicious masterpieces. "Good evening."

Birgit turns to spy me over her shoulder. With red rosy cheeks from the heat and a bright smile, she asks, "Arabelle, you're looking so lovely. How are you doing?"

"I'm good. Tame tonight," I reply with our inside joke. It never mattered what they heard about me, they only saw the good. Knowing I had their support gave me the strength to be true to myself.

Gerhart chuckles. "That's a shame."

"Eh, I'm plotting good times ahead. I just have to survive tonight. What are you creating?" They trained me young to see food as an experiment for the taste buds. So they don't make, they create.

"Prime rib was requested by your father. The rest is up to us. We have a few surprises—fresh apples from the orchard for the most divinely tasting dressing with the tail end of the summer crisp lettuces from the village. Marinated cherries in brandy over molten chocolate cake. Oh, and your mother has requested a fish option."

"That does sound amazing." Rubbing my hand over my grumbling stomach, I remember I only had fruit for lunch. "I'm starving."

"You should join the others. It's too hot in here for your pretty hair to withstand, and your cheeks are turning pink. Hurry along. The sooner everyone arrives, we can serve the meal."

"I'll see you tomorrow?"

Birgit smiles with pride at me as if I'm one of her own brood. They have one son, Gregor. When I was younger, he was so friendly and treated Marielle and me with care not generally shown of boys his age.

We took the horses out once and got caught in a rainstorm. He tied his own horse to a tree and rode as fast as he could to return Marielle to the palace safely.

Now he runs the stables. I haven't seen him in a few weeks since I've been buried beneath expectations and acclimating back into our society.

Birgit says, "Stop by around two o'clock on Sunday if you want to learn about bread. It's been a few years, but if I recall correctly, that's where we left off before you left for the States."

"I will. Have a great night." I grab a baby carrot and escape into the butler's prep area before they have a chance to protest, but Gerhart still does. I can hear him all the way out here, which makes me laugh.

I'd rather spend the evening in the hot kitchen with them than entertaining business guests. I sigh, ready for this night to be over.

Princess Arabelle

"Boo!" My sister pops around the corner, startling me.

I gasp, curses sucked in with the alarmed breath I take. "Good lord, Marielle. Are you trying to scare the bejesus out of me?"

"Some things never change. Why do you always wait in here before parties?" Even in the dim light, I can see the sparkle of the tiara on her head.

I hear the low murmur of conversation from the formal living room echoing into the dark and vacant staff space. The bustling kitchen and butler's room on one side, then the dinner guests across the entry hall greeting each other with polite conversation. "I was visiting with Birgit and Gerhart."

Her head tilts just as her eyes roll. "Why do you still do that when you've been told not to?"

I pull her around the corner so nobody spots us. I'm not ready to face the guests yet. "Why do you not? They're amazing people if you'd give them a chance."

"I'm sure they are, but we're not supposed to be in the kitchen. You know the rules."

"The rules can fuck themselves."

"Belle! You have not changed one bit. I actually think you've gotten worse."

"Well, get used to it because I'm not changing anytime soon. What are you doing here anyway?"

She leans her shoulder against the dark wallpaper that's been here at least a century, maybe more. It's tattered in places, but I like the imperfections. I just wish it wasn't so dark and dreary. "Mother's looking for you."

"Why?" She taps her tiara, her eyebrow going up as if it's obvious. I huff. "For real?"

"I know you refuse to act like a princess, but heaven forbid you look like one."

My mother's shadow reaches the room before she does. Her disappointment is clear, though it's hidden in her darkened silhouette. The chandelier hanging high above could light up the village, but its golden glow never reaches this room. "There you are, Arabelle." She moves into the shadows with us and pats Marielle with her free hand. "Join the guests. They have all arrived."

Marielle goes quickly and in silence, demure as a mouse. Makes me want to scream if only to see my mother's reaction. I don't, though. My mother is an amazing queen when she wants to be. But I've never felt she would have applied for the job if she'd had the choice.

When we're alone, she holds up a tiara. "This was your grandmother's. I thought with all these lovely baguettes surrounding the teardrop black diamond in the center, it would complement the dress."

I used to admire my mother's crown the most. It's delicate jeweling and pretty blue stones. I would sneak into the vault when her stylist would venture in to pick her jewelry.

She would catch me and let me stay as long as she did. "It is. It's very beautiful. I've never worn it before."

"I thought it was time we started treating you like the future queen you'll be. I wore the same tiara at twenty-five. There are three others that I can show you as well as teach you the history of each and the meaning behind them."

"I'd like that. As for tonight, I thought this was just a business meeting? A meal to get to know the guests better so you could decide who will cover the coronation?"

"There is not 'just a business meeting' when it comes to giving outsiders access to our private world. This will be an agreement that will span the coronation as well as coverage of your wedding and the first introduction of your children to the rest of the world. It's an association we would like to build once and maintain for your lifetime. So you see, dear Arabelle, it's not just a meeting, but a relationship forming."

I underestimated the pace of my ceremonial rise. Talk of weddings and children twists my gut while my mind only thinks of one man. My lips tingle with our last kisses, my body aching for his touch once more. That last night had been incredibly wonderful but stupid on my part. I'd felt selfish asking so much from him, especially when I understood that he truly wanted more with me. Yet how could I leave without saying goodbye? Without feeling his touch once more?

I'd only canceled our weekend together because of the pressure of returning home, and how I didn't want to grow any closer to him than I already had. But then I had to see him one last time. Had to be kissed and loved by him. *Something to cling to during the lonely nights.* Seeing his beautiful face when I told him I loved him? *Forlorn and heartbroken?* That nearly tore me in two. *How unkind of fate to provide me a man to love that I can never have?* And now all I'll have are memories.

My mother sets the tiara on my head and secures it with two clips to my hair. "Keep your shoulders straight, your chin up, and the tiara should remain level on top of your head."

I do as she says because I'm not always the rebel and I do have a role to play. My mother's beauty rivals Grace Kelly's, and I've been told I resemble her. It's a compliment I've always held on to. No matter what happens, I'm protected by name and looks from the worst of the attacks.

But also, she's my mom, and growing up, I wanted to be just like her. I just didn't realize that came with the title of queen.

She slips out of the room as quietly as she entered with the expectation for me to follow. I don't keep her waiting. When she walks into the living room with the guests, I pause, though, allowing them to greet the queen so I can enter without so much pomp.

I sneak a glass of champagne from a passing tray and finish it before stepping into the doorway. It doesn't take more than a second for my heart to start beating again as it once did.

How?

I haven't felt a rush like this in so long, too long, and it's all from the sight of a man I never thought I'd see again.

It must be an illusion?
My mind playing tricks on me?
Champagne gone to my head?
How can it be him?

And of all people he's talking to—he's having a laugh with the man I'm supposed to marry.

My breath catches as I watch Hutton Everest own the room with all eyes on him. He's wearing a tailored white dinner jacket over black pants, and James Bond doesn't hold a candle to this man in a tux. His warm and inviting eyes find me across the heads of the other guests, and a slow smile works across his mouth like the one I remember seeing in the moonlight slipping inside the hotel room.

Seeing him again makes me wonder how I ever had the willpower to leave, much less stay away. I feel the slide of the jewels on my head, so I adjust my tiara and tilt my chin up. The bad girl wants to come out and play.

My arm is caught just as I take two big strides toward him. "Oh no, you don't," Margie says, shaking her head.

My best friend knows all my secrets, including Hutton since she was in Austin with me. "Did you see who's here?"

"I did, and you're to pretend you don't."

"What? Why?"

Angling us back toward the hall, she says, "Because your parents will flip out if they know you . . ." She stops and looks over my shoulder.

"Don't worry. The coast is clear."

Margie coughs, then whispers, "You know *that* will disqualify you from ascending to the crown."

The decree to end all others. The most powerful law in our land in this day and age. It's the only decree that can officially remove me from taking my rightful place on the throne. Effective only toward the queen—we must be pure virginal white on our wedding night—or we lose all our rights.

I whisper, "But we'll never tell, and just speaking with him won't give that away."

"But your body language will." *How am I supposed to suppress how my body reacts to this sexy and endearing man?* She adjusts my crown. "Look at you already crumpling over his presence. You must stand tall, Belle. Don't let anyone know."

She's right. I swallow down the happiness that I'd started

feeling and put on the mask of the royal I'm supposed to be. "I'll be fine."

"He's here with his brother."

"Why? Why are they here?"

She says, "His company is one of the contenders for the media deal."

As I glance back at him over my shoulder, his eyes find mine again so easily like he always did in a crowded and loud bar back when we seemed like a good idea. Temporary, but always so good.

"That makes no sense. He's in finance and works for his father in Houston."

She eyes him, her expression souring. "Not anymore."

I know it's only to protect me, but I do wish she liked him. I guarded my time with him from her. She was a gray cloud on a sunny day trying to dampen my parade. I've been known to speak before I think, but the last few years I've learned to hold my tongue, to keep secrets. All because she never approved.

It's not gone unnoticed how happy she's been since we've been back. I can't help but wonder if she'll turn on me again now that he's here through business or fate, now that he's back in my life.

"Don't do anything you shouldn't and the night will go smoothly."

I practically majored in doing things I shouldn't, so tonight will be a test. It was never easy with her guarding my legacy like a pit bull, but I was never clearheaded around him. Something about that man makes me lose my better senses. A lot like seeing him wearing that tux is doing.

I turn back to Margie. "Do I look okay?"

"Like a queen."

It's something she's always said to me since we were little. "You look pretty."

Smiling, she does a little curtsy for me. "Why, thank you, my queen."

"Those are treasonous words."

"Then don't tell your mother."

We giggle just as the guests are summoned to dinner.

As much as I want to run into his arms like I did that last morning in Austin, I restrain myself and walk with Margie to the dining room near the kitchen. It's where smaller gatherings dine, and since tonight we only have twenty guests, the more intimate of rooms was chosen.

The gentlemen wait while the queen and my father, the prince, take their seats, and then stand by while the rest of the royal family finds their place cards. It's always a mystery who I'll be stuck talking to for the evening. My mom loves a good mix up of people to liven the conversations. I get it, but it's easy for her to sit at the head and preside than to be in the thick of it.

I find my card next and look left and then right, disappointed not to find the name I want placed on either side of me. I wait until the two men arrive at their seats. Mr. Bixby, an Englishman, pulls out my seat for me while Mr. Yamagata from California waits politely until I'm tucked between them.

When I look up, I'm face to face with Margie, who is great, but the dinner guest to her left is whom I'm most pleased to see.

Hutton greets me with a smile. "Princess."

"Mr. Everest."

"I didn't know you knew my name."

"You're very memorable."

"I wouldn't have thought so."

Fine. I deserve that dig, but it's still not going to stop me from savoring every minute of this dinner. Food being the last thing on my mind. I point at his place card. "Actually, your name is on the back."

"Ah. And here I thought you knew me."

"I guess not."

"Pity."

"Is it? We have tonight to get to know each other better."

I almost forget that there's a world of people around us. I've always been so caught up in him that it's easy to forget. I wish it were just us again. *Privately.* My gaze dips to his hands, and I'm reminded of the deliciously sinful ways he uses them on me, in me, all over me.

A half-smile is better than nothing, but it's the devious glint in his eyes that has my body humming. He says, "Here's to getting to know each other better."

"My apologies. I don't have wine to cheers to that toast."

"I'll take your word for it."

Why does he have to be so gorgeous and so utterly maddening? "I'm good for my word. Good as gold."

"I suspected as much." His shoulders drop as he relaxes.

Mr. Bixby says, "Chin-chin to all of us getting to know you better, Princess Arabelle."

My wine glass is filled, so I reach for it and tap it against his glass and then to Mr. Yamagata's before I turn to Hutton. "I gave you my word, but I still owe you a proper toast." Our glasses come together across the large table, and our eyes stay fixed on each other.

Glaring at me from three seats down and across, Marielle says, "I hope you're not going to monopolize Mr. Everest's attention all night, sister. I would like to socialize without yelling to include the entire table of guests."

Jealousy spreads through my chest. "I wasn't monopolizing his time. I was simply becoming acquainted."

She touches his arm, says, "I have so many questions

about your business . . ." and continues to flirt with him over four courses.

By dessert, my favorite part of the meal, I've lost my appetite.

I stare at them, not hearing anything Bixby or Yamagata has said to me. My blinders are on, my full focus on the man sitting catty-corner. Margie's kicked the toe of my shoes twice, but even that couldn't rally a reminder of the role of the joyous and charming princess I'm supposed to be playing. Instead, I've relegated myself to the expectations of my youth—pretty and quiet—as my heart sinks to the pit of my stomach.

Is his interest in her more than surface deep? Marielle doesn't have the same obligations that I have to the crown. She's held to entirely different standards. Is that something that Hutton finds attractive? Could his affections really transfer from me to her?

I take a deep breath, because I no longer have any claim on him, and that's heartbreaking.

My sister has never cared about business dinners or the people who attended them. *Until now.* Not only has she stolen Hutton's attention with talk of media coverage and ratings, but she's smiling at the man I love as though she could fall in love with him as well. If only my heart could behave like the poised and detached shell I'm portraying.

Not with him.

Never with him.

10

Hutton

FUCK.

I don't know how much more I can take of this torture.

She's so close.

But just out of reach.

Ally looks incredible. I can imagine taking that dress off her, the strapless bra she's hiding beneath the silky fabric that reveals the curve of her body my hands remember so well.

Shifting in my seat, I'm careful not to look at her for more than a few seconds, or I'll give my thoughts life and expose both of us.

I wonder if she's wearing a thong or lacy underpants, maybe even the pale pink cotton panties that used to drive me wild. Naked or dressed, she's always driven me crazy. I've never had a craving to be with a woman more than I do her. Feelings of possessiveness tighten my chest every time Bixby speaks to her, Yamagata smiles at her, or that asshole down at the other end of the table across from my brother calls her name as if he has some damn claim to her.

Fuck him.

The asshole needs to learn some fucking respect. She's not just a princess; she's the woman who holds my heart in her hands, and she makes it so damn hard to figure out if I want it back or I want her instead.

Her.

When I look up, her blue eyes are just as vibrant as ever. For a brief second, I think back on the photos I've seen online over the last month where there was no luster or life in them.

Did I bring the life back to her eyes, or is she acclimating into her fairy tale again? I hope it's the former, but I'm pretty sure it's the latter.

After dinner, we're led to another fancy gilded room with a roaring fire in a fireplace large enough to fit my kitchen island. I guess that's all they had to stay warm back in the day. It's still hard for me to wrap my head around the fact that I'm in a palace in the middle of Europe and my ex-girl —*my Ally*—is a princess standing ten feet from me.

Bennett brings me a drink, though I have no idea where the bar is. He says, "Dinner was interesting."

"Very."

"Did you close the deal?"

"I couldn't get time alone with her."

He scrunches his face. "I meant the media deal, not your ex."

Ex. I hate that fucking term.

She's my now.

She's my next.

She's my always.

Damn it. "Don't worry. I talked about the company all night to Marielle."

"I saw you scored the princesses at your end. I met their brother, Jakob. He's taking us out tomorrow night. Seems like a cool guy, plus I think he's part of the team making the actual final decision."

Sipping my drink, I look across the room at my princess with the crooked tiara. I like that she's not perfect in appearance, though I find her perfect for me. The only problem is so do half the men here. You would think this dinner is to find a suitor instead of a business deal. But maybe with royal families, that's one and the same.

"I was talking to Tracey Learnings at dinner. She's based out of London and said Bixby seems unassuming, but he's a shark in sales. I think she was trying to intimidate us. She doesn't understand that as Everests we don't give up, and we definitely don't back away from a challenge."

My gaze keeps gravitating to Ally, wishing she'd come talk to me. Bennett points in her direction with his glass in hand. "That guy with your girl is an asshole."

"She's not my girl. And he's most definitely an asshole. What company is he with? I want to fucking take 'em down."

"He's not with a company."

"Who is he then?" When he doesn't answer, I ask, "Bennett?"

Hemming and hawing, he shuffles around looking more uncomfortable than I've ever seen him. "Look, Hut, you were right. It's probably best if you and Ally don't try to work things out. She left, and she had her reasons."

"That's not what I said, and what reasons are those?"

He turns his back to the room and lowers his voice. "He says he's with Princess Arabelle. That they're engaged, but it hasn't been announced."

A punch to the gut would have been less of a blow. "That guy? The asshole?" I turn to look at them again. Nothing in her body language suggests they're together, much less getting married. "What the fuck?"

"I know. I tried to get more details, but Tracey wanted to talk business, so I let her run most of the show." Nudging my shoulder, he adds, "But don't forget, Jakob's introducing us to the local party scene tomorrow night. We can get the deets then."

"Does anyone still say deets?"

"I do," he replies unapologetically.

"That's fair."

Giving the beauty my full attention, I stare at her—red lips, long dress, heels I'd tell her to leave on. Her hair is longer than before, and there's not a tangle in sight. When my gaze shifts to the asshole, I try to see him in a new light, but I can't. He still looks like the same drunken jerk yelling across the table at her, but this time, he's pawing at her.

Fuck that.

I start for them, but Bennett grabs my arm. "Hey."

"What?"

"Don't blow the deal." My brother is a lot like me. He likes to have a good time and a lot of laughs, but when he's focused, he's serious. Right now, he's serious.

Standing there, I take the time to look around, noticing another pair of eyes latched on me. Ally's roommate, Margie, didn't like me in Austin, and she sure as shit doesn't seem to like me any better in Brudenbourg. Her lips are curled into a snarl, and her arms are crossed over her chest.

Maybe she's hot for me.

"I won't blow it."

I cut across the room and see Ally's eyes go wide as she peeks over the asshole's shoulder. "Hello again," I say, not giving one shit about what this guy thinks.

Ally smiles, though I can tell she tries not to. "Hello again," she says, setting that gorgeous smile free for the whole world to see.

Moving around to include me in the group, she asks,

"Have you met the Duke of Wenig, a small southern province off our east coast?"

"Wenig means little. We like to say our province might be little, but it's mighty. Wenig at one time was the first line of defense in protecting our small country, so we're a proud folk."

Duke? *What-the-fuck-ever.* "Everest. Like the," *fucking,* "mountain. Hutton Everest." We shake hands, but I make sure he knows who the alpha is in this pack.

"Another American," he says in some haughty accent. "The Sutcliffes have taken a liking to the States, it seems. I was just telling the princess that she lost the Bruden accent. Her short time away seemed to bulldoze right over our traditional pronunciations of our English speaking words."

"*Al*—Princess Arabelle has a lovely accent. I agree that she could have hidden in plain sight in the States by the way she spoke. But hearing her tonight, my ears can pick up the delicate lilt at the end of certain words, much like the British."

"All hope is not lost then, now is it? Duke Richard Vaughn, but you can call me Dick."

Asshole. "Dick." *Whatever.* They both work the same.

"So I hear you've had a spot of trouble recently in America. Has that been sorted?"

"Huh? I'm not sure what you're referring to."

"The lawsuit. The company. The model and the drugs."

Wow. What a fucking tool. "Actually, I wasn't involved in that situation. It was a dirty mess. My brother was dragged through the mud—"

"And the press from what I read," he says, squeezing her cheek. "Much like my little Arabelle here."

I'm a quarter second from popping this douche when Ally turns her head, and says, "I'm full from dinner and would like to rest. I'm going to retire for the night."

Douche Dick says, "Would you like me to walk with you?"

"To my room?" Her voice scales up two octaves. "No." Seeming to catch herself, in a calmer voice she adds, "I'll be fine."

I step forward, though I know I shouldn't. My body connected to hers as if she never left that hotel room. "I was hoping to speak to you, Princess Arabelle."

Dick says, "You can call her secretary, right, Arabelle? But I'm not sure regarding what you would need to speak with her. I'll be part of the committee that decides on the winning bid after much review."

I want to throw out my plea to give me five minutes, but I can tell it won't work tonight. The Dick of Wenig—I mean Duke—is an obstacle to be dealt with. The man is completely annoying, but more so, disrespectful to Ally. Looking at her, I'm bewildered. How does she put up with him? How can I get time alone with her?

The dick gets sidetracked by the queen. Bumping Ally's arm, he says, "See you tomorrow," as he dashes across the room.

Ally asks, "Will you walk with me, Mr. Everest? It's not far, but we can talk."

Holding my elbow out for her, she takes hold of me, the current that has always connected us set on fire again. "A few minutes isn't enough," I whisper as we stroll toward the hall.

She smiles at Mr. Yamagata, bringing one to his face as well. "It's all we have." She looks at me as if the act itself was done on a dare. "I can't believe you're here."

"I never thought I'd see you again."

"But you knew. You must have known you were coming to Brudenbourg, and that I was here."

"I did. I read plenty of articles online. I knew where you

were. I just wanted you to be the one who wanted to see me again."

We reach the hallway, and there's nowhere left for us to go, just like before. "Can we take a walk outside?"

"I can't have the other guests or my parents seeing us leave together."

"Not even for a walk?"

She looks back at the party. Dick is chuckling it up with Bixby and his business partner, Tracey. Her parents seemed to be making the rounds to say good night. Bennett is with Marielle, and Margie is still scowling at me.

The other guests have either retired already or are deep in conversation near the fire. I add, "No one is watching us."

"My parents and Marielle are. She seemed quite taken with you at dinner."

"Are you jealous?"

"Yes."

"Good. So am I. Want to tell me about Little Dick?"

"What about him?"

I almost laugh that she instantly knows who I'm referring to. "He told Bennett that he's your fiancé."

"What?"

Her parents look our way when her voice echoes through the expansive space. Unfortunately, that brings them our way. Ally and I go quiet, but her mother says, "I hope you enjoyed dinner and had a lovely evening, Mr. Everest."

"I did." I nod my head to bow like I was shown. "Thank you for the evening meal and for having me here in the palace. It's an incredible place."

"I call it home," she says. Turning toward her daughter, she mouths, "Chin up," before adding, "We're going to retire to our quarters. Will you be staying, Arabelle?"

"I was going to show Mr. Everest how to get to his wing

of the palace. As you know, it can be quite confusing to an outsider."

"Yes, it can. If you need more assistance, make sure to call one of the butlers. They're here to make your stay more pleasant as well as run the home, so please don't hesitate to contact them if you need anything. There's a button on the phone in your room if you do."

"Thank you again."

"You're very welcome, Mr. Everest," her father says with a voice bordering on hoarse. We shake hands before he nods and takes his wife's hand.

As soon as they head toward the elevator, Ally looks at me. "Guess I have my parents' permission. Come on. I'll show around the house."

As I look around, this is not like any place I ever called a house before, but I finally have time alone with her again. "I can't wait."

11

Princess Arabelle

IN FRONT of the last door at the end of the west wing on the second floor, I stop. "This is your room."

"How did you know that?" he asks, his voice much more seductive when we're alone. Or maybe it's always that way, but I'm starting to fall under his spell again. God, those lips. I want to kiss them, and I want them to kiss me, and—"Ally?"

I let my gaze slide above those full lips that I've sucked on and look right into the eyes that frequent my dreams. "Yes," I reply, my throat dry and my breath coming less easy.

"How did you know this was my room?"

"You told me your room is white with blue pillows."

"And you knew which room it was based on that?"

I nod. "I have them all memorized. This was our playground, our hide-and-go-seek wonderland. The winters are cold, and when we weren't allowed outside, we played inside. Each room has a different color scheme, and your room is one of my favorites, decorated in yellow. I used to sneak off and sleep in there. The most beautiful sunrises can be seen through those windows."

"Did you know I was coming?"

"No." I hold out my hand. "Key please."

He hands it to me, and I unlock the room, wanting to see it again. He remains outside the door and looks back down the hall. "Is this allowed? I'm not going to be beheaded, am I?"

"Don't be silly. We haven't done that in thirty years."

"What?"

"The look of horror on your face was worth the joke." I roll my eyes and wave him inside. "We never believed in death as punishment, but then again, we aren't a country of high crime, so I don't think it was ever necessary."

There's a hesitation to his steps, discomfort as if he's breaking an unspoken rule. "It's okay. No one will see us. We can even leave the door open if you don't want to be alone with me. I understand."

With distance still between us, he says, "You don't understand. I'm not afraid of being caught with you. I'm afraid of being alone with you."

"Why?" I hate the way my voice betrays me, dipping into seduction from one word spoken. I have no control around him. He stimulates my mind and tempts my body with ease. He doesn't treat me like a doll that is easily broken or like a woman here for his pleasure. My pleasure *is* his pleasure, and his pleasure is mine.

He would never choose a pretty face over insightful conversation. But most of all, he would never expect me to be quiet.

Hutton looks out the door as if debating, but when he turns back to me, his mind is made up. "That last night together in Austin was the first time I realized what you meant to me. It had been so simple to keep things casual when we were living in different cities, but when I saw you, I knew what I wanted."

"You wanted me?"

"I still do, Ally."

The name warms me like a wool blanket in winter. "I missed that name. I missed you saying it. I missed so much." I laugh lightly, looking down, almost embarrassed by my silly confession. Almost. But he never makes me feel awkward or uncomfortable sharing my feelings. I peek back up, and his interest is set in the depths of his soulful eyes.

"Then why did you leave suddenly? Why are we here pretending we don't know each other better than anyone else?"

"I'll be queen one day, and I can't rule my own country from Austin, Texas."

"I understand that, but what I don't understand is why you didn't tell me."

"I wasn't allowed." I turn away from him, not wanting his eyes dissecting my lies. I can't tell him I was escaping a past of my own doing, and that I almost lost my chance at the throne because of my bad decisions. I can't tell him that loving him would hurt me in the end. I can't put that burden on him to carry. So I'll carry it instead. "It's complicated, Hutton."

When I turn around, he shoves his hands in his pockets, looking drop-dead debonair in his tuxedo. "Clearly, but that doesn't answer the question."

"It's late. I should go before the rumors start."

"Let them—"

"No. I've traveled that route before. I'll take the less scenic way this time." I move to pass him, but he reaches out, catching me by the waist. I'm slow to allow myself this last look to indulge, but weak to this man, I do and angle my chin up. The tiara begins to slip, but he catches it. "You wouldn't want to lose that."

"What's a few jewels when I've lost so much more already?"

"Speaking in riddles won't get us anywhere but lost again."

"That's where I'm best when it comes to you." I take a step just out of his reach but turn back, and whisper, "No one can know about us."

"What happens if they find out?"

His tone isn't bitter, but more curious. "I lose everything." I walk to the door and take the knob in hand. Just before I close it, I add, "Good night, Hutton."

"Good night, Ally."

I take the cozy name and shut his door, and then carry it in my heart all the way to my room on the third floor. By the time I'm climbing in bed, my mind is whirling with thoughts of tonight, my heart both full and confused, and my belly hungry. Watching my sister and Hutton hit it off like a house on fire at dinner caused me to lose my appetite, so I'm actually starving.

Tossing and turning for more than two hours leaves me depleted, so I take matters into my own hands. I flip the covers off and slip on sleep shorts before I grab my Crow Brothers T-shirt to wear downstairs since I'm traveling down memory lane already. I take the back stairs and halls, tiptoeing in bare feet, boxer shorts, and my shirt with no bra. My hair is twisted on top of my head and my face free of makeup.

I don't worry about seeing anyone or running into the staff. Everyone's been asleep for at least an hour. Slipping into the kitchen, I'm met by the light of one of the refrigerators and a dark silhouette rummaging through the food inside. "Hello?"

When he leans back, I recognize that body—broad shoulders, carved biceps made of steel, hair that is short enough to look professional but long enough to mess up during sex. *And that ass . . .*

I could write poetry about Hutton Everest's ass.

As a matter of fact, I have.

Roses are red.

Violets are blue.

I want to bite his ass and squeeze it too.

I didn't say it was good poetry. Just an *ode to* sort of thing.

"Is that you, Ally?"

As much as it pains me to say, I have to. "You need to stop calling me that."

He sets a block of cheese and a jar of mustard on the steel countertop and grabs a knife from the butcher block. His lack of response has my reactions going into overdrive. I know he heard me, but he pulls a cutting board from the stack in the corner as though he didn't. As he digs the knife into the cheese, he pauses and looks my way. "I like it."

Deep.

Husky.

His voice fits the night and the sneaking around we're both doing. The dulcet tones strike straight to my core. I grip the counter, the cold metal steeling my shaken willpower. "I'm a princess, and one day, I'll be queen." I hate how whiny I sound as if my saying it makes it real for him. It doesn't. I'm still Ally from Austin in his eyes. The thought makes me smile, but I can't, or he'll never see me for who I am now. "Acknowledging my title is a sign of respect."

"Respect is an interesting word, isn't it? One could argue that you didn't respect what we had. Someone else, maybe yourself, could argue that you respected me enough to let me go. So respect seems to be relative to the person using the term. What do you think?" The blade of the knife hits the cutting board with a thud.

What do I think? "I think this is too deep for one thirty in the morning."

"Let's go with something less philosophical. Mustard or mayo? I don't know which one you prefer. Weird, right?"

"Mustard."

"A girl after my own heart."

Hutton's made himself at home, working around the kitchen with such comfort and helping himself as if he owns the place. To my annoyance, it also comforts me. He's so sure of himself, so utterly sexy and cocky Hutton. *Grrr* . . . Seeing him make sandwiches shirtless has me after something, but at this moment, it's not his heart. "Are one of those sandwiches for me?"

His eyes find mine through the moonlight, and a smirk appears. Damn him. He never did play fair. He uses everything he's got to get what he wants. I'm just not sure if it's that sandwich or me he's vying for, though. I move to his side and pull the bread from the sealed container. He takes a bread knife and slices the loaf, then lays the pieces on the board. Like a pastry chef, he leans over his creation, spooning the mustard on the four slices.

He's so close that I'm warmed from the heat emanating off him. I move against him, the side of my chest pressed to his arm and then rest my cheek against his bicep. Hutton stills and stays. "What are you doing, princess?"

I know he's not calling me by my title but how he called me by the nickname he used to use. His rebellious ways speak to me on such a personal level that I lose my train of thought. "I don't know."

That rogue smile appears again, but this time, he turns my way, putting the slightest of distances between our bodies. "At dinner, all I wanted was to ask you a million questions just to hear your voice speaking only to me again. Despite the answers, I would have taken the hit to have your undivided attention. When you were in my room, all I wanted to do was kiss you. I felt you near before I saw you here. Do you know how hard it is not to touch you? Not to bend you over this surface and do what I've been craving for months?"

Breathless, I ask, "Months?"

"Months. Tell me, Ally. Tell me you can't let go of me like I haven't been able to let go of you." He's so much stronger than I am. His emotions come on the wings of a confession, but his body stays just far enough away from mine to make me miss his heat.

"What do you want me to say, Hutton? Because what I want and what I can tell you aren't the same things." I look down, my heart hurting. "I can't be with you."

"Why?"

Raising my eyes along with my chin, I reply, "I've told you. I'll lose everything. This country and the throne are rightfully mine. What do you want me to do? Toss that away like it means nothing."

"So you'll toss me away instead? *Princess*?" The difference in his usage is apparent as his defenses go up. He puts cheese on one of the sandwiches and then tops it with bread.

"You don't want me to answer." And I don't want to say the words either. I've craved his touch, his kisses, lying in his arms in the early morning hours when the rest of the world is sleeping. Being so close to him now, feeling the coarse hairs rub against my skin, is breaking my heart. I need to be stronger than this . . . *and he deserves a better answer than I can give him. He deserves not to be taunted because I can't give him anything.*

"You're right. I want a sandwich, and then I'm going to bed. The meetings should only take a few days. I appreciate the hospitality your country has shown me." With his eyes staring into mine, he takes a bite of the sandwich, and with a full mouth, I'm sure just to bother me, he says, "Good night, princess," and walks into the dark.

The swinging door is the only sound heard, and I turn, resting my palms on the metal counter, hoping it can cool me down. When I look down, I see his creation. I read what is written in mustard on one piece of bread, "We once said," and then read the other, "I love you."

We did, and I meant those words.

I'm not allowed to mean them anymore, but as much as I want to deny tasting the words on my tongue, I can't suppress the feelings I have for him inside.

"Oh, Hutton." I sigh, then slap cheese on the bread and take a bite of the sandwich, forever hiding the truth inside.

12

Hutton

"Relax," Bennett says, at ease in a burgundy leather wingback.

Sitting in a matching chair across from him, I lean forward to stop my knee from bouncing by resting my forearms on my legs. "Bixby and Tracey. What are we dealing with?"

He looks over at the pair across the library from us. They've been whispering frantically for the past hour while staring at a laptop.

"They'll be cut first."

"Why do you say that?"

Shrugging, he says, "Hunch."

I shake my head and then rub my temples. I didn't sleep well, though it's not the bed's fault. That mattress was amazing and the pillows comfortable. My mind kept me up, my body itching to find Ally making me restless. I finally stopped the tossing and turning torture and went for a run around the palace grounds.

The fog was thick, but the ground dry. The crunch under my sneakers was the only sound I heard for four miles. I ran hard, wanting to dampen the memories. I ran fast, needing to escape my traitorous heart. I ran as far as I could just to feel my heartbeat for any reason other than the sleeping beauty behind me.

With exhaustion filling my muscles, I ask, "Are you ready for round one?"

"I'm always ready."

He is too. Bennett's a machine. It doesn't matter if he parties late or works overtime, he's always the first to rally. It's time to be on top of my game. I was requested to attend this submission process to back the groundwork laid by my brother. Being the numbers guy, they didn't want to waste time going over irrelevant details of Everest Enterprises. My proposal is solid. My brother's pitch is spot-on. We're prepared for this meeting.

But we still have to sit out here and wait. While Bennett scrolls on the screen of his phone, I stand in front of the modern prose section of shelves. The library is impressive in size, but the collection of rare books far exceeds any I've ever seen or even heard about.

My left eye twitches when I find Shakespeare shelved here. "What the hell?"

"What is it?" Ben asks.

I should let it go, but I'm tempted to move them. Then again, the classic literature of Shakespeare wasn't considered classic back then. Of course, his talent wasn't recognized at the time either, making these dusty editions more confusing than ever. I almost pick one up to check which edition this is, but that's going too far, so I take my seat again. "Nothing. Let's go over the presentation."

Thirty minutes later, Mr. Yamagata and his assistant leave

the library across the hall with big smiles on their face. He seems like a confident man in general, but his expression is almost celebratory.

Shit.

A petite, gray-haired woman with square heels and pointed glasses stands at the entrance to the library tapping the eraser end of a pencil on a clipboard. I feel like I'm back in school, and I'm being called into the principal's office.

We stand, and I follow Bennett into the meeting room. He's the lead, but I'm his point person.

"I can't say much, but I liked what you said today." Jakob Sutcliffe isn't anything like what I would think a prince would be like. He's looking back at us from the passenger seat of one of their badass SUVs.

Bennett asks, "Is this armored?"

"Bullet and explosion proof. Of course, if something tries to blow up the vehicle, you have other concerns on your hands."

I bring us back to the meeting. "Do you think we'll make it to the next round, or are you taking us out because you feel sorry we were already cut?"

Jakob laughs. "You weren't cut. We really did like the package plan you put together. Yours is the only one fully customizable. The other bids were specific but had no flexibility. I think you have a good shot of winning this bid."

I pat his shoulder. "Good news."

He adds, "We'll celebrate Everest Media moving to the next round."

Bennett says, "Yeah, we will. So tell us, anything we need to know before meeting women here?"

"No," he replies, "nothing different from when I was in Los Angeles."

Bennett's interest is piqued, and he sits up. "You were in LA? I lived there for a few years."

"I studied at Pepperdine."

"Damn, that's a prime location."

"Yeah. It was nice. Those California girls will get you in trouble, though."

We laugh, but it hits home with Bennett. "Ain't that the truth."

Jakob says, "Video surfaced of me skinny-dipping in the ocean my tenth year of school. My ass is brighter than the moon at night, so I was quickly identified. My parents weren't amused. My sister was vocal when the media tried to release the footage, or as she called it to tease me, the *ass-age*, and it was suppressed."

"Princess Arabelle or Marielle?" I ask, suddenly with a vested interest.

"Belle. She gets a bad rap, but she's got a good heart."

Ally with a bad rap? That doesn't make sense. "A bad rap for what?"

"She's very . . ." He pauses, then says, "Strong-willed."

"Feisty," I mumble, getting a clearer picture of the woman I know and the princess he's talking about.

Looking at me curiously, he says, "Yes. Precisely."

"Yeah." I look out the window and see tiny lanterns lighting the cobbled streets. I know she is firsthand. She's torn between duty to her country and duty to her heart. They don't mix. "I heard your sister went to the University of Texas in Austin. Bennett and I both went there too. Small world."

The SUV pulls over, and Jakob hops out. When we get out, he says, "The pub's up here."

"You can just walk around without security?"

He shrugs. "Most of the time. We're a small country and half of it's family."

"And the other half?" Bennett asks.

"Tourists. We get some of the hottest women in Europe visiting our shores. There won't be a lack of females tonight. They outnumber us."

"Why is that?"

Gripping my shoulder, he asks, "Haven't you heard, Hutton?"

"Guess not."

"Women rule here. We've only had one king. King Sutcliffe. He had five daughters and refused to give up the kingdom he worked so hard to establish to a man who would change the name and take over."

I must have missed that tidbit. Knowing there's a queen is one thing, but realizing the reason behind it is a whole other thing. "Fascinating."

We reach a door that looks more like it leads to a dungeon than a pub. Pulling it open, Jakob continues as we walk inside, "He decreed only women rule in Brudenbourg. So the firstborn daughter always ascends to the throne." Nodding at the bartender, he apparently hangs out here enough to know the important people.

"Probably wise."

Jakob laughs. "Probably. With hearts of lions, women are still the fairer sex in looks and in measure."

Sitting around a square table off to the side near a dartboard, Bennett asks, "What happens if she only has sons?"

"It falls to the next female in line for the throne. A sister. A cousin. An aunt. Who knows really? It's never happened."

"Amazing. So if Princess Arabelle chose a different path—"

"She won't," he answers casually as if this is common knowledge. "She was born and bred for this life. She only rebels because there's a restless fire inside her. Once she's crowned, she'll settle down."

I like that fire inside her. I'd hate to see it extinguished. "What do you mean?"

He says, "Texas was Belle's get out of Dodge card. Although she could get into the business program on her own merits, my parents pulled strings since it was past the deadline. She was here on a Friday and there by Sunday."

"Why?"

"Several things, but mainly it was decided she needed an image makeover. The people of Brudenbourg love her because they feel like she's one of them. She fucked up a few times. Dated cads. Drank too much. Partied too hard."

"Don't we all?"

"Not when you're the future queen."

I have so many questions, but two pitchers arrive with three pint glasses and an eyeful of cleavage that, by the looks of it, wants to bust free from the green ruffled shirt squeezing them. Since she's bending over me, I try to be polite and not look, but the waitress is proud and brushes her tits on my shoulder. "Can I get ye anything else?"

"We're good," I reply, keeping my eyes forward. Her tits come to rest against me as she leans down and says, "Jakob Sutcliffe brought me the delicious meats tonight. Don't go gettin' too drunk, all right, handsome?"

Wow. "I think we should order another round now."

My back is whacked. "He's funny too."

Jakob is laughing, but Bennett has his eyes on her ass as she walks away. Jakob says, "Sabine Rosalie is fucking fine, but her daddy has a shotgun longer than my leg that he rigged into a four barrel."

"I can see why," Bennett says. "She is . . . wow."

I add, "And friendly. *Very* friendly."

My brother can't seem to put his eyes back in their sockets, though he manages to form a complete question. "Are all Bruden women that hot? Your sisters sure are."

I half expect Jakob to throw a punch. The guys I know back home are protective over their little sisters. Jakob just drinks his beer. When he sets it down, he says, "I'm afraid so, and stay away from my sisters." He gets up, and says, "I'll be back."

Bennett laughs a little too hard. "Too late."

As soon as he's gone, a grin I recognize as trouble slides into place. "What did you do?" When he keeps grinning like the cat who ate the canary, it dawns on me. "You didn't. Tell me you didn't, Ben."

"I didn't."

I exhale, relieved. "Keep your distance from Marielle, or we could lose this whole deal."

"Look at her, though, Hut. She sure is fine." He adds, "One little make-out sesh won't harm anything."

"The fuck it won't," I say, running my hand through my hair. "Stay away from her. Don't fuck this up for us."

"Why are you griping at me? You're the one banging his other sister."

"I'm not banging her; that's why I have a case of royal blue balls, fucker. He doesn't know about Ally and me nor will he."

"No wonder you've been so fucking uptight lately. You've lost your sense of humor, and you have no patience. The doctor prescribes a night of fucking to ease the pain."

"Haven't you ever cared about anyone? What about . . ." I snap my fingers as I try to recall her name. "What's her face? You brought over for the Super Bowl."

"Ashley? She was crazy. Like fucking psycho crazy. I once woke up to her trimming my toenails and storing them in a jar that had nails in it, and she talked to me in this baby voice. What a fucking dick softener that is."

Starla comes to mind. "I hate that, too."

"The baby voice disturbs you more than the creepy toenail collection?"

Chuckling, I correct, "Both behaviors send me running."

"Thought so. So I know you're all wound up about Belle—"

"Ally."

"Whatever, dude. But that Sabine Rosalie." He whistles and plucks the front of his shirt. "She's a looker, and for some odd reason, she seems partial to you. So it seems to me that you're caught between Sabine Rosalie and a hard place. Why don't you find a soft place to land for the night? I spy two very large soft spots coming our way now."

Sabine Rosalie drops another pitcher on the table and pours the remainder of the first into the second while pressing against me. "You're Americans?"

"We are," I reply, looking at the full pitcher of beer.

"Like movie stars. Are you staying at the palace with Jakob or in Luxum tonight?"

Bennett asks, "What do you recommend, Sabine Rosalie?"

She takes the empty seat next to me and rests her chin on the palm of her hand. Batting her eyelashes, she says, "I know a cozy place just down the road from here. What's your name, handsome?"

"Hutton?"

Shit. Of all the times I hear my name roll off her tongue, it has to be when another woman is flirting with me? *Fuck.*

Sabine Rosalie pops up from the seat and curtsies. "Princess."

Ally nods once, but says, "Sabine Rosalie. Long time, no see."

"Yes, ma'am." With tension flaring, she bounces out as

soon as she stands. There's definitely a story given the chill between them.

I start at the heels that highlight Ally's toned calves and work my way up, slowly taking in every inch and enjoying the journey over her bare legs. Up higher, I'm met with a very short dark blue suede skirt. *Fuck me.* Last night was torture to my cock when she was in the kitchen in those boxer shorts, but this? It's almost too much. Talk about kicking a man when he's down. She hits hard and looks so good doing it.

A fitted white T-shirt gives a sneak peek of a lacy bra underneath. Makes me curious if it matches her panties.

Her hands are on her hips, and I remember another time she stood like that. The biggest difference between then and now? Clothes.

It's not gone unnoticed that she's looking better than the last time I saw her in Austin. She may carry new burdens, but her body is incredible. I stand, letting my gaze glide up her body to appreciate those curves I love to trace . . . with my tongue. "Princess." See? I can play along.

The daggers in her eyes disappear as the heat from her anger cools. "What are you doing here?"

Jakob shows back up. "I brought them. What are you two doing here?"

"Girls' night."

Jakob's mouth drops open. "Is that—"

"Marielle," Ally replies with a proud grin. "I finally got her in a pair of jeans."

Standing, Jakob says, "I don't think it's a good idea to have her here, Belle." He walks around her and heads straight for his younger sister.

"What's wrong with jeans?" I ask, watching Marielle argue with her brother.

Ally looks back but shows no real concern. "We're

supposed to dress demurely," she mumbles. "Screw the rules. At least for tonight."

She's too fucking hot for demure. "Because of the whole royal family thing?"

"Pretty much," she says, taking the chair that Sabine Rosalie briefly occupied. "Hey, Bennett."

"Hey, Al."

My mouth falls open as I sit down. "How come he gets to call you that? What happened to the whole princess respect thing?"

"I loosen up under the influence of a good stout."

She sets her almost empty glass of dark beer on the table, and says, "Want to buy me another?"

"Sure thing," I snap. "Bennett."

He rolls his eyes and grumbles, "Fine," but still heads for the bar.

With only a few minutes alone, I decide to take her in. She's different here. Mixed up. Hard to read. Completely vexing.

She's not dressed quite like how she used to in Austin, but it's miles away from the black-tie affair from last night. "I hear you're the rebel of the family. How does that work if you're going to be queen one day?"

"I sneak out occasionally to have a few beers."

"You used to drink vodka."

"I usually do, but tonight felt like a beer night." She finishes off the liquid and sets the glass down with an air of cockiness. "If you get to ask a question, I do."

"Go for it. You know me," I announce, raising my arms wide. "Open book."

Leaning forward, I catch her eyes lingering on my mouth. She does that a lot. I lick them just to tease her. Her lips part just enough to take an audible breath, and then she looks me in the eyes. "You said you're here for business. That means you didn't come for me."

I'm pretty sure there's a question in there, but the sadness that tears into her words rips into my heart, making it pound in my chest. "You ended us and left me piecing together the puzzle of what we were and what we never could be. You left me no options."

"It's best you let me go. I had dreaded that goodbye for months. I didn't want to hurt you, yet I did anyway."

"That's why you didn't come and stay with me in Houston?"

She nods. "Distance was supposed to help you forget about me, but then you came to Austin, and I knew I had to see you again. I'm a very selfish person, and you paid the price for that."

I touch her leg. I'm not sure what the rules are—here in this country regarding her or the ones between us—but I'm willing to break them, just as she is. "You're not selfish. I think you've spent a lot of time denying what we had was real, or that it was nothing more than sex, but it was. We were. We still are." If we were anywhere else, I'd kiss her. "I should have come after you."

"I can't blame you." She smiles softly. "I told you not to."

"I should have listened to my gut instead of the words you were saying. I know you were trying to spare me the trouble, but I thought you were done with me."

"That's just it, Hutton. I've tried, but I don't think I'll ever be done with you." Her gaze falls to the floor, sinking like the edges of her shoulders. "I beg of you to please be done with me."

"I can give you anything but that."

When she looks back up, it's as if she's seeing a new me, not the version that almost broke. As if she's reassuring herself, she says, "I'm going to be queen."

"What does that mean for us?"

"My destiny was determined the day I was born. I never thought you'd come here."

"I'm here."

"I don't know what to say. I just know that we can never be."

13

Hutton

WHEN ALLY SAID we can never be, I'm guessing by how handsy she was with me, she means starting tomorrow.

Signals are not just mixed.

They're completely scrambled.

A table for four turned into two tables for eight and then three tables for twelve until the whole pub was drunk and sharing pitchers all on Everest Media. Bennett and I had become the most popular people in town. Who knew all it took were a few rounds of beer?

We did.

Even though I had no intention of getting Ally and her siblings drunk, it's been a positive side effect. For me. She's relaxed and covertly touching every chance she gets, tempting me to take her into the bathroom and lock the door for an hour. Well, an hour might be my ego speaking because I never could last long with her.

Laughter fills the place as fiddlers and a guitarist enliven it even more with music. "I feel like I'm caught in the middle of Hansel and Gretel."

"It's like a fairy tale here." Her smile fades too fast, though, and she looks at our hands touching on the bench between us. Her pinky lifts and rests on top of mine. It's the littlest of acts, not one that anyone else would notice, but I know what she's doing.

I lean over, and whisper, "I miss you."

She nods but remains quiet, letting inhibitions she never had in Austin creep in. Why does she hold back? Where's the spirited woman I know her to be? I want to pressure her into saying those three words again in hopes of hearing another three right after. But we're in a public place, so I know I'm living in my own fairy tale if I expect more from her.

Jakob calls from the other side of the bar, "Hey, Everest?"

Bennett's been missing for a bit, so I guess that's me. "What's up?"

"Now that you've been to a proper Bruden bar, what do you think?"

"I like this place."

Another guy shouts with a thick accent, "Come on. We don't care about the pub. Share your latest conquest of the female variety." Holding his hands in front of his chest, he adds, "And tell us if everything's bigger in Texas like we hear."

I could go with my standard answer of my package, but I'm not in college anymore, and I don't need to impress this guy. I just nod, letting the comment pass as the crowd gets lost in their own circles again while laughter rings through the small place. But then I hear Ally ask, "How have you been?"

Seeing those sky-blue eyes on me again gives me a strength that was starting to weaken. It's such a personal question to ask in the middle of a public setting, but I get it.

It's safe here. No matter how personal we get verbally, physically we're still countries apart. I say, "The morning you left plays on repeat in my head. Every day. All day long." *While I slept the air has become stale—her scent fading too fast—the warmth she brought gone, leaving the room cold. I pull the covers down and finally face reality. Ally Edwards is gone.*

"Hutton . . ." Her head falls forward as her pain sneaks out, and her eyes dip closed. "I'm sorry."

"Look at me." When she does, I say, "You don't have to apologize for hiding this side of your life. I just wish you wouldn't have let me fall so far, knowing you were leaving."

"I was selfish. With you, I was selfish."

Honesty is seen in her eyes and heard in her tone, but we shouldn't get this heavy when we've been drinking, so I rub her leg. Tears sparkle in her eyes, tempting me to kiss her pain away. "Why are you crying? This is what you wanted, right?"

Her hand slips under mine, and our fingers fold together. "Because I still . . . love you. I don't know how to turn that off, but I can't have you and Brudenbourg. I want my cake and to be able to eat it too."

I could crack a joke about that, but this is the most real we've been with each other since she left, so I hold the jokes and hold her to the fire. "Why can't you?"

"Because no one can know about us."

"What's the big deal? Will your parents not approve?" I can't believe I just asked that as if I'm a fucking teenager. At thirty-one, I never thought parent approval would be an obstacle keeping me from the woman I love.

There's not enough time to tell her how empty my life has been without her—not being able to text her during the day, the loss of our long-distance calls at night, the weekends she used to fill now so lonely. With this trip soon coming to an end, I can't waste the time we do have together.

I decide to spill my feelings onto the splintering wood table before us. "It doesn't matter what I say, you have an automatic response. This situation, like us, is unique. I hear what you keep telling me. I understand you want to be queen one day. That's incredible. So much so that I can't even wrap my head around your reality. But here's the thing. I don't have to wrap my head around it. I just have to support you and what you want, but where does that leave me and what I want?"

With her guard down, I can see the sympathy in her eyes. "What do you want, Hutton?"

"It's simple. I want to be with you. *Again*." I put my hand up to stop her from repeating her canned response. "I know we can't be, but that doesn't mean I don't want it, that I don't want you. I guess I'm a fool for feeling so much for you all this time when you had already closed off the option for us."

I'm not sure what this woman has done to me. I suddenly sound as pathetic as I feel. Fuck this. I start to stand, but her hand tightens around mine, her plea creating a line between her brows I've never seen. "Hutton, please." I sit back down and wait to hear what she has to say as if I've waited my whole life. She says, "It's not been like that at all for me. I've cried myself to sleep every night we've been apart. It's a reality I struggle to accept. You once asked me why I didn't show up for our weekend in Houston."

That she's still holding on to me so tightly makes me want to give her this chance to cleanse her soul of the sins she needs to free.

"If I had come—"

The cracking of wood ends the conversation abruptly. A chair is broken when two dudes start throwing punches. I jump up and lift Ally to her feet, standing to protect her from the chaos. "This way." I wrap myself around her, covering her from the flying glasses and anything else being thrown as the entire pub joins in the fight. When we reach the far wall, I use my body as a shield until we reach the door and I can get her out of here.

The quiet street and late hour stand in stark contrast to the bright light streaming through the open door as we hurry to a doorway and hide in the shadows. I press her against it, using my body to protect her from harm.

"You're my hero." Her arms come around my middle, and she holds me from behind. She feels so good.

"Not a hero."

"You are to me."

"Where do we go?" I ask, turning around when it seems we're at a safe distance from the fighting.

She remains wrapped around me but now has her cheek against my chest. "Back six months, so I can tell you how I feel about you sooner." Looking up into my eyes, she says, "When I said I love you, I meant it. But—"

"But when you said you can't be with me, you meant that too."

Ally nods, her gorgeous face grief-stricken under the confirmation. I hate seeing her in pain, especially if I'm the cause of it even if it is at my expense. Caressing her soft cheek, I say, "We don't have a future, but we have tonight."

"Do we?"

"That's up to you, princess."

Her arms tighten around me. All the signs I used to notice when I knew she wanted more than she was getting, more than she could voice she wanted, are bubbling to the surface.

Heavier breath, causing her chest to push against mine.

Lips licked and bitten with such an innocence that we never were.

Pupils widening, the lighter blue being taken over by darker thoughts.

Hands that slide under my clothes without hesitation, journeying to their final destination without a road map.

"If you're offering . . ." she starts. Words are spoken standing on the cliffs of breathlessness. "I want tonight."

My lips are on hers like time will turn to ash if I don't. If our relationship is doomed to go up in flames, we might as well be the ones who start the fire. There's no slow when it comes to us. We were never into foreplay because we'd rather fuck instead.

We were flames to ashes in a flash.

My jeans constrain my cock, which is hard as a fucking rock. Holding this woman again, kissing her, thinking about the possibility of being with her again doesn't just sober me, but energizes every part of my body.

I press my body to hers in the corner of this closed shoe shop. Her fingers tangle into my hair, pulling me closer. Keeping her mouth against mine, she whispers, "I want you so much. I missed this connection, your touch, the feel of your body controlling mine."

Control.

Her body is mine to play, to tweak, to bend to my will and elicit the perfect pitch of an orgasm. She's my playground, my fever, my every wild day tamed from my lion ways. I don't pace the cage when she's near. Bars can't keep us apart, only her obligations.

Closing my eyes, I take in her soft floral scent as I kiss the delicate curve of her neck. Her lips at my ear urge me for more, her murmurs little kitten purrs. Her hands lower from my back to my ass as one diverts to rub the front of my pants. "Careful," I warn, my restraint not as strong as the denim of my jeans which is currently cutting off circulation.

"Or what?" *There she is. There's my spitfire.*

I pull back to let the light from the lamp across the street brighten the dark corner we're in. "Or we're going to be fucking right here."

Her eyes are fixed on mine. "Would that be so bad?"

"You're a very naughty princess."

Her tongue dips out and wets the corner of her mouth. "I may not want to own it, but I earned my reputation."

Shaking my head. "I don't think so, but you're about to." I'm about to turn her around and tell her to hold the wall, but Bennett's obnoxious whistle fills the air. It's a call into the night we always used to use to find each other in our party days. "We need to go."

"What? No," she says, desperation manipulating her fingers to fist my shirt and hold me in place.

A chuckle escapes, echoing along with the sirens arriving on the scene down the street. I take her hand and kiss her wrist. "We're going to leave, but I'm not leaving you tonight." I run my hand into her hair and hold her head so her eyes stay on mine. "Not until I've tasted every part of you, inside and out."

"We can't—"

"We can, and we will, because I see how you look at me, how you want me. I feel how you touch me. You gave me no choice before, but now that I'm here, I'm not walking away without a fight, because no matter what I thought you meant in Austin, I'll never be done with you either," I reply, dropping to my knees before her. "My princess."

14

Hutton

With every fiber of my being, I was absolutely sure of one thing. I was not walking away. Ally means everything to me. But before telling her I'd accept us living in two different cities, two countries worlds away, if that means we can see each other fairly regularly, I need to take inventory of the situation.

I'll start by finding out what's under that little skirt of hers. *The tease.*

Sitting in the back of the SUV, I ask, "You dressed like that for someone else?"

"I dressed in what made me feel like me again."

"You look like the woman I know."

"I feel like Ally, and I haven't felt like her in a long time."

I run my hand over her bare thigh, teasing just under the hem of her skirt. "You're gorgeous as ever."

Her hand covers mine and encourages me to go farther. "Touch me," she whispers.

With my palm pressed between her thighs, I say, "I am. How far do you want to go?"

"Make me come, Hutton." Looking at Marielle and Bennett chatting in the middle row and then at Jakob in the passenger seat up front with our driver from the other day, everyone seems occupied. Laughter and stories about the end of the bar fight bring an excitement to the small space.

Ally brings excitement to our small space. I reach a finger out and touch the softness between her legs. She spreads her legs enough to let the largeness of my hand in.

Warm.

Wet.

Welcoming.

I get the answer to my earlier quandary. Her panties aren't lace to match her bra because she's not wearing any at all. *Fuck.*

Leaning toward her, I make sure she gives me her complete attention when I say, "I'm going to make you feel so good, baby."

"You always did."

"Remember that, Belle?" Jakob calls from the front. "Crazy night."

We weren't listening, so she wings it. "Yeah, crazy night. Hey, turn up the music. I love this song."

He continues chatting with the driver, continuing a story about his youth. When the music gets louder, I make my move. "Sit back. Just a little and keep your eyes on me. When I say something, I want you to acknowledge me like we're talking."

Capturing her hand, I kiss the underside of her wrist.

Surveying the scene ahead while I lower her hand to her lap and bump my hand between her thighs. "Open for me." I return to that warm place that begs to be touched, to be loved, sucked if I could without being busted, and fucked even if we were.

As I swipe roughly through her soft lips, curls that weren't there before tickle my fingers. She takes a quiet breath and then releases it, but it comes out as a soft moan. I catch her gaze and silently mouth for her to be quiet.

"I'm going to fuck you with my fingers until you come all over my hand. Does that sound good to you?" I whisper so she can hear me, but the words stay between us, sounding like casual conversation to the rest of the passengers.

"More than good."

My pride sneaks out, my girl making me smile. She can't hide her wild side from me just as I can't hide mine from her. She's the one that brings it out in me. I toy with her, working her up, and get her wetter until she's starting to squirm. It's not the best angle for me, but it's fucking hot, so I'm not stopping. *I can hear how wet she is even over the music.*

I could probably fuck her right here, judging by how she's looking at me. Her lids are heavy, a sex-induced glassy gaze settling in as she leans back to give me more of herself.

She said I disrespected her, but that was nothing compared to what I'm about to do to her. I plunge in, going as deep as I can with one finger. A deliciously sweet moan I would normally steal from her tongue is exhaled, so I quickly cover her mouth and warn, "You must be quiet, Princess, and don't move. Or do you want them to know their future queen is being finger fucked in the back of this SUV?"

Her eyes snap to mine. "Twenty minutes left, and I haven't come yet."

I glance out the window as we pass through another village. The challenge doesn't intimidate me. I've had her on her knees begging for more in less time. Her pussy's tight, and a caveman sense of ownership grows inside my chest. I slip in another finger and start slower this time, letting her adjust and stretch.

Those sweet ruby lips part, and her eyelids momentarily dip closed. One of her hands starts to grip me over my jeans, but I move it. My dick is solid steel, and that's going to be hard enough to hide, so I don't want to add a cum spot that I can't disguise. Never one to listen, her fingers weave through my hair, her nails scraping lightly over my scalp before she returns it to my leg.

I'm not worried about the time we have left; I just want to get her off to remind her how good we are together. To bring her release. I thrust and swirl, using my thumb to dote on her clit. Her chest heaves, and her mouth hangs open.

She hikes her skirt to her hips and takes my fingers and squeezes before releasing for another round.

"How do I feel inside you again?" A jagged breath replaces an answer I'm going to demand of her even if she struggles to come back down from this high again. "Use your words, Ally."

"Like you should have never left." She pushes down, her body begging for more. "God, I'm so close. I need you to go faster."

"No. I've waited too long to rush this. I'm going to enjoy every second."

"Please, Hutton."

"Take what you want. Take it, baby. I'll give it to you. All you have to do is take what you need."

"I need you."

Fuck me. I want to kiss her to take all of her like she wants me to, like I need to, but I'm reminded we're not alone and we're not supposed to be doing this when Bennett pops open a bottle of beer and looks back. "Want a beer, Hut?"

"No." My death glare is enough for him to glance at Ally who's stiff with my fingers still inside her.

He would only have to look down to see everything, but he gets the wordless message. Marielle starts to say something to her sister, but he sidetracks her by touching her hair. She snaps, "What are you doing?" and pulls back, her eyes wide as she stares at him.

"You had a leaf in your hair," he replies, winging it; something my brother is very good at doing. Their conversation takes the heat off us, and I start moving my hand again.

Within seconds, her hands are holding mine, and her body is clenching around me. Her exhales come as restrained rough breaths, and her body releases the sins she's kept pent-up. "Hutton," comes with her body as she closes her eyes.

My heart pounds, and my cock throbs for relief, but I steady my body, staying still while she works her way through a universe of sensations.

When her body begins to loosen, her eyes opening as her tense muscles relax, I slowly pull out and watch as those castle walls she built while we were apart start to crumble. Brick and mortar can't keep me from invading her heart. Neither can distance nor tradition.

I bring my fingers to my mouth and suck them clean of her nectar. I'm not going down without a fight because the forbidden fruit always tastes the sweetest.

She tugs her skirt down, not giving me the satisfaction of boosting my ego or stroking my pride with a smile of satiation. She doesn't have to. My ego is not that fragile, and I don't need her to tell me what I saw or what I see in her eyes now. The fire between us still burns brightly. Hers needs to be fanned and stoked the right way, so she'll try to find a way for us to be together.

That's a job I was made for. Anyway, I told her to take what she needs, and she did. There's nothing sexier than a woman who knows how to get herself off other than one who gets me off. It's not my turn right now, but I know she won't leave me hanging.

Her sister turns around, and says, "How are we sneaking in?"

"The kitchen," Ally replies flatly.

When Marielle turns back, I watch Ally. I sense her anger as she stares out the window. Trying to bring her back to me, to feeling good again, I touch her hand. "Hey, look at me." When she does, I say, "You're amazing."

"I don't feel amazing." Her gaze goes to our hands barely touching between us. "I feel terrible."

"I'm that good, huh?"

It's small, but I'll take the smile she gives me. Looking at me again, she says, "I want to be with you freely, to touch you, and to make you feel like you make me feel."

"How is that?"

"Like my sins don't matter."

"What have you done that's so bad?"

"Broke the rules. I've been paying for it ever since, so I can't step out of line again. I can't have a hair out of place. I have to marry who they tell me to. This role is what I've been groomed to fill. It's all I know."

My hand hasn't dried from being coated in her pleasure before I'm hit with anger at why we can't be together again. "So that's it then? After I just told you how I feel about you, Ally?"

"You can't call me that . . . if someone overhears—"

"I don't give a fuck if someone hears."

"I do."

The SUV pulls to a stop at the back of the palace. The doors open, and she starts to slide across the same leather I had her squirming on moments ago. I grab the same wrist that I kissed earlier. When she turns back, I say, "You sure didn't mind when I was fucking you with my fingers five minutes ago."

"I mind now."

"Why?"

"Because I'm Ally to you, but I have to prove myself to everyone else. Please don't push on a matter that barely affects you but can destroy me."

"Barely affects?" I can't believe it. "Two steps forward. Ten steps back. Wow, Princess Arabelle."

Our eyes stay locked in a standoff until I release her and let her go. I don't have to force anyone to be with me. "You'll make a fine queen."

"Why do I feel like that's not sincere?"

"Read between the lines, sweetheart. But if you need it spelled out—you have the cold heart and iron fist part down pat."

Being on two different pages, even if it is the same book, isn't doing either of us any favors. We both need a night to think about what this is between us and not only what's best for her, but for me. If there really is no hope for anything, can I really step back and let her go like she asked me to do?

I get out of the vehicle and join the group at the back entrance. Jakob opens the door, and we all file inside what appears to be a receiving area for parcels and food deliveries.

The group is quiet as we wind our way through several rooms and end up in the kitchen. Marielle says good night, but her eyes stay on Bennett as if having a private conversation the rest of us aren't privy to. Jakob tells Bennett and me to follow "Belle" the back way up the stairs, but fuck that.

I know my way back to my room, and I'm not fucking sneaking around to get to it. I'm not under house arrest. Let them scatter like rats so their parents don't catch them drunk and sneaking in from a night out. I'm taking the main stairs.

Jakob pushes through the far door, leaving the three of us

standing in the same place where I made sandwiches the other night.

Her expression falls, and the princess starts, "Hut—"

"Don't worry about your image. I have no intention of tarnishing it. What you said back there," I grit out, "message received. Loud and fucking clear."

Shoving the door, I walk through one room that leads me to the great entry hall. I can't think in this place. It's too big. I need to ruminate someplace where my thoughts can't float away so easily. The front door is to my right, tempting me to get the fuck out of this place. The stairs are to my left, calling me to bed.

I need to take my own advice and let things lie for tonight. Bed it is.

15

Princess Arabelle

HUTTON SEES RIGHT THROUGH ME.

He sees *me*.

No one else does.

I've put on a mask each morning so they see who they want me to be.

Tricks and games don't work on him. Not that I'm trying to play any, but he refuses to see me for anyone other than Ally. That mask falls the moment his warm browns find me, melting my cold heart.

He doesn't understand I can't be Ally, not even for him. She's not who I am anymore, no matter how good it feels to be free from the shackles wrapped around me as Arabelle.

I still feel like crap after he made me feel so good. I want to return the favor, not just for him but for me. I like pleasing him. I like the way he looks at me like I'm a good girl when I'm doing bad things.

The beat of my heart picks up while I work my way up the dark back staircase to the second floor. Cutting down the staff wing, no one will hear me. These are full front doors to apartments, not bedrooms. I round the corner and look across the long hall and then slide through the shadows of the mural of a family picnicking in a park. It's one of my favorites, but I don't stop to admire the details.

Instead, I find myself standing in front of the room I told him was the one where I spent many nights sleeping, mornings watching the sunrise, and hours hiding when I was supposed to be in finishing lessons. It's the reason I still can't seem to balance a crown on my head.

Should I knock?

He was mad. "*You have the cold heart and iron fist part down pat.*" I can't blame him for lashing out. If it doesn't all make sense to me, how would it make sense to him?

Should I go in?

We can talk.

Unsure what to do, I pause to decide if I should go in, but the wood-paneled door swings open, and I'm pulled inside, pinned to the wall, and kissed as if he'll never have the chance again. I understand the feeling, the desperation connecting us.

My lip is tugged and released when he pulls back in angry debate. His head lowers to mine until our temples align. "Why do you torture me?" His lips are quick to my ear. "I have you, and then I don't. I taste you, and then I'm left wanting more. It's never enough, and then you tell me we can't be together like I can walk away unscathed. Like I can somehow forget that this fire between us hasn't burned my soul to ashes already."

He's right. "So right," I whisper into the agony that I've caused. "We're not over as long as we hold on to each other." His pain becomes my own. His passion gives me strength. I knew the moment I saw him again, I couldn't walk away forever. *But what do I do? How do I keep him?*

My arms go around his neck as his body moves against me. The light switch stabs into my back, the pain worth this pleasure. Our teeth clash as he takes over my mouth, making me forget the apologies and niceties I owed him. Like every other time we're together, everything becomes about lust and desire, pleasure and release.

I tug the hem of his shirt up until his mouth releases mine, and he pulls it off along with mine. The lace covering my breasts is pulled down roughly, scraping against my nipples and sending a shiver up my spine. His lips are on me, sucking the skin of one breast as his fingers tease the nipple of the other, eliciting a moan that shoots straight up from my pelvis.

"I want you so much, so much . . ." My tone is only a ghost of my voice, want taking over as I hold his head, messing his hair. He made me feel so good in the SUV, even if we were constrained by the situation.

Paybacks are deliciously devilish.

Pushing him by the shoulders, I put distance between us. We pant, breathless as the intensity of lust links us through eye contact. I've never seen him look more carnal or animalistic as he begins to pace while watching me, ready to devour me, wanting me more than he knows how to feel, more than he knows how to control.

I feel the same. I'm just better at hiding it. Until I can't any longer. Moving to him, I press my hands flat against him, tracing my nails through the hair covering his chest. When he leans into me, I kiss him once on his chest over his heart and again on the other side. I say, "Stay right here."

"Okay."

As I kneel before him wearing my wedge heels and skirt, my breasts suspended over the cups of my bra, he pushes my hair away from my face. Our eyes meet as I work his belt and pants open.

Shoes come off.

Pants.

Underwear.

When he stands in front of me naked, I swallow from the sight of his erection. Built from kings, Hutton Everest has always lived up to his last name and exceeds it when it comes to his size. I start like he does, with no buildup or foreplay. I take him deep into my mouth and listen to the moans he can't hold in. Grabbing his ass, I pick up speed. Hearing his melody again makes my center tighten, my pussy wet, and causes me to tighten my lips around him. I can still picture how my red lipstick stained him, claimed him as mine, the last time I was on my knees to pleasure him.

His hand tightens around my hair, my body reacting—wet, hard, need—taking over. I love when he takes control. When he takes.

I love giving to him—me, my body, my power—and watching him fall apart from greed. Tonight is no different. It doesn't take long before his erection pulses, and I swallow every last drop he gives me.

I've needed this release—his is mine, and I take it happily. I've never felt so good being bad, so myself than when I'm with him. Freed from propriety's restraints, I bask in the euphoria.

He pulls my hair, and I suck in a deep breath while running my gaze languidly up his body until our eyes meet again. "My dirty little princess. Tell me you've only done that for me."

"Only you."

Taking me by the elbows, he lifts me to my feet. He pulls the cups of my bra up until the lace is covering me again and then caresses my cheek. Tilting closer, our lips almost touch, but he stops and says, "Such a good girl." His hand slides under my skirt to discover how wet I am for him. "You get off on satisfying me, don't you?"

"So much."

"Open your mouth." Bringing his fingers up, he holds them in front of me. "Taste how much you love pleasing me." He's about to touch my tongue but pulls back and licks me off him slowly, his gaze glued to mine. "I don't share you with anyone, not even you. You taste too good not to hoard all to myself."

Then he kisses me, and I realize he will share but on his terms. Licking my lips when ours part, he asks, "Shall we fuck?" My phone buzzes. "Ignore it," he says.

"No one texts me at midnight. It might be an emergency."

"Okay."

I'm released, a whoosh of cold air coming between us as he goes silently into the bathroom. I grab the phone from my back pocket and see a text from my sister: *Emergency.*

Me: *What's wrong?*

Marielle: *Where are you?*

I lie: *I was hungry. I came back to the kitchen.*

Marielle: *I need to talk.*

Me: *Right now? What's wrong?*

Marielle: *Not in text.*

I glance at the bathroom door, and the light slipping out from under it. *God, I want him.*

But my sister and I have become close since I've returned. Closer than we ever were before. I can't let her down now. I also can't tell her what I've been doing with Hutton.

Me: *Okay. I'll come to your room.*

Marielle: *I'm in your room. I'll wait. Please hurry.*

Me: *Be there in five.*

Tucking my phone into my back pocket, I walk to the closed door. "Hutton?" I whisper.

The light is turned off, and the door opens. "We're going to have to take advantage of that counter and mirror and that huge shower." A happy glint enters his eyes along with a smirk sliding into place as he takes me by the hips. "And the tub."

I rub his shoulders. "We will. I promise, but my sister needs me."

Concern colors his expression. "Is everything all right?"

"I don't know, but she's in my room."

"Ah. And your room is currently empty because you're in mine." He kisses my cheek. "I have an idea. How about we find a room that's ours?"

He's not just handsome. He's cute and really sweet to me when he's not sexually dominating me. We're a complicated pair, to say the least. "I'd love that, but there's just a little matter of the monarchy and that I'm not supposed to be with you at all."

"Screw the kingdom."

Poking his side, I say, "I think that's why Marie Antoinette got beheaded."

He chuckles but knows it's time for me to go and steps around me. *Totally nude.* Strapping. Confident. Sexy. Muscular. I've never known or seen a more handsome man than Hutton. And he owns each of the six feet four inches of his large build. Just as he owns me—heart and soul—although, for his sake, that's something he can never know.

Picking my shirt up from the floor, he comes to me and slips it carefully over my arms and head, giving it a little tug so it hangs in place. It doesn't matter how rough we are sexually or how our roles seesaw between submission and domination, when it's just the two of us, we're always Hutton and Ally. That's when my heart is happiest, because it knows what true love is.

But then his thoughtfulness and the way he makes sure I

look okay break my heart all over again. Will the man I marry do the same for me? Take care of me with such gentleness with that four-letter word resting easy in his eyes like it does in Hutton's?

Duke Dick doesn't love me.

He loves the power marriage to me offers.

Hutton asks, "Can you come back tonight?"

"I'm not sure how long I'll be, but if there's a chance to come for an hour or more, I'll be here. I promise."

I'm kissed sweetly on the lips. "Do what you need to do, Ally. You know where to find me. Now go before your sister worries."

Walking me to the door, he opens it. I almost tell him I had fun, but I think we know we're well past that. "Wait," he says, reaching for me. "You have a little makeup smeared under your eyes." With the skill of a surgeon, he uses the pads of his thumbs to carefully wipe the makeup away. "All good. Pretty as ever."

He doesn't realize he's making everything so much harder for me. Why can't he be an asshole I can fuck and forget? Why can't he be like the other guys I dated and make it easy not to love every single thing about him?

Saliva thickens in my throat, stopping me from telling him how I really feel, but the tears don't want to stay in the harbor of my eyes. So I look down and say, "Good night," and then walk away.

"Good night, Princess." This time, when he uses my title with the respect I demanded of him earlier, I'd rather hear Ally.

16

Princess Arabelle

LIKE A CAT, I'm stealthy and make it to my bedroom in a flash. When I open the door, Marielle is lying dramatically across my chaise with her forearm draped over her forehead. "Should I get the fainting salts?" I ask sarcastically, shutting the door behind me.

"Maybe. What do they do?"

I roll my eyes. "What's the emergency?"

She sits up abruptly. "I kissed Bennett, but it gets worse." With her hands pressed into the velvet, she just stares at me.

Drama queen. "Worse? Is he a bad kisser?"

"No," she replies, looking at me like I just sprouted a second head. "The opposite. He's an amazing kisser."

"Then what's worse?"

"He kissed me back." She takes another deep breath. "And just now before I went into my room." Pushing up, she starts walking in a circle around my room. "What am I going to do?"

Since the emergency is not a crisis, I stand in front of the vanity mirror and start taking off my earrings. "Well, if it were me, I'd be kissing him. A lot."

She scoffs, and when I find her in the reflection, her arms are crossed. "That's why you've been in so much trouble."

"I'm not in trouble." I turn around and head for the bathroom.

When I pass her, she pinches her nose, and, "You smell."

"I know," I reply with a smirk. I smell of Hutton and unadulterated lust. Since she's only here to figure out how to deal with her feelings versus what she's been told she's allowed to do, I figure I have enough time to shower and get back to Hutton before he falls asleep.

"Gross, Belle. Anyway, back to me."

"Yes, let's get back to you and the kissing." I lean against the doorframe. "What's the big deal? Bennett's so cute." I spin into the bathroom to turn the shower on.

She giggles. "He is." When I peek back out, she's touching her lips. "But we kissed, Belle. What's going to happen?"

"What do you mean what's going to happen?"

A quizzical look creases her brow as she stares at me.

My mouth drops open. Oh my God. "Is Bennett the first guy you've ever kissed?" Tears spring to her eyes, and she starts nodding like a crazed person. How is that possible? She's grown up attending parties and balls and socializing with men. She's pretty and charming, a perfect princess. She's had ample opportunity to kiss and be kissed. For crying out loud, how did she get through school and remain unkissed? Remarkable and quite astonishing. "Awww, Marielle, I had no idea." I go to her, clasping her face in my hands. "How is that possible? You're gorgeous. You're *twenty-three*."

"I took our bylaws seriously."

"Those were written six hundred years ago." I sit on the

end of the mattress. "They don't expect us to follow laws originally put in place to keep women under a man's control."

"What are you talking about? Yes, they do. We're supposed to." She gasps, her hand covering her mouth. "I know you've kissed boys, Belle, but have you—" She gasps again.

"Stop doing that," I snap, standing up.

"Please tell me you haven't broken the law."

"Broken the law? Good lord, Marielle. What are they going to do to me for kissing someone?" A memory flashes— *I take him deep into my mouth and listen to the moans he can't keep quiet*—as I move around my room, aimlessly looking for a distraction from the current conversation. "Throw me in the dungeon?"

"Yes. Or worse. They could keep you from becoming queen."

I worked hard to earn my degrees, but that was to use the knowledge from the throne, to know how to keep world relations as well as understand Brudenbourg's economy. Being queen is not a backup plan. It is THE plan. The only plan I've made. There are no contingencies in place. I never regretted my actions before, but I'm beginning to. But that means regretting being with Hutton, and I don't have that capability.

But I do start questioning if I can trust my sister, which makes me feel awful. No, not Marielle. She doesn't have a mean bone in her body. I've seen too many royalty themed movies. "They wouldn't do that."

"What if they do?"

I stare at her, my eyes narrowing. "Then you would become queen." The sound of the shower brings me out of my suspicions. "We don't have to worry about that, though."

"You're still a virgin?"

"Of course," I reply nonchalantly, lying between my teeth. "I wouldn't break the law. A kiss won't get me knocked from my rightful place." I walk back to the bathroom.

"Right."

"But you wouldn't tell, right, Marielle?"

"No. I wouldn't. You won't tell on me, right?"

"Of course not. You're my sister. If we can't trust each other, we can't trust anyone." I hug her. "I have your back." I do too, but my gut twists all the same.

"I have yours, too." She hugs me tightly. "I love you, but you need to shower. You really stink."

My smirk returns. "I'm going. I'm going." *Right back to Hutton*. Before I close the door, I say, "Just enjoy that kiss and the innocence of it. And nothing is going to happen. If you like him, kiss him again. If you want more . . . do what you want. When I'm queen, I'm getting rid of those stupid bylaws anyway. Be happy, sister."

When she touches her lips again, a sweet smile graces her pink lips. "Thank you for taking me out tonight."

"I'm glad you came. Night."

"Good night."

I don't rush in the shower. My skin feels raw and alive, his fingerprints still searing my body. It's easy to wash away the memory of what we did earlier when I know we'll be making more tonight.

I'm not sure how fate worked her magic, but she managed to bring us back together. Should I be looking at this differently? Believe a future together *might* be possible?

The laws are stupid and sexist, and I can't believe my mom has kept them in place. She's had thirty years to change them and hasn't. Why? What bothers me more is if I bring the subject up to her, they'll question why I care. Basically, I'd be busting myself.

My father would see it as giving us permission to do the

deed. Who cares if I have if the man I marry doesn't? And I have no intentions of marrying a man who I haven't been with like that. One thing Hutton has taught me is that chemistry in the bedroom is vital. I have it in spades with him, so why would I settle for less?

Duke Dick floods my thoughts. *Ugh.* He makes me feel dirty, but not in the fun way Hutton does.

I'm quick to dry off and get dressed. I don't bother with underwear or a bra. They'll be off again as soon as I step into Hutton's room. I work my way back down to his quarters and knock lightly. Maybe I should have texted him first. When there's no answer, I slowly turn the knob. "Hutton?"

No response.

My hope falls until I see him asleep in the bed. I close the door, lock it, and tiptoe around to the side of the bed I remember him always choosing, even when he has a king-sized bed to spread out on. Kneeling beside the bed, I watch him sleep for a few seconds before kissing his forehead, keeping it light so I don't wake him up.

His eyes slowly open anyway, and a smile appears. "Hi," he says, his voice caught between sleep and awake. Deep and sexy.

"Hi."

"You came back."

"I didn't want to stay away."

"You smell good."

I smile. "I took a shower."

His heavy-lidded eyes take me in. "Come to bed. Stay with me."

Checking the clock on the nightstand, I calculate the latest I can stay before the staff wakes and moves about the palace. "Maybe three hours?"

He lifts the covers, opening his arms for me. I take off

my sweatshirt and then pull down my pants, stepping out of them. "You are a very dirty princess."

"Maybe." *But everything about being with you feels right, not dirty.* His arms pull me in as soon as I lie down. He's wrapped in the blanket. I'm wrapped up in him, loving it. My heart beats to let me know he's close but is steadily soaking in the peace he provides. The back of my neck is kissed, but his hands don't roam. Not yet. His warm breath covers me, and he asks, "Do you want to rest or . . ."

As much as he always turns me on, I feel like we've turned a corner. We have time. We'll make sure we do as long as he's here, if I can make my parents see how amazing he is, then we *can* possibly have the rest of our lives together. If they approve of him, we won't have to live every second like it's our last. I close my eyes and snuggle in his hold. "Maybe I can sneak in a little catnap." I mean, I still want him. I'm not going to say no to sex with him or anything. He's damn incredible.

"Get some rest, princess."

He can't see since he's behind me, but I'm smiling because I hear the tease in the title. I'll take it.

I'd normally blame exhaustion for my foul mood, but I know the truth. I don't want to leave Hutton. His arm is heavy like a weight, but one I don't want to lift. I like how strong he is, how big he is, hiding me from the rest of the world while in his embrace. But the sun is coming up over the fields in the distance, so I need to go.

As I slip from his hold, he continues to slumber peacefully, which makes me smile. Maybe he can be happy here with me in Brudenbourg, in the palace, living his days without the worries of his work while he sits on the throne next to me.

He can't be king, but he can be my prince just like he's been my Prince Charming all along. This could work. He loves me. And I love him, so much that it hurts to have to leave. I'm about to lean down to kiss him, but I stop myself this time. He woke up last night when I did, so I kiss his shoulder instead, hoping he stays asleep.

I return to my room without running into any staff and shut the door. I lean against it smiling, never feeling happier. Today is a glorious day. Best day ever.

"Where have you been?"

I jump, but with my hand over my heart, I say, "You scared me, Margie. What are you doing here?"

"I work here."

"Not at five fifteen in the morning."

She gets up from the chair by the window and holds her phone out. "My phone was blowing up."

"*Wiiith?*" I start to get annoyed. It's way too early for this. I'm grumpy and tired.

"See for yourself."

I look at the screen, and read, "Reckless Royals Cause Bar Brawl." Defensively, I screech, "We did not! We got out of there as soon as it broke out."

"Who's we?"

Rolling my hand in the air, I reply, "It's the royal we."

"Very funny, Belle, but for real. I don't know how to get ahead of this if I don't know what I'm covering up."

A yawn escapes. "I'm really tired. There's nothing to get ahead of. We didn't do anything wrong."

"You being there was wrong. Why did you go out?"

I enter the bathroom and shut the door for privacy. "I've been good the whole time I've been back. I wanted one night of fun. Is that so bad?"

After washing my hands, I open the door to find her sitting on the bench at the end of my bed. She says, "Yes. Your party days are over. We can't have stories like this coming out. Your parents were very direct when they told you how they expected you to act."

Walking a wide berth around her, I climb into bed and lie back. "It was one time, Margie. That's it."

She turns around and leans on the mattress. "Swear to me, Belle."

Damn her. "Whose side are you on anyway?"

"Yours. That's why I'm here."

"And here I thought you were my best friend."

Grabbing my foot over the covers, she says, "I am." Her voice is less professional, and I start to hear my friend in there again. "I'm always your best friend, and I'll always look out for you—personally or professionally—Belle. But when it comes to my job, I work hard. Work with me and make it a little easier."

I start thinking about the bar and going with my sister. Propping up on an elbow, I ask, "Are you upset I didn't invite you?"

"No," she replies, shrugging. "But since when did Marielle start partying?"

Thinking about my sister and how she had her first kiss, I know she doesn't. "I promised to spend more time with her, and she promised to wear a pair of my jeans."

It's the first time I'm really getting a good look at Margie. Her hair is pulled back in a pretty chignon, and she's wearing a pearl necklace. She says, "Wow, really? That girl is never casual. How did she look?"

"Sexy. Caught every guy's eye who was there." Thinking of Hutton, I add, "Almost every guy."

"Almost? Who wasn't looking at her?"

"My brother."

"Jakob went?" She looks confused and sits up. "He was at a business dinner last night in the Village with Everest Media. *Oh*. Tell me you didn't see him, Belle."

"Why would I lie? I did see Hutton there, but it was pure coincidence. I had no idea he would be there. That was all Jakob."

"So you didn't hook up with him?"

"No, there was no hooking up. We were all hanging out one minute, and then the next, there was a full-on fight. We escaped and came home."

"Where have you been since you clearly haven't been in your room?"

"In the kitchen getting food." At least my bed looks ruffled from where Marielle threw herself across it at one point, but the high of my cuddle session with Hutton has completely worn off. "I'm going to sleep. You're welcome to get a few more Zs if you want."

She stands, and I've never been happier to see my friend go. "I have a long list of things to get done. I'll see you in a few hours."

"Yes, I'll be right on it." My eyelids grow heavy, and I finally close them. I wish I still had the weight of Hutton wrapped around me. "Talk later."

"Yes, Princess. Have sweet dreams."

I plan on it.

17

Hutton

AFTER THE CONTRACT contenders have toured the palace and the grounds, they load in an SUV to head to the castle. We're being shown possibilities for the filming of movies, news coverage, tourism commercials, and everything royal—from births to marriages to deaths. I try not to let the simplified sales pitch bother me. This contract has ballooning to cover other events over a twenty-five year period.

It's an incredible opportunity worth a fortune, one that would net the company billions. My other work has been put on hold until this deal is secured, but I can only afford another day before I need to return. I won't let the current clients suffer if this gets dragged out.

The princess hasn't been seen around this morning. Not at breakfast and not in any of the places we've been visiting.

I already miss her.

She's easy to get addicted to. When she smiles, it's genuine. Her laughter comes from the inside as though she can't contain it. She's flirty and so fucking sexy. When we talk, she listens—really listens. She doesn't always agree with me, but that's because she knows her opinion is important too. Our games were never about who we were, so I know she never set out to hurt me. I didn't know about the life she was trying to hide, but at least I know she never hid the real person from me.

The combination of her determination, strong will, and intelligence is a mental turn-on. *Feisty and frisky.* Those might the best words to describe the contradiction that is Ally Edwards versus Princess Arabelle Sutcliffe.

But with the breaking of a new day, the problems come out from the darkness that nighttime cloaks and become clearer. *What happens next for us?* We really need to talk somewhere that allows us to talk about something deeper than the weather.

When we arrive at the castle, I see Dick standing in full Duke regalia next to a horse. He shoos away the stable boy, who leads the horse away, while he greets us. *Asshole.*

I'm still not sure what part he plays. He says one thing when it comes to Ally, and she says another. I need to dig a little deeper.

As he explains the history of the castle and the moat, we cross the bridge that leads to the drawbridge. Inside the castle walls, Yamagata leaves the group to take a call. I tell Bennett, Jakob, and Dick that I need to make a call, and I'm given permission to wander the grounds without them.

I walk down a corridor and then down a rounded stairwell. Intrigued into the darker recesses of the underground, I look for a cell signal but realize I lost it when I came down here.

"Are you lost?"

Turning around, my beauty stands near a lamp with a flickering bulb that needs changing. "Endlessly without you."

After closing the distance between us, she caresses her

hands over my head and then wraps her arms around my neck. "You're found now, my love."

I kiss her quickly, and then say, "You say such sweet things when I know the bitterness of fate will soon come from those very lips."

"Am I that cruel, sir?"

"Crueler, but that's just to my heart."

"It's strong and handles anything little ole me can throw its way."

I take a moment to look at her in the dim light. "What about others?"

"You've never had trouble handling yourself before, Mr. Everest."

In case we have to leave before I get another chance, I kiss her. This time I'm not quick or thinking of time. I'm just feeling, taking in, and savoring what this is like. "Explain to me how the marriage thing works."

A sly smile slips into place. "Well, sometimes when one person meets the person they're meant to be with, they get married, strengthening their bond under the law of that land."

"You're cute. A comedian. But I'm talking about you and how things work here in Brudenbourg. Dick is here, and by all appearances, he looks confident in his role as duke. He treats your employees like they're beneath him."

When her arms begin to loosen, I grab her to keep her in place, and say, "I'm not letting you escape. We need to talk, Ally. I need to know the real situation and what's going on. I can't fight against the unknown."

"You need to understand that anyone who works for us is an employee—paid and free to leave at any time."

"I sense a *but* coming."

"Let's walk down here." She takes my hand and leads me farther into the bowels of the castle. The women I've dated in the past would be scared in such a dank, dark, and dingy place. It gets colder the farther we walk. "The but is, they are beneath him in title only."

"Not when it comes to humanity. I wouldn't treat my employees how he so comfortably treats yours. Considering you're in line for the throne, I've never seen you dismiss or treat anyone rudely. Even Sabine Rosalie. The ice was thick between you two at the pub, but you still weren't rude."

"Sabine Rosalie is . . . how do I say this? She's very popular with men."

"You know this for sure, or is this just gossip?"

Walking ahead of me, she's almost far enough that I momentarily lose sight of her. "She and the senior dance king were caught in the back of his carriage getting it on." I reach her, wrapping my arm around her waist and holding her close.

I say, "Two things. First, a carriage as in a horse-drawn carriage?"

"Yes." She giggles. "That's what we take to dances. It's our version of limos."

"Secondly, who cares who she was getting it on with?"

"I did." When her lips purse, I think I've hit a raw nerve. "He wasn't just my date. He was my boyfriend."

"Wait a minute. Back up. He gave up being king of a country for sex in a carriage?"

She rolls her eyes, but it's playful and followed by a laugh. "Pretty much, but let me explain how things work here in Brudenbourg. There are no kings. Only queens. So he might have been a crowned prince if I had kept him around."

"Ah yes, Jakob told me."

"To be honest, when I caught them, I was relieved. He was kind of an asshole. He'd been pressuring me for sex for months even though he knew the law."

"What law?"

"The chastity law."

"What the fuck is that?"

She spins out of my hold, catching my hand, and pulling me with her. "Not so loud." Up ahead, I see where light sneaks in through a hole in the brick, and she whispers, "We're almost there."

Whispering, I repeat, "What's the chastity law?"

"Just what it sounds like." Her voice goes even softer. "I'm supposed to be virginal, sacrificed for the first time at the altar of my husband."

"That's quite the visual."

She giggles. "I have a flair sometimes."

"Yes, you do. That law is utter bullshit. Only a weak man would subscribe to something put in place to protect a delicate ego." So she'd be judged for sleeping with me. I mutter under my breath, "Bullshit." Glancing at her silhouette, I don't want what we've done to hinder her in any way. "How are you going to get aroun—?"

Fingers are pressed to my mouth. How can she even fucking see me? "Shhh. Don't say anything more. The walls could have ears."

Alert, I look around, willing my eyes to adjust better to the dim light. "That's creepy as fuck."

Standing close enough to see her shrug, I want to laugh that even the suggestion doesn't seem to bother her. As far as the women I've known, she's a true anomaly. No wonder I haven't been able to get her out of my head.

Once we pass the light, it goes dark again. I don't know how she can see anything more than a foot in front of us. My eyes haven't adjusted, and I'm tempted to pull my phone out to use as a flashlight since it's getting even darker the farther we go.

I'm pulled into a room and pinned to a cold wall built from stone. I can't see a fucking thing, but I can feel. Ally presses against me, her lips lightly on mine. "I want you inside me, Hutton. Not your fingers and not your mouth, though it's magical. I want your cock." My dick is grabbed, halting my breath in my chest. Her hand feels good, so I release a heavy exhale. "I've missed the fullness. I've missed you so much. Make love to me."

"Here?"

"Yes. No one even knows I'm here. No one knows you're with me or where we are. It's been too long. It will be fast and—"

"Ally." I may not be able to see her, but I know her body well. I caress her face and lean my head against hers. "It has been too long, baby, but I don't want it fast. I want to take my time with you. Not in a wet and musty dungeon, but on a bed where I can spend hours appreciating you without interruptions."

"Hutton—"

"Ally," I say again, taking her hand from below and bringing it to my mouth. "You're so tempting, and I'm going to regret this as soon as we leave, but it wouldn't be making love down here." I kiss her wrist. "Tonight, I'll make love to you all night because I want to do it when I can see your eyes, your gorgeous face, and those lips. Fuck, those lips are incredible. And whatever you want, I'll give to you. I promise."

Her lips crash into mine, causing me to hit my head on the stone. Our tongues meet in a sudden rush together, and I'm now thinking I could be persuaded to take her hard and fast in this pitch-black room. She pushes off me, pulling out of my grasp, and says, "Tonight. All night."

Her warmth covers me again, and I hear the excitement in her voice even if I can't see it, making me smile. "All night."

"I can't wait. Come on." She takes my hand and leads me

out of the room. The light in the far distance is enough to guide us back the thirty or so yards we traveled. When we reach the stairwell, she smiles, admiring me. Running the pad of her palm over my cheek, she says, "That's better."

I don't mind her marking me any way she wants to, but the guys might wonder what I've been up to if she doesn't wipe off her lipstick this time. Giddy, she lifts up and down on her tiptoes several times. "See you later."

"See you later, Princess."

She waves and then runs into the dark. This is the creepiest-ass place I've ever been, and she knows every part of it. Damn, is this what royal kids do for fun when they're little? Or is it required learning from the book *Beginners Guide to Being a Queen*—learn the secret passages in your castle?

Something buzzes by my ear, so I rush up the stairs, wanting to get the fuck out of here as I swat whatever it is away. When I reach the ground floor, I walk back toward the entrance but pull my phone out and call Ethan.

"Thought you were avoiding me," he answers light-heartedly.

"No," I reply, stopping in the courtyard inside the tall walls. "We've been buried here. I emailed you about making it to the next round, but Yamagata is working them hard to bring them to his firm."

"He's solid competition. With his remarkable career, I'm surprised our startup has made it as far as we have. You and Bennett must be doing something right."

"Bennett may be a real pain the ass sometimes, but he's been an asset in the meetings. He's a real innovator. He's creative like you."

"You underestimate yourself."

"I appreciate the compliment, but I'm a numbers guy and happy to be so. I've shown Everest Enterprises is a solid investment, but Bennett's given them a lot of new ideas to consider, projects that we can take the lead on for them to bring them into the digital age and make money doing it."

"The reports are great. I'm comfortable with the numbers you've sent for the bid. What will it take to close the deal?"

"I should have a better feel of where we stand by the end of the day. I think it comes down to experience versus vision and feelings. I hate to say that since feelings are the last thing that should come into play in business, but if the connection isn't there on an emotional level, we won't get it."

I see the guys return from an arched doorway. I nod once. Ethan asks, "Should I ask about Ally?"

"Depends on what you want to hear."

"How about starting with how are you doing?"

Kicking up dirt with the toe of my shoe, I smile, feeling ridiculous. I guess being happy over the girl you like liking you back makes you do crazy stuff, and feelings are the last thing that makes sense, so I go with it and stop overthinking. "Unexpected."

Ethan laughs. "Okay, care to elaborate?"

"No. Not quite yet. I'm cautiously optimistic."

"I hope you're more than cautious when it comes to the optimism of the deal."

Now I chuckle. "Don't worry. My head's in the game."

"Good. Hey," he starts, shuffling some papers, "I have a meeting to get to. Shoot me an email in the morning."

"I will."

"Oh, and when are you returning?"

"I'm here through tomorrow, then I catch my flight early the next morning. I'll stop by the office before I go home."

"No, it's fine. Come over for dinner. Singer's dying for an update. You know how much she loves to read romance books. Hate to put the pressure on, but you're like a real-life fairy tale for her."

"Are you slacking, bro? Romance the woman and then she won't worry about my love life so much."

"Hey, hey, go easy. But you're right. The woman's a saint for putting up with me. I already made surprise plans for her this weekend, but I think I'll bump them up. Hey Cheryl, cancel my six o'clock meeting and all my meetings tomorrow."

"That's a step in the right direction."

"By the time we return to Manhattan, she will have forgotten all about you and the princess. Gotta go."

I chuckle. "Have fun."

"I plan to."

Hanging up, I walk toward the drawbridge. There's unfinished business with Ally, but I need to close the media deal first. Time to put the Everest negotiation and innovative skills to work. "Hey Dick, what exactly does your Duke-ship entail? Do you own the coastline or rent it or what?"

"Well, it's not true ownership. Queen Aemilia owns all the land. As Duke of Wenig, I'm the guardian of the province."

"And you are the first duke in your family?"

"It's an inherited title. My son will be the guardian after I pass."

I watch with rapt fascination as this drawbridge that's more than six hundred years old lowers before us from a pulley and chain manpower system. "And if you have a daughter?"

"Which is likely in these parts," he says with a goofy laugh and a nudge to my arm. "The Vaughns have managed to outwit the Bruden waters and birth males." In irritation, he motions for one of the guards to latch the chain. Seeming satisfied, his untrustworthy smile returns and he says, "I'll carry on that tradition, although the weaker sex must be birthed to rule Brudenbourg."

My eyebrows shoot the sky. The weaker sex? If I wasn't so angry, I'd laugh in his face. He doesn't understand women at all. If he did, he'd know they hold all the cards.

He continues even though I wish he wouldn't. "I'm hoping to work on changing the worthless law that prevents a king from taking the throne."

Arrogant. Small-minded. Little Dick just like his name says. That law is in place for that exact reason—to protect women from the little dicks—and even bigger assholes—of the world. And as if I wasn't irritated enough, I decide to push some more buttons. "How do you feel about the chastity law?"

Just inside the castle walls, he stops and looks at the cloudless sky, seeming to think before he speaks. That's a good sign. Maybe he's not too far up his own ass yet. "Reputation matters." *And then he speaks.* "If she has a bad reputation, it can stain your own. The Vaughn family name will not be tarnished on my watch . . ." He stops to gripe at a man with a clipboard, then claps his hands to make him hustle. Asshole. "I would think you, Mr. Everest, would be well informed on the matter of reckless women wreaking havoc on the family name, considering your brother's misfortune."

"A woman having sex prior to marriage isn't a stain on my name. Only I can ruin that."

Though I have the height advantage, his eyes stay on mine. "Very well. I've just never been inclined toward loose women."

Wow.

Bennett comes through the entry to the fortress with Jakob trailing while on the phone. "So what are we discussing, gentlemen?"

When I don't reply, Dick does. "Loose women and the volatile nature of their emotional cycles."

"Whoa!" Bennett's hands go up. "I was not expecting that."

Then Dick has the balls to finish. "Women are too volatile to rule fairly."

I hate him. I hate every fucking little thing about him. How can her parents believe this egotistical dickwad should marry their daughter?

I check to see if Jakob heard. He's busy on a call still, but I imagine Dick wouldn't be so cavalier about women rulers if Jakob were here. I ask, "And that's what you would do if you were the crowned prince? Rule fairly?" By how he treats everyone around him, I think the answer is obvious, but I poke the bear anyway.

"That's what I *will* do," he insists. "I just have to handle the situation delicately."

Situation? Is he referring to my Ally as a situation? His arrogance needs to be cut off at the knees. I'm about to knock the fucker in the face when Bennett steps in, and says, "Let's talk business," and leads the Duke off to chat with Jakob.

I stand there, turning my back to them. Three deep breaths and three exhales to dispel the anger that's built up. *Business.* I need to focus on business because personally, I will never let him marry Ally.

That is a deal I'm willing to wager my life on.

18

Princess Arabelle

SOMETHING IS WRONG.

A last-minute meeting was called when normally my parents would be napping before supper. And the fact that Margie, in her secretarial role, summons me makes me nervous. "Are you sure you don't know what it's about?" I ask her before we reach my father's office.

"I don't know. No clue at all." She looks as worried as I feel and holds her tablet to her chest. "Your father just rang me and asked me to bring you."

"Maybe it's good news. Maybe they're moving forward with the coronation."

She nods enthusiastically. "That could be it. This could finally be what we've been waiting for." My mother isn't ready to retire anytime soon, being quite youthful for a queen, but she has to put the plan in place just in case.

It's a little thing that is big to me, but seeing her excited for me gives me hope that we can get our friendship back on track. We've had a lot of ups and downs in the past few years.

She hated being in Texas because she hated living the lie we both had to for me to be there. I even asked my parents to let her return, but as is customary, I had to travel with a companion, which meant she was stuck with me. Heaven forbid I'm allowed to live a life without the watchful eyes of the monarchy.

She was bitter because when I was exiled, sent away, or whatever nicer term my parents used, she was basically banned too. I looked at it as an adventure. She viewed it as a punishment. We still were making the most of it.

I became Ally, and Margitte became Margie. Over the two years I was there earning my master's degree, our once thick-as-thieves friendship started to unravel. Soon, she wasn't my friend but my babysitter. *Or at times, my gatekeeper.*

When we'd first arrived, it had felt like us versus them. We spoke our own language, ate our own style of food, and went out together. Over time, especially as I made more friends, she began to resent me. She saw our time in the States as *my* time where only I got to spread my wings, which was essentially true. And at times, I didn't make her job easy, and I knew that. But once I met Hutton, she turned on me completely.

Margie saw how I felt about him from the beginning. Hutton and I were fireworks waiting to explode. Since we've been back in Brudenbourg, the tension has lessened, but it hurts my heart to know we may never get our friendship back.

As the family's official secretary, a job she inherited from her mother, she manages all of our schedules. Sometimes I miss her just being my friend. Like how before we became adults and took on life's responsibilities and before I experienced new things.

"Real quick." Tapping on her tablet, she then turns it

toward me. "You'll be wearing this emerald dress tonight. I've had it steamed, and your shoes are pulled. Your mother told me you're to wear your great-grandmother's tiara. I'll receive it from the vault right before dinner, and I'll bring it up when you're ready to leave. Just text me."

"When's my pee break?"

"Not funny," she singsongs, but we still laugh because it is.

That's not ominous at all . . . My brow furrows. I see a color-coded chart on the tablet, and from the looks of it, each color is a member of the royal family. "You're very organized." Taking the grand stairs to the lower level, I ask, "Jeez, what else is on that thing?"

"Everything." She pulls up a different chart. "Not to creep you out, but we even track your menstrual cycle."

"What?" I stop and look down at it. "How do you know that?"

"You don't even want to know."

"Who's we anyway?"

"Everyone who needs to know."

I try not to freak out that the staff and I can only assume my doctors and parents are all in cahoots when it comes to what my body is doing. But I have bigger concerns than worrying if they're digging through my trash.

Down the blue hall, I see the gilded double doors at the end that lead to my father's office. Butterflies begin to flutter in my stomach. Margie's a nice distraction. She says, "I've updated the entire system. We're not living in the Stone Age anymore." We reach the closed doors, and she adds, "Fingers crossed."

"Yeah, fingers crossed." I straighten my shoulders and raise my chin as I knock on the door.

"Come in," my father calls from the other side. He's a very formal man—not the most cuddly but always caring. I walk in and close the door behind me quietly. Quiet. So quiet like a lady is supposed to be.

I stand with my hands clasped behind my back until my parents look up. "Come in. Come in," my father says impatiently, waving me over.

Sitting on the couch opposite the one they occupy, I quickly take a mental note of the surroundings: a fire roars in the fireplace in the middle of summer, and books are stacked in the corner ready to tip over. My mother's ankles are crossed, so I cross mine to match. My dad pushes a pair of reading glasses up the bridge of his nose but still manages to look at me over the top of them. "Dear Arabelle, how are you acclimating to Brudenbourg since you've been back?"

"Quite well. Thank you."

He opens a file on the coffee table dividing us, flips through a few pages, and then says, "We want to discuss the coronation."

"Yes, I'm ready to discuss it."

Sitting back, he grasps my mother's hand, and says, "As you're well aware, we're young at heart and hopefully have a lot of years ahead of us, but we are getting older. Now that Marielle is twenty-three and seems to be on a good path, and Jakob is doing a fine job handling our family's affairs, those are years we would like to spend traveling and relaxing a bit more than we can with our current situation."

When he pauses, I speak up, "Yes, you've both worked very hard for a long time now. Taking time to relax and do what you want would be a wonderful way to spend life."

My mother says, "We agree, but we're not quite sure what to do about you."

"What do you mean?"

"As you know, your role in the family is much more complicated."

"I'm very aware of my role in the family. It's one I've been training for my entire life." I hate feeling like I have to defend myself, but I will if it helps me.

I hate the pauses in conversation. I see where Marielle gets it from. My mom finally says, "We've had several offers come in—"

"Offers? For what?"

She studies me, and then my father replies, "For your hand in marriage."

"What? What do you mean? What offers? From whom?"

He continues, "Two actually."

"I had five," my mother interjects. "You're very beautiful, Arabelle, but I have to say I expected more."

"Two or twenty. It doesn't matter to me. I'm not flattered. Those offers didn't come because of my looks. They came because they want the connection, the throne, the money, and to take over our country."

"Don't be so dramatic, Arabelle," my father says.

"Me? Have you met your middle child?" I know I shouldn't have said it. Sarcasm is probably not the best route to take with this conversation. After all, I'm trying to figure out why the hell I'm here.

"Please be good," my mother says. *Good?* She adds, "We've been reading the decrees and bylaws, and although we've read them a million times, we wanted to make sure everything was in order before we spoke with you."

My stomach turns from the tone she's using. It's not filled with the happiness it should be. It's the opposite, in fact.

"Speak to me about what?"

She shuffles papers from the file, and then I see an image of me drinking beer from the pub in Luxum. "We thought you had made the necessary changes for us to move forward with our early retirement, but clearly, you're not ready to wear the crown."

Panic fills my veins. "It was a beer. That's all."

"It's not just the beer," my father says. "There are rumors you were seen in an alley with a strange man." When I start to speak, he holds his hand up to stop me. "I don't care if the rumors are true, but we can't have stories circulating about our queen. Let me correct that. We do care if the rumors are true. Were you in an alley with some strange man that night?"

"No," I plead. "I wasn't." A dark doorway? Yes, absolutely, but the man is not a stranger. But none of that matters as I see my inherited future slipping through my fingers. "What are you saying?"

Sympathy shines like tears in my mother's eyes, and she leans on my father's shoulder. He says, "We've accepted one of the offers."

"What? No." I stand, my hands fisting at my side. "You can't."

"Yes, we can. It's for the betterment of Brudenbourg. You know that your time away was to curb your rebellious ways, but it seems your behavior hasn't changed. Judging by these photos, you'll still be viewed as a princess with a tarnished crown, so that leaves no choice but to marry you into a prominent family."

"Prominent family? Not for love. Not for my dignity. You're marrying me off for image alone?"

"Yes, to fix yours."

"Then tell me." Anger courses through me. "Who is deemed worthy enough to save me?"

My father says, "God save the Queen and if he doesn't, we will."

"That's enough, Werner. And calm down, Arabelle. You will still be queen," my mother says, probably attempting to placate me. But I'm incensed. "But you'll have a marriage partner who accepts your missteps and bad choices."

"All of them?" I ask snarky, "Or just the ones they deem forgivable?"

"That's for you and him to work out. Preferably privately." She holds my father's hand again. "I found love through a marriage match. You can too if you give the relationship your full effort and your husband the commitment he deserves."

Maybe I'm being rude, but I can tell they're avoiding the question, so I push back. "I asked who?" I'd almost concede the fight if it weren't for two things—I feel sick already knowing who they've made this royal match with, but most importantly, because it's not to Hutton.

"The Duke of Wenig will make a fine husband—"

"No!" No. No. *No.* My arms tighten over my stomach.

"You should feel grateful that you have offers with the ruckus you've caused. You're a smart girl, but it's time to step up and be a strong woman and a leader. The role of queen should never be taken lightly or in jest. The world is watching your next move, so what will it be?"

"Not living a loveless marriage. He'll take over the decision-making just like he takes over conversations."

"Dear," my mother starts, "he's a man in charge of an important province, and he's done a fine job for us. He'll take a lot of the burden off you with his experience."

"I bet he will . . . Have you told him?"

"He's feeling confident—"

"Arrogant," I correct.

"We asked him to wrap up the communications deal so we could tend to other business."

"Me? I'm the other *business*." I roll my eyes. Yelling at them will get me nowhere, and it's clear that my feelings on the duke are irrelevant. I feel lightheaded for the first time in my life, but the thought of Hutton steadies me. "The deal . . . has anyone been chosen?"

"No one just yet," my father says. "But I think the committee is leaning toward The Yamagata Group."

"No!"

Startled, my parents jump. "What is wrong with you?" I realize I just protested louder regarding the deal than my marriage. My mother comes to me and puts the back of her hand to my forehead. "Are you not feeling well?"

"Everest Media is a better choice."

Staring at me, my father is intrigued. "Why is that?"

I need to be careful. Gathering my thoughts together, I sit. I control the pitch of my tone and reply, "Because they're innovative and have a youthful ambition, strong work ethic, and a vision for the future of how our country is represented."

"How do you know all this?"

"I sat in with Jakob going over the reels and submission documents."

He smiles, giving me the affirmation I've needed from him for years. "Yamagata has experience and has handled the communications and representation of image for other countries. We can't overlook the trust he's been given to handle their presence on the world scene."

"You can't deny the impact Everest Enterprises has made. *Hint.* It's more than a splash."

"You're right," he says, "but I'm concerned with their day-to-day operations. I think we need to visit each of their headquarters to see the real operation behind the men."

"You're going to New York?"

"That's what I'm thinking."

"I volunteer. I'll go."

Standing up to move back to his desk, he says, "I had planned to send Jakob."

"Send him to Los Angeles to inspect Yamagata's setup."

"Why?" my mom asks.

"This is what I studied in school. I can contribute in more ways than just looking pretty." Making sure my head is held high, I add, "And because this will affect my reign. I want a say in it." My parents stare at me. "I insist."

She smiles, pride in her eyes, but waits for my father's reply. I never understood why she handed him all the power she holds. Can she hate her station enough to sit idly in the passenger seat of her own life while someone else drives? And now, particularly about who her daughter will spend the rest of her life with?

Her reluctance to own her inherited position drives me to want it more. I've never been power hungry, but I still intend to rule wisely and intentionally.

He looks at me, and then says, "That's fair. The Everests are leaving the day after next. We'll have the plane secured, and you can fly with them. You have four days, and then we need to make a final decision."

"That's all I'll need."

"Very well. A princess involved in business could be very good for our country." It's not a dig at mom. She's happy to let him handle business even if he doesn't get the glory of the title. Nonetheless, something about her situation makes me sad.

I start for the door but wonder if I should bring up the chastity law. The same reasons I never did before stop me now. Anything that slips out could be used against me, just like the past is. "See you at supper."

"Yes," my mom calls behind me. "Wear the tiara, Arabelle."

"Will do." I'm about to shut the door when I see Margie down the hall wanting to burst with a squeal.

"Please don't talk in slang," my mother slips in before I can close it. "It's so unbecoming."

"All righty."

I shut the door and laugh at myself, but it's cut short when Margie stands from a chair in the hall, and asks, "How did it go?"

"Depends."

"On?" she asks as we walk toward the grand stairs.

"How New York goes."

"New York? What's in New York?" *Hutton.* But I don't say that. I know exactly where her feelings lie when it comes to him. Maybe I can change her mind now that we're home, and she can see him for the good man he is instead of assuming he was a guy I was only hooking up with.

He wasn't.

He was always so much more. I tried to separate my heart from the attraction, but now that he's near again, I realize my heart is attached to him. We were never just a physical attraction. We're so much more than a fleeting connection. We always were.

We're two chains linked together in a circle. We shared a slow and steadily blossoming love, one so delicate I foolishly thought we weren't meant to last more than a season. The moment I saw him again, hope renewed and our perennial love bloomed again.

I need to talk to him about what he wants. We can show the world how much we love each other and prove to my mother that love ultimately rules. With his financial knowledge and charisma and my understanding of our land and socioeconomic needs, Hutton and I will not only work to benefit the Bruden people, but our country will continue to flourish.

Yes, I really need to speak with Hutton. I don't know about the life he leads in New York, but does it compete with a life here? He says he wants to be with me and is well aware where I intend to be, but we still need to have that conversation.

I've lived my life in this fishbowl. He's lived his freely. Is it possible he won't want to give up that freedom in exchange for me?

No. Surely, we're on the same page. We're forever. No matter what my parents say about my "offer," I won't settle for less love than I've been given. Hutton is mine, and I'll fight for him. I just have to be very careful in front of them for now. "I'm going to close this deal."

"Is that why they called you in? Jakob can't do his job?" Her perturbed tone surprises me. She's always liked Jakob, even when he was pestering us as youngsters.

"Jakob's going to California to visit the Yamagata headquarters. I volunteered to go to New York and report back."

She stops two steps below me, and says, "This seems like a stretch. What do you know about business?"

Like a slap, I flinch and look back. "What do I know about business? I have a master's degree in business communications, or did you forget what we were doing in Texas?"

"I didn't. I just thought you had."

Fury flames hot inside me. I'm shocked and hurt and angry she would speak to me so harshly. I take a deep breath, wanting to calm the storm brewing inside. I exhale, and then say, "I understand that you want to get ahead, but does it have to be at the expense of our friendship?"

"My apologies, Princess. I shouldn't have spoken to you like that. I was out of line."

Princess, not Belle.

"*Okaaaay*, I see how this is going down." In flames apparently. I start walking again. "I'll see you at dinner."

I stop when she asks, "When are we leaving for New York?" *Shoot.* I hadn't thought of that.

Slowly, I turn around. "I'm not sure you'll be my companion this trip."

With a finger still pressed to the screen of the tablet, she says, "Be careful, Belle."

My grip tightens on the banister. "Are you threatening me?"

"No. I'm looking out for you."

"Guess it's all perspective."

She comes to one step below mine and looks up at me. Whispering, she says, "I know what you're up to. You know I do. As your friend, I'm asking you to please be careful and don't do what I know you're doing."

"What am I doing, Margitte?"

"This is about Hutton. You don't lie as well as you think you do."

"I'm not lying. I'm going to New York to see their head-quarters and to see if they can supply what they say they can."

"All right." Her eyes squeeze closed quickly before she adds, "You can lie to yourself, but I know the truth."

"What truth is that?"

"That you're in love with him. Is he in love with you, or is he just another guy who wants part of your legacy?"

"You don't know him at all. If you did, you would have seen all he wants is me. That's all he's wanted all along."

Her mocking laughter echoes around us. "God, Belle, what are you doing? If he didn't meet you that night on Fourth Street, he would have met someone else. You weren't special. You were just easy." *What? Who is this stranger?*

My heart hurts. My eyes begin to water, stunned by how far our friendship has deteriorated. I knew she was unhappy having to follow me around for my schooling, but as my friend, I thought it was an opportunity. "When you turned a cold shoulder to me in Texas, I looked to others. It's incredible how you can't see that you're the one who forced me to find new allies." She has so much ammunition she can use against me, but I refuse to cower. Raising my chin and straightening my shoulders, I do what I've always been told. "I'll see you with the tiara. Good afternoon."

"Belle," she says, grabbing my arm.

I stop, my gaze going to her hand.

She's quick to remove it as if she's touched fire for the first time.

She has.

She just doesn't realize how hot I can burn.

19

Princess Arabelle

ME: *I miss you.*

Hutton: *I miss you more.*

Me: *Come see me.*

Hutton: *And risk being sent to the pillory?*

Me: *Look at you with all your fancy words.*

Hutton: *I have other words.*

Me: *Like?*

Resting back, I feel close to him through this exchange, but I need him here. I need to see him. So much has happened in such a short time, and it makes me wonder what would have happened if I had given into a real relationship a long time ago. What if I had gone to Houston instead of trying to save my heart the hurt of saying goodbye? What if I hadn't stood him up and instead said hello.

Hutton: *You. Soul. Affection. Mouth. Blue. Key.*

Me: *Key?*

Hutton: *To my heart.*

Right here on my bed, I become a puddle of melted swoon.

Me: *Come see me. Please.*

Hutton: *Already on my way.*

Me: *At the top of the stairs, swing right and then stay close to the blue and white striped curtains. It's a blind spot for the camera.*

Hutton: *Do I even want to know how you know this?*

Me: *No. I'll leave the door unlocked for you.*

I giggle as I push send on the text message, then I wait impatiently for a reply while lying in bed. My eyes are puffy and burn from the tears I've cried.

Being betrayed by my best friend this afternoon . . . again . . . is not something I expected to happen. We have been two peas in a pod since we were born. Margie and I even dressed up as peas and carrots one year, Miss Piggy and Kermit another year . . . the costume worked for the brief but awkward stage I was going through at the time.

We were supposed to be better in Brudenbourg, not enemies. What makes me madder is I feel weak crying over her. She doesn't deserve my tears or kindness. Margitte hasn't supported me personally or professionally in a long time. She may have kept her trap shut about my "activities" in Texas and a few of my wild nights here as a teen, but how much can I really trust her?

A light knock on the door drags me out of my suspicions, but when the door opens and the most handsome man I've ever seen is standing there, I sit up to take in the full view. Holding the phone up, Hutton asks, "You summoned?"

That roguish grin. His rugged good looks. How they help me forget my troubles. "I missed you."

Closing the door, he crosses the large room and sits next to me on the bed. Stroking my hair back, he narrows his eyes as he looks at me. "Why have you been crying, beautiful?"

"It's not important."

He kicks off his shoes and then stands to undress. As much as he's distracting—perfection and Greek god-like—his expression is gentle when he looks at me. "It is important if it affected you enough to cry."

"I need to grow up anyway. I can't stay a little girl forever and being here, where I'm treated like one, doesn't help. I have no power, not even over myself."

He climbs under the covers and holds me to his chest. I love hearing his heart—the strong, steady beat—enveloped by arms that make me feel safe and protected in a way that I don't in my home anymore.

How did I ever taste pure bliss and then walk away like I didn't care? I thought I could, but I failed. Not a day, not even an hour has passed that Hutton hasn't crossed my mind. The memories we made have stayed with me as if the images could make them real again.

But here he is in my bed, wrapped around me, willing to take on my problems and regrets as if they're his own. "You have more power than you know. You hold all the power over me."

"Do I?" I ask, surprised by his admission.

"You always did. We once asked each other if we were dating others. I told you I wasn't. What you didn't know was that I didn't want to. I wanted you, but I couldn't have you."

"If you had me, what would you have done?"

"Anything you asked."

Tilting up, I expect to see a smile on his face or hear laughter—something that would signify he's humoring me. But I don't find it, and his honesty is evident in his soulful eyes. I push up and rest on my palm, still looking at him and half expecting him to tell me he's just kidding. "You're serious."

"I am," he replies casually, tucking a few stray strands of my hair behind my ear.

"How are you so sure of yourself?"

"I'm not. I'm sure of you."

My arm weakens under his sweetness. Bending down, I kiss him. Margie's words from earlier haunt me, placing doubt where there was none. "Why did you talk to me the first time we met?"

"How could I not? You were the most beautiful woman I had ever seen. You still are." He kisses my cheek and then my chin.

"There were plenty of pretty women around, including Margie. She has so many admirers."

"That's just looks."

"But you said that's what drew you to me?" I'm confused and getting frustrated. Is she right? Am I nothing but a pretty face? An easy target or, worse, an easy lay?

"Who said I was talking about your looks? My attraction to you was . . . soul deep. I was simply and inexplicably drawn to you."

He must be able to hear my heart thundering from happiness. "Soul deep?"

"Yes, princess," he says, his smile smug. "I like more about you than just your body." He leans down and pushes the hem of my tank up, exposing my breasts. "Although your body is so fucking fantastic."

Running my hands over the deep wells of his carved biceps and the hills of his shoulders, I feel so much strength and power in his every move, and I see it in his steady strides. Even when he looks at me, I feel the hold he has on me.

But it's not just his looks that keep me entangled in him, either. I find him so utterly sexy when I listen to him talk business, numbers, and facts rolling off his tongue from ingrained memories. His passion for the company is undeniable when he speaks of their vision and the impact they've already made.

"Do you know what turns me on, Hutton?"

His hand sneaks between my thighs. "Yes, Ally, I do. I know exactly what turns you on and what gets you off."

I can't hide my smile, and I don't want to. I feel free when I'm with him and captivated by him. I don't stop his hand, but he does. Looking in my eyes, he asks, "What turns you on?"

"Watching you achieve everything you dreamed of."

"I haven't achieved them all." Kissing my neck, he gently sucks, causing me to ease into it until it tickles too much. "Not. Quite. Yet."

"What dreams do you have left to achieve?"

"Everything that has to do with you." His answer is just as confident as always.

My cheeks hurt from smiling so much around him. "How close are you to achieving it?"

"You tell me."

"Pretty damn close. I'm coming to New York with you."

He pulls back suddenly, the covers hiding us from the world outside—the world that makes *us* an impossibility. He'd be denied as a true contender for my hand if he decided to apply.

Too bad for them.

I refuse to walk away now that I'm in his arms again. In his life again. *How can I?*

"What do you mean?"

"I talked my parents into letting me be a part of the communications team. I'm traveling to New York, and you can show me around your headquarters."

"What happened to Jakob?"

"Do you not want me to come?"

A wry grin appears. "I always want you to come, princess.

I also want you in New York. I'm just surprised. When did this happen?"

"This afternoon." I don't tell him about the rest of the conversation, not about Margie, or about the offers, and my match. It will never happen. Not if I have a say, and I will have my voice heard even if I have to demand it. "I volunteered."

"I like you volunteering for the job. Are you up for it?"

Cocking an eyebrow to match his, I reply, "I'm so up for it. Are you?"

"I'm about to be." I love the feel of his weight on me. He doesn't put his full weight on me, but enough for me to savor the size of this large man. I wrap my arms around him, and whisper, "I guess I'll have Margie book a hotel."

"Fuck that. You're staying with me."

Margie will love that . . . *not.* "I don't even know where you live."

"I'll show you, and then I'll take you to my favorite places. Wait, what is the security setup?"

"Most people don't even know about my country."

"Enough know for me to be concerned about your safety."

"I'm not famous like the Royals from England. Even on official business, I rarely need a bodyguard. This trip will be no different. But Margie might be there."

"She hates me."

"She does." Why bother lying? "If I can get the clearance, I won't need her by my side."

"New York is amazing. If I can have you there with me . . . We can walk in the park. You'll love Central Park. We can see a show. We can do whatever you want to do."

He still doesn't realize that spending time with him is all I want, and I'm starting to think it might be all I need. He might be all I need, but I see the excitement in his eyes when he speaks of the city. What if he really doesn't want to be here, even if it's with me? *But what about the crown? My life-long schooling?*

I lean my head against his cheek, wanting to hide from what I might be asking of him and the home he might not be willing to leave. Winding my fingers through his hair, I pull him down until our lips meet. A gentle kiss turns into more, and I deepen it, holding on to him as our lips part and our tongues greet.

Soon, he takes hold of me and turns us over, our bodies tangled together. Mixed up in the covers, he tugs the blanket out from under me and pulls it over us until we're buried under the fluffy cotton.

So sexy.

His golden skin is in stark contrast to the white blanket. White teeth highlighted by full lips that spread like wildfire into a heart-melting smile.

Hutton Everest is a bright knight in my dark nights.

Like him, I don't rush the love we're creating. Slow is not something we often do, but in the unrushed acts, I feel cherished. His hand covers the curve of my waist, and he lifts to look me in the eyes. "How long will I get you in New York?"

"I have four days."

"It's going to be the best damn four days of our lives."

"You don't have to do anything special. I'm happy I get to spend time with you."

"I need to pull out all the stops. Roll out the royal red carpet. I have a princess to impress."

I run my hand over the prickly scruff of his jaw. "She's already impressed, but what can I do for you?"

"You're doing it. Time alone with you is all I can ask for."

"Until the clock strikes midnight. Then—"

"No thens or worries of the future. Just give me four days

of Ally again. Don't put restraints on our time before we've even left."

"I won't, but my family will. I can't promise I'll be traveling alone."

He pauses his argument, and he shifts his gaze to the sheets. "Margie?"

"We'll see. My parents have recently expanded her role. She's pretty busy."

"She hates me."

"It doesn't matter. What I think does, and you know how I feel about you, so let's not worry about her right now."

"How?" Dipping his head to the side, he kisses my throat to my collarbone.

"I love you."

"I love you. I also know how much you love when I kiss this spot right here."

"I do love it."

"You do." *Kiss.* "And just like that, you're putty in my hands."

"God, yes, I am." That traveling hand makes it to my hips before it detours between my legs. Like wings, I flutter open for him. Remembering how good his hand felt in the SUV, I crave the same roughness, the same desire, but this time, I don't need his hand. I need him. "Make love to me, Hutton."

20

Hutton

ALLY'S DISCOUNTED because of her looks. In the few days I've been here, I've witnessed men talking over her more than once and dismissing her ideas as silly. These assholes are missing the big picture of what makes her beautiful. I wonder how many of them have a master's in business and international relations. My guess is none.

She's not just a pretty princess to be admired for her looks. Ally has so much more to offer the world than sitting on a throne as a headpiece. With her master's degree, she could give guidance not only to the committee regarding this deal, but she could also use her studies in international relations to extend olive branches to other countries. She's the full package, and they don't even see it.

The duke speaks of her with no consequence. Mr. Yamagata pays her no mind as he tries to impress her father. No value is given to those with beauty.

What they don't know and what I won't show anyone— since I want her all to myself—is that true beauty is found in the quiet moments. Here, with me, she's vulnerable, and her guard is down with her arms open and her spirit strong. She thinks she's weak for crying, but her strength is in her determination. Everything she wants doesn't always make sense with how she wants to live her life, but she doesn't shy away from her ambition. She's impressive.

I have no idea how I'd fit into this life, or if I'll even be allowed. It's a life I never imagined before, and I haven't had time to measure the pros and cons. I need to calculate how I saw my life going—life in New York, growing the media division—with possibly staying in Brudenbourg doing I don't know what.

Frustration has set in. Hers. Mine. *Ours.*

The increasing concern I see in her eyes growing with an excitement that still resides in the clear blue shows the tension she's feeling. Does she really see me as her Prince Charming? Who knew a costume would lead to this? Not me. That's for sure. But now that we're here in the second act of our story, we're going to have to decide who sacrifices their life for our love to survive.

One day, she'll prove she's already a queen, ready to reign. But to me, she'll always be my Ally.

I stroke my fingers through her desire. Under the heat of the blanket and pressed against her warmth, I keep my voice low. "Let me take care of you first, baby. I don't want to hurt you."

"You won't. I want to feel the stretch. I want the burn. I want to sit at dinner and feel how my body has changed from being with you."

Kissing between her breasts, I trail my tongue along the curve of her cleavage. I move back, planting my forearms on either side of her pretty face. We've had sex a lot and done everything between sin and making amends, but this lump in my throat, the one that formed when I saw her tear-streaked cheeks, makes me want to replace her pain with something tangible. "When I told you I loved you . . ." She can't touch love, but hers has touched me. Setting my eyes on her bright blues, I want her to know what she means to me. I need her to feel the words, not just hear them. "I meant it."

"So did I." She lifts up and kisses me before lying back down and wrapping her arms around my neck. We don't say those three words again, maybe soon, but I see them in her eyes, and I hope she feels them from me.

With her legs open for me, I press myself against her. My natural inclination is to thrust fast and deep, but that's not what she needs. I push in, keeping my eyes locked on hers. The heat from her welcoming body spreads, spanning from our connection.

When her mouth opens, I kiss the corner, inhaling her scent. Her eyes close, and her arms tighten around me. A warm breath covers my neck, and she kisses the underside of my jaw as I move with intention—slow enough to feel every inch being engulfed but fast enough to touch the satisfaction we're striving for.

Her nails scrape down my back, my skin alive like a live wire.

The words come as easy as breathing when I'm with her. "Beautiful."

I kiss her forehead.

"Loving."

Rising into a pushup, I thrust faster. Her body glistens as it syncs to our own music.

"Graceful."

Little moans fill the large bed, and the covers are tossed off me. My shoulders are grabbed as my body moves from instinct—hunt, gather, devour—take. Take. *Take.*

I run my nose along her neck, her chest against mine, her

breath in my ear. She says, "Please," as if it's all too much. It is. I start to lose myself but want to give. Give. *Give.*

Her body tenses, her breath sucked in like the rough-edged rocks of the castle—sharp—and then as she crumbles into a million pieces, letting her body sink into the ecstasy, and I fall apart right after.

My soul's peace is in her arms as she holds me so tight that I wonder if she thinks I'll disappear. I lift my head from her shoulder. "Hey, I'm right here. I'm not going anywhere."

Her hold loosens, and a languid smile graces her lips. When her eyes open, she says, "I don't want to lose this."

"If you're referring to me, you won't. If you're referring to my body, well, your parents might not be happy to see me still inside you if we head to dinner like this."

She bursts out laughing, her arms falling wide open on the mattress. "Fine. I won't cling to you like a spider monkey."

"Strictly for the sake of the other guests. For me, spider monkey away."

"So what you're saying is when I'm in New York, I can cling to your back, and you'll carry me around?"

"Yep."

Squealing in delight, she hugs me again. "Can't wait."

The two of us, alone, out from under the pressure she feels here. "I can't wait either." I kiss the tip of her nose and then get out of bed. "Dinner is soon. I'm going to use your bathroom and then head back to mine to shower."

Propped up on her hand, she says, "You could stay. We could blow off dinner and make love all night."

"Yeah, that'd go over well. I'd be thrown in that dungeon of yours before the night was over."

Laughing, she says, "I'd take care of you even down there. You know, bread, water, blow jobs. The necessities."

I look back, impressed by my girl's rebellious side. Before

I disappear into the bathroom, I tell her, "Never change, okay?"

Flopping back, she laughs. "Yeah, okay."

"I'm serious." Her smile lightens, and she takes another look at me. I say, "When you become queen, promise me you'll always stay who you are. Don't change for anyone."

"What about you?"

"Not even me. I adore you exactly how you are."

"Why are you such a charmer?" Crossing her legs, her foot bounces in the air as she tucks her hands behind her head.

I cross the threshold and flip on the bathroom light. "Just telling you the truth."

"I like your truth, hot stuff."

"Good because I like you."

I'm closing the door when she says, "The mustard told me otherwise."

Stopping where I stand, I smile. I'd always wondered what she thought about that sandwich. "What can I say? It was made with love."

After taking a piss, I wash my hands and then splash water on my face. I've been fighting jet lag for days, but once I saw her again, there was no way I was going to miss a chance to spend time with her.

The tie that binds us is stronger than ever. Knowing Ally's going home with me is more than I could have hoped for. As for the media deal, I need to talk to Bennett because I might need to recuse myself. I want the deal to go through for him and Ethan. I need to talk to Ally about it, too, to hear what she thinks.

After I finish in the bathroom, I come out and give her a few kisses while getting dressed. Sitting down next to her, I kiss her, and then say, "I'll see you downstairs, beautiful."

"I'll be the one in the green dress."

Sending her a wink, I run my hand over her cheek as I get up. "Looking forward to seeing the dress . . . on the floor of this bedroom later."

"You're so bad—"

"Don't forget hot." I stand and head for the door.

"And humble. Don't forget humble."

I chuckle. "Can't forget that." With my hand on the knob, I add, "And by the way, you're more amazing than I remember, and I have incredible fucking memories of you."

This time, she doesn't smile from my jokes or any of my arrogant antics. Her smile is genuine and drop-dead gorgeous. It's Ally, not the cool-as-ice princess. "Everything about you is unforgettable."

"You got some lines there, Princess." When I open the door, I peek out.

"Hey, Hut?" Looking back, she says, "Thank you."

"For what?"

"Reminding me how to smile."

She melts my heart when I see said smile, wishing I could stay longer. "My pleasure."

"Stick to the outside edges of the walkway, and the camera won't catch you. And staff doesn't come up here unless something is requested or taken care of when we're not here."

"Beyond me having major issues with the lack of security around you, I'm going to try to push that aside since it gives me easy access while I'm here."

Giggling, she replies, "Probably best. I'll see you later, sexy."

I give her a wink and slip out of the room, sticking to the edges. The coast is clear, so I hurry out and down the long hall. Once I'm on the stairs, I feel home free.

I'm used to wearing suits in New York. I wear them to work every day. But here in Brudenbourg, I've stepped up my suit game—fine fabrics and impeccable tailoring.

Ally usually can't keep her hands off me, but I have a feeling the restraint she's shown in public while here is going to crumble before dessert is served. At least that's what I'm counting on.

With our physical bond stronger than ever, I'm glad we'll have New York to get to know each other without an audience. We've never had the option. Margie was in Texas, and here, she's surrounded all the time. The problems of a future queen have become my problems when I just want to date her. Love her.

I meet Bennett in the corridor. "How does it work dating a future queen?"

"Hello to you too. And I was just wondering the same thing."

"You were banging her in Austin, and you're trying, if you haven't succeeded yet, to bang her in her own palace, but dating seems to be off the table?"

"Stop calling it banging. We're not seventeen." We continue to the stairs to take them to the first floor. "And get the fuck out of my head. I have enough to worry about without you reiterating my every thought on the situation."

"Is that what she is? A situation?" We start down the large staircase. "And damn, dude. If you're banging in a fucking palace, it's only downhill from here."

"You're such an ass sometimes, Ben."

He shrugs. "I don't hide my likes, and I like women a lot. I like having sex with them even more. No apologies."

"You haven't met the right one yet. If you had, you'd be content just being in their mere presence."

"Mere presence? Okay, Shakespeare. Whatever. And let's

talk about that 'right one' you just threw out there like you have met her. Is Ally your right one?"

My brothers and I don't hide stuff from each other, not professionally or in our personal lives, but feeling like I'm constantly under scrutiny here, there's a sense of protectiveness that comes over me. It's wrong when I'm with my family. I can tell him anything, and he'd have my back no matter what.

I stop before we reach the bottom step. "I never got over her."

The jokes and smiles cease. He walks down and looks back up at me. "You're serious, aren't you?"

I nod, my throat tightening from the confession, my chest feeling exposed. "Well, let's get you the girl then."

"It's complicated."

"It always is."

"I'm referring to her being next in line to the crown."

Now he nods. Crossing his arms over his chest, he says, "It does make things more complicated but not impossible. I see how she looks at you. The duke doesn't stand a chance."

"I don't have land to offer her."

"Buy some."

He makes it sound so simple. Thinking about it a little deeper, maybe it is that simple. "I can buy land. What about a title?"

"Everest is a pretty damn good start, but who needs a title when you'll be the crowned prince if you marry her?"

"Marry her?" I repeat, letting the words roll around in my conscience. "I could marry her."

"Do you think you both are ready for that?"

"By how much time I spent thinking about her when she was gone, yes." *Marriage. I'm thirty-one years old, and before now, I hadn't really given marriage a huge amount of thought. Sure it crossed my mind when my mom asked me. That was easy enough to blow off, though, since I wasn't dating anyone seriously.*

Now really isn't the time to do that thinking, but it does need careful consideration. I don't know the rules or laws in her country. *What if I legally cannot marry Ally? What would it mean for my job if I can? My . . . my life? The life I'm building back in the US.*

Later, Everest. Think about this later. "I'll get a better feel for where her head is at in New York."

"I got the news earlier. How much work and how much play are we talking here?"

"Ten-ninety split?"

He laughs. "I had a feeling." Stopping once more before we join the others in the library, he says, "Ethan wants to see you happy as much as I do, but this isn't the same woman you met in Austin. She's in a whole other league with problems of her own that come along with her position. Be careful, brother."

"I will." I'm about to walk in but take a detour. "I'll be right back."

Heading into the dining hall, I want to make sure tonight goes as planned. I learned my lesson the hard way last time. I swap my place card with Bennett's, which now puts him next to Marielle. Figure he'll owe me one for that score. And I make one other change before I leave.

Margie's place card is currently directly across from Ally, so I move her next to Yamagata and Ally's father at the other end of the table, keeping Duke Dick centered for two reasons —not to be too obvious with the changes and to keep my eye on him. He's friendly to me because he doesn't realize who I am to Ally. Once he does, his ego is swollen enough for me to know that he'll be trouble.

21

Princess Arabelle

HUTTON EVEREST IS TRYING to kill me one suit at a time. Seeing that fine wool fitted to his athletic build is a glorious way to die.

The melted chocolate of his eyes causes my body to quiver under the intense gaze. There's no question who my body belongs to, and my heart made up its mind back in Austin, too. I'm tempted to run into his arms and jump on him, mount him, kiss him all over, and mark that man as mine for everyone to see, but I have to be sensible. Act with propriety, as is expected of a future queen.

He speaks with my parents briefly and then heads my way. With a glass of wine in my hand, I've had the luxury of enjoying a few minutes of solitude by the fire. I'm happy to have him invade my space. "Princess Arabelle," he greets, kissing my hand, then quickly placing one on the underside of my wrist. The gentle gesture always makes me weak in the knees. "You're breathtakingly beautiful."

Reaching up, I'm about to touch his tie but think better

of it. Too many witnesses, and I'm so close to New York I can taste it. I'm not blowing it now. "You look incredibly debonair, Mr. Everest."

"You clean up nicely, but I prefer you dirty."

I giggle. *Giggle like a schoolgirl.* He does that to me. "My sister doesn't. She told me I smelled after spending time with you. I should say she didn't know we had been together or what we had done, but if I could, I would wear your scent all over me for days." I sip my wine, not ashamed at all.

As he tucks his hands in his pockets, I wonder if he struggles not to touch me. Is he as weak to me as I am to him?

My mother joins us, her hands clasped in front of her. "Good evening, Mr. Everest."

"Good evening, Queen Aemelia," Hutton replies with a bow. He's so charming.

I can tell my mother thinks so by the way she smiles at him. It's a less-guarded grin reaching her eyes. She says, "You have quite the cheerleaders in your corner regarding the communications package and media deal."

"Is that right?"

"Jakob has been very impressed with your innovative way of approaching our needs."

His eyes glance at me. "I try to meet any needs before they arise."

"It seems. Then our lovely Arabelle will be joining you in New York City to be our eyes on the ground."

"I'm looking forward to showing her around. It's quite a large operation."

My mother replies, "I'm sure she can handle it."

He smirks. "I know she can handle large operations."

And I die . . .

With interest, he angles more toward her. "I'm curious

what you want Princess Arabelle to see while she's in the city. I like to be prepared. The corporate office might be uneventful unless . . ." He looks at me with the kindness of someone looking out for me, someone who cares about my well-being. My insides warm, and I know it's not from the fire. "Seeing employees hard at work is of particular interest. Our network is housed in New Jersey, but since the princess has an interest in communications, I think she'll enjoy seeing the studio we're building in Brooklyn. It's a fifty-million-dollar project that will be finished next year. It will also be where our media broadcasting division will be moved. So when we sign the deal—"

"If," the queen corrects.

He chuckles, charming her like he did me. "I prefer when."

"I'm sure you do, Mr. Everest." Her tone is playful, matching her expression.

"There's never been anything built like this. It's under lock and key, protecting the top-secret technology. It's quite a sight."

"I'm sure it is. I look forward to my daughter reporting back."

He says, "I think this trip will be quite productive," and glances at me. "Hopefully helping the committee decide." The queen looks pleased. Score one for Hutton and me. "Mr. Everest." Looking toward the grand hallway, she adds, "Dinner is ready. Shall we?" When she levers her hand toward him, he picks up on the signal and offers his elbow. What he doesn't realize is she's just made a bold statement, elevating him to the next hierarchy of royal prestige. No one can walk in front of her, except her guards, but not just anyone can walk next to her either.

"I'd be honored, Queen Aemilia."

Hutton looks at me and offers his other elbow, but I

shake my head subtly. I stick to protocol and stay three feet behind her, following them to the dining room.

He escorts her to the head of the table and then with swagger makes his way to my seat, reaching it as quickly as I find it as if he already knew where I'd be. "You're very good, Mr. Everest."

"So I'm told."

"Again, and humble."

He pulls my chair out for me, and I slip my hands under my dress to straighten before I sit. He leans down as he scoots me in, and whispers, "It's hard to be humble when one is built to please a queen."

"I hope you're referring to a future queen over a sitting royal."

Laughing, he says, "Only a future and forever queen for me," making my body tingle. He'd helped me work up quite the appetite earlier, but all I can think about is getting back in bed with him.

When he sits across from me, I start laughing. Margie says, "What is so funny, Princess Arabelle? I could really use a good laugh today."

The guests, all seated, turn to me as I look at Margie. "Just happy."

She flattens her napkin on her lap, eyeing me. "It's wonderful to see you so happy again. Any particular reason?"

I'd shoot her a glare, but everyone is silently waiting for an answer as if I'd discovered the fountain of youth. My mother says, "My Arabelle always did love to travel to far-off lands."

My father interjects, "Even if in her own head."

I feel the pressure of Hutton's shoe against the tip of mine. When I look up, I'm met with the kindest eyes I've ever seen. My mouth opens, but I catch myself before I speak.

He loves me. I feel it. I can see it. Does anyone else?

My mother continues as if my father never spoke a word. "She's always wanted to travel to New York."

"Yes, Mother, I can't wait."

"I've been cleared to travel with you." Margie is smiling as if she just won some grand prize—pretty on the surface and fake as fuck underneath.

"Oh, I assumed you'd be too busy working."

"Never too busy for you, Princess."

The soup is served like it's my saving grace. My gaze dips to the bowl in front of me. To the server, I whisper, "Thank you." The knot that's suddenly formed fills my stomach, making me worry. I've been so naïve. I need to stop acting like a princess and start thinking like a queen. Did I ever really think I'd get to spend this trip alone with him? Will Hutton and I have time alone, or will I be babysat the entire time?

Think like a queen.

Margie doesn't control me. And if I'm careful, she won't ever know a thing. I'll formulate a new plan by morning.

Hutton says, "Trust me. It's going to be an amazing trip."

Through the courses, I start to realize Margie has no power over me or Hutton or our relationship. It doesn't matter if we had a fight. I know when it comes down to our friendship that she'll back me. Ultimately, she wants what I do, and that's what's best for our country and for me. If that's Hutton, which my heart believes it is, then she'll support us.

She just doesn't realize that I've already fallen for him.

Fallen for him.

With my heart lumped in my throat, my gaze travels to the man on the other side of the table from me. Fallen for him . . . I haven't fallen for Hutton Everest. I've crashed and burned for him.

I now wonder . . . did I subconsciously believe he could

be the man who might sit next to me on the throne one day? I've always known the type of man I should marry—and that it was part of being queen—so had I already noted those qualities of respect and leadership in him from the beginning? *The qualities I want in my life permanently.*

Giving.

Caring.

Patient.

Loving.

Kind.

Respectful.

I don't think I've ever seen him treat anyone with disrespect. I laugh to myself, inwardly rolling my eyes. The only exception is me when he's pushing my buttons. I love the way he challenges me.

He doesn't treat me like a princess he has to bow down to. He treats me with honor while also treating me as an equal.

"Did you save room for dessert, Princess?"

When my eyes meet his, I feel the heat from our connection rising inside and coloring my cheeks. "I always save room . . . for dessert."

Magnetic.

He commands a room like no other man has tonight. Everyone is drawn to the dark-haired knight. Even his biggest rival is fascinated by Hutton's charisma. He's entertained us and has conversations with my father, the prince, and competitors as if they're longtime friends, holding his own.

Hardworking.

Intelligent.

Supportive.

Maybe he's not fully adjusted to the idea of me being a royal, but even as Ally, he was proud of my accomplishments.

He's the type of man who wouldn't lose sight of who he is, and he's not threatened by who I am.

"Arabelle?"

I turn to the sound of my name. My father says, "The duke asked you a question."

Shifting to look toward the other end of the table, Duke Dick says, "I was asking if you were free for a stroll around the gardens after dinner."

My eyes glance to my father, my stomach starting to sink. My father replies, "I informed him that you're free to speak on your own behalf."

"Am I?" The question is met with ire in my father's eyes. Turning away to avoid him, I swallow hard and try not to look at the only ones I want to see. I know the answer to the question asked of me. I just don't want to say it because, despite my father claiming I have free will, I know better. "Yes, sir."

The duke says, "Splendid. As soon as Queen Aemilia is finished, we can head out. It's supposed to be a full moon tonight."

My mother stands, cheerily. "I'm finished. Please don't let me keep you."

Staring at Hutton's hands, I keep my eyes locked down.

His fingers twitch, and then they're gone, a napkin tossed in their place.

I'm dragged out from under the table by the chair being pulled back suddenly. *What the hell?* The duke holds out his hand for me. "Princess Arabelle." *A demand, not a request.*

I don't want to do this because I know what this is leading to. If the scene hadn't been set for a proposal, my mother's happy tone was a giveaway. Reaching up, I set mine in his, and it's wrong. All wrong. Cold and kind of clammy. Thin and bony. Weak, like his personality.

When I dare to look up, Hutton's eyes are caught on my

hand that Dick is holding to help me up. Even though I whisk it away, Hutton says, "Please excuse me," and walks out of the room, heaviness in every step. The other guests follow as if there's entertainment in another room.

I can't imagine Hutton will go to his room, but maybe his anger gets the best of him. I just hope he's not angry with me.

Laughter echoes through the grand hallway where the dinner guests take their drinks and wander across to the library where this evening began. The duke stands, waiting on me, appearing pleased as punch as I get my glass topped to the brim with red wine before I leave with him.

I don't take the offered elbow. Not his. I walk with my wine and my head held high, trying everything I can do to deter him from doing what I think he's about to.

We walk through the arched doors to the veranda. The sky is clear. The moon is full and bright. The only chill in the air is the vibe I'm sending into the world. This better be snappy. I have an angry alpha to tend to . . .

Dick says, "You look lovely tonight, Arabelle."

"Thank you. I prefer Princess."

"Yes." He chuckles. "You'll make a beautiful queen. Speaking of, I spoke with the queen and prince this morning before I took our guests to Sutcliffe Castle." He walks ahead of me, which in itself is considered ill-mannered, and I chug a good fourth of my wine before he turns back. "They said they would speak with you."

"They did. I'm going to New York on Friday."

"Oh." His expression sours. "I was not informed of this decision."

"Why would you be?"

"Well, I thought we'd start making the proper arrangements."

He makes it sound like a funeral. It feels like one to me.

"The only arrangements I'm making are for this business deal to close so we can move on in life."

Dick says, "I agree. Put the pieces in place so when our engagement is announced, they'll be ready for our first official appearance. Something about the Everests rubs me wrong." Ironic because everything about Hutton rubs me right. "I'm leaning toward Yamagata."

There's so much I want to say about what he just did, but I need to get myself out of this situation. "Please be open-minded when it comes to the deal. I'll send back a report with my thoughts, so everyone has all the necessary details to make an informed decision." I take two gulps, not being ladylike at all in my rush to get out of here. "As for us, that's tabled too. My parents advise. They don't force."

"But, Princess, this match was made the day you were born."

Holding one hand up, I shake my head. "I will not be bartered or given in trade for the highest dowry. I'll rule as I live—with thought and care. It's the same for who I *choose* to marry."

He scoffs. "You act as if your choice—*love*—plays a role in this decision."

"For me, it does."

"Tread lightly, Princess. You don't have many offers on the table."

He makes my blood boil. Remembering what Hutton told me about the manner in which the duke spoke to the staff makes me angry all over again. He doesn't respect them, and he'll never respect me either. *Fuck him.* He needs a swift reminder. Preferably to his little dick. *Fuck him.* "What are you saying? That no one wants me? You'd be wrong, sir."

I turn away to go inside, but he snatches my arm, and I'm pulled back against him—his mouth to my ear—so fast that shock stiffens my muscles. "You're as spoiled as your reputation." His fingers dig into my arm. "You'd be lucky to marry into the Vaughns, *Belle*. So consider this my formal proposal."

Yanking my arm from his clutches, I stay close to make sure he hears. "Speaking of treading lightly, watch how you speak to me, *Duke*, or that might be the last time you retain that name."

I put my back to him and start up the stairs to the veranda. On the third step, I turn back, and say, "Just in case I wasn't clear enough for you, the answer to your proposal is a resounding and permanent no."

22

Hutton

Pacing my room got me nowhere. Literally. It didn't cool the anger I felt either. That fucker couldn't wait to get my Ally out of there.

I've been doing things wrong, not playing the game. I should have taken this royal situation more seriously. While I was busy picking up where Ally and I left off, this dick was making his move on her parents. Did I lose focus?

No. What Ally thinks is all that matters.

As soon as I enter the library, the butler tells me that the guests have moved to the media room. I wait for a bourbon neat, needing a strong drink to calm me. My mind is in overdrive, wondering what Dick and Ally are doing and what they're talking about that couldn't be said in front of us.

With a drink in hand, I head in to join the others. When I enter the room, Bennett waves me over, but I see her father, the crowned prince, sitting around a poker table with Jakob and Mr. Yamagata.

"Bennett." I nod toward the table. When he joins my side, he says, "I'm more of a dice man."

"You're a poker man tonight. C'mon."

"We saved two seats, gentlemen." Jakob welcomes us over. "Willing to wager?"

"I sure am." I sit down. "What's the ante?"

Mr. Yamagata replies, "Ten thousand US."

"I really suck at poker," Bennett says, dragging his hands down his pants before he sits. He orders a lager and two shots when a butler delivers drinks.

Looking at my glass, I'm going to need another. I want Ally back here and away from that asshat. The longer she's gone, the antsier I get. "Another, please." Leaning over, I tell Bennett, "I'll cover your debts tonight, but play big."

"Why?"

Chips are set down in front of us. I pick up one of the one-hundred-thousand-dollar stacks and set it next to the others. While the others discuss soccer, I lean over, and whisper, "Because we need to kick everyone's ass and show them we're not going down without a fight."

"Are we talking about poker, the deal, or are you talking about the princess?"

"Keep your voice down."

"Princess it is."

I'm not a gambling man by nature, but tonight I am. "Ante."

We toss our chips in and wait for the cards to be dealt. Our drinks are served, and our empties collected. I did well before becoming part owner of Everest Enterprises, but now I have money to burn and, apparently, an ax to grind. I'm invested balls deep in this game.

Jakob calls the round before I have time to think about my hand. Fuck me. There goes ten K without a second thought. "A pair of queens." *Ironically.*

"Full house," Bennett says, laughing. "Maybe I do need to be a card man." Winning the pot, he pulls the chips to his pile and stacks his winnings while the next hand is dealt.

I lose fifty thousand before I feel like I'm getting in the swing of things again. Although the bourbon warms me, I feel Ally's father's ice-cold stare between hands. I finally wager more than money. "Something on your mind, Prince Werner?"

"Actually there is. I've tried to work my way through what I've heard from Jakob versus—"

"Versus?"

"We've had some information brought to our attention," he says, organizing his cards. Glancing up, he looks at me. "Brudenbourg is a small country but a proud people. We trust each other by their word, and a handshake is as strong as a binding contract. We're fiercely protective of our image because our tourism and revenue are based on how the world views us. When problems arise, we deal with it." His eyes return to his cards, and new ones replace our discards.

"Has a problem arisen?"

He shows his hand. "It was brought to our attention that you were arrested for disorderly conduct."

"Whoa. I did not see that coming." I glance at my poker opponents, landing lastly on Bennett, who shakes his head, disappointed, no doubt, that this has been brought up.

He says, "That was four years ago."

Laying my cards down, I say, "I would have thought your initial background check would have spotted that blemish."

"We were looking into your current life in New York and assets. Upon further investigation, it seems we missed what you call blemishes." Her father is not wearing the crown, but he might as well be by how high and fucking mighty he sits on that imaginary pedestal.

Another losing hand feels fitting for this conversation. I

take a drink and then show my own hand—my life—laying it all out for him to see. "I was arrested when my brother was cheap-shotted in the back while helping a woman trying to get away from her abusive boyfriend."

Mr. Yamagata asks, "What is cheap-shotted? This is not a term I've heard before."

Bennett replies, "It's when someone hits you when you're not looking. I was punched in the back."

Yamagata says, "Ah, yes, a low blow."

I nod. "Yep, it was definitely a low blow. That's why I couldn't let him get away with it. I stand by my brothers. They're not only family, but they're also my best friends. Attacking one of us is the same as attacking all of us."

Jakob sits forward, his cards on the table. "My sister did that for me."

I know he means Ally, because that is true to her character. Before I can ask to hear the story, his father snaps, "Your sister hasn't been arrested." Ally's dad stands, clearly agitated, judging by the angry lines carved into his brow. "Please stay out of this, Jakob." His father presses his fingers into the green felt-top table, whitening the tips. "As I was saying, our image and tourism are everything. Brudenbourg won't survive if our reputation is tarnished, even if by association."

"Are you saying—?"

"Princess Arabelle," Bennett says, standing up.

In a piss-poor mood, I turn around. *Oh fuck.* Her tiara is crooked, her hair messier than when she left, and black has seeped into the skin under her eyes. *What the fuck?* I'm on my feet and about to rush to her, but something in her eyes, a plea and small shake of her head tells me to stay. "Al —*Princess?*"

"Please don't get up for me." Her hands wave at us to continue as though my heart isn't beating out of my chest to reach hers. "I only stopped by to say good night."

Jakob and Mr. Yamagata wish her a good night as if she's not standing there falling apart inside. Bennett steps forward, concerned as well. Not even looking at his daughter, her father dismisses her as if she's a bother. "Night."

Our eyes catch once more when she turns to leave. The door closes, and I'm on the move. "I'm retiring for the night. Bennett will handle the chips. Good night, gentlemen."

Swinging the door open, I run into Duke Dick's smug grin and shiny gold epaulets. "Where are you rushing off to, Everest?"

"Pardon me." I push past him because I don't give a shit about him. Only Ally.

"Stay and play a few hands. I was hoping to take your money."

His arrogance seems to be amped up tonight. Why's he so fucking cocky? I stop to get a real good look at him. "Where have you been?"

Bennett appears in the doorway when Dick's grin turns down. "Strolling with the princess."

"Strolling, huh?"

"That's what we're calling it."

A click of the tongue and boys' club wink are about to send me charging into him, but Bennett grabs his arm and tugs him into the room. "We've been waiting for you." My brother kicks the door closed, and I'm left with this anger boiling inside.

If he touched one hair on her head, I'll end that moth-erfucker.

Fuck him.

I need her.

Taking the stairs by three to the second floor, I stop on the landing, knowing I'm not supposed to be on the third floor, much less knocking on her door. Her words come back to me. "*Stick to the outside edges of the walkway and the camera won't catch you.*"

I rush toward the red curtains on this floor as I decide if it's best to take the stairs or find another way when I hear, "Psst."

Looking around, I don't see anyone at first, but when I hear it again, I make out a small woman at the far end of the floor, closer to my door. With deep red cheeks and messy blond hair sprouting out from under a white handkerchief, she smiles.

"Me?" I ask, pointing at my chest as I move quickly in that direction.

"Yes, you're Hutton."

She's not asking me, but I feel the need to still confirm. "Yes, I'm Hutton."

"Come here," she demands, waving me over to her. I bend down, and she squeezes my cheek. What the hell? "You're just as handsome as our Belle said."

Ally's talked about me? *I like that.* "She did, huh?"

"She's sweet on you."

Grabbing my hand, she pulls me down a hall. "That's good to hear because I'm sweet on her." She can't be more than five foot, but she's ox strong. "Who are you?"

"Birgit. I'm head cook for the Sutcliffes. Have been since Queen Aemilia was a princess herself."

Her joy is contagious when I shake her hand, and I smile in response. "Nice to meet you, Birgit. Now where are you taking me?"

"To the staff stairs." She opens a door, and I walk inside. "You won't get caught by the family or any of the other guests if you use this stairwell."

The stairs are black, and the cream-colored walls have many years' worth of handprints staining them. "Will I get in trouble for using these stairs?"

"Belle used these stairs her whole life when she wanted to get around without being seen."

We climb slowly to the next floor. She's not quick, but Birgit is friendly, entertaining, and I like that she protects Ally. I open the door on the third floor for her, but she shoos me. "Go. Be quick, and no one should see you."

"Thank you. It was nice to meet you." I'm not sure what to do—shake a hand, walk away, or hug her.

Beating me to the punch, she says. "I'm a married woman. Keep your googly eyes on Belle."

I laugh, but then realize I need to keep my voice down. Whispering, I say, "He's a lucky man."

"Toot scootin', he is. Like you. You're a very lucky man to have caught not only her eyes but also her heart. Take care of it. It's softer than folks realize."

I realize. "I will."

Checking this floor for any movement, I don't see any, so I make a run for Ally's door. I knock once, and then again before it swings opens, and I'm pulled in.

Pressed against the wood paneling, she rests against me, putting her head on my chest. "I'm so glad you're here, Hutton."

"Are you all right?" My arms wrap around her, and I hold her tight. She's so small in my arms, even smaller when she's sad. "What's wrong, sweetheart?"

"Sweetheart?" She rests her chin on my chest and looks at me with the true youth of her years residing in her eyes.

"My Ally. My girl. My baby. My princess. My sweetheart. You're all those things and more to me."

"Your girl?" she says, her emotions choking her.

I kiss the tip of her nose and then caress her cheeks and kiss her forehead. "Definitely my girl." When she begins to tear up, I say, "Tell me what's wrong."

"I was a fool. I thought all fairy tales had happy endings."

"Ours does." My words are quieter, and although I know what I'm saying, tasting the words means so much more.

Innocence. Trust. Love. Her irises are filled with everything she feels for me. "I wish we were going to New York sooner. I want to escape, to leave this place for a little while."

"We can go anytime you want."

Excitement gleams in her skies. "We can?"

"I only have to make a phone call, and the jet will be ready when we are." It's the first time I've gotten a good look of her in the low light of the room. She's washed her face clean of makeup, and her hair is down and silky brown. But her fingers twist around my shirt, tugging it free. "I want to be with you."

"I'm here." Tilting my head to the side, I want to see her eyes. Desperation colors her expression, so I stroke her cheek, hoping to ease whatever aches she's feeling inside. "I'm here for you. What do you need, baby?"

"You. Always. Kiss me, Hutton."

When I do kiss her, her lips take mine, and my tie is pushed to the side, and my shirt is yanked up. As much as I love being with her, having her desire me, something about this doesn't sit well. I stop the frenzy and hold her hands between us. "What's wrong? What happened with Dick?"

Her panting breaths heat my chest as she stares straight ahead. "Nothing. I just missed you."

"Then why aren't you looking me in the eyes?"

She never shies away from a challenge. Her bright eyes find mine, and she angles her chin up. "I am."

"Now. You are now, but something is wrong. Tell me."

"There's nothing to tell. I want to have sex with you. Is that not good enough?"

"Good enough?" What a fucking strange way to put it. "You're good enough. If anything's not, it's me even having a chance to spend time with you. So you wanting me is more than good, but something else is going on with you. Something happened, and we're not burying this conversation under a physical act. Tell me what happened that has upset you so much. What happened with Dick?"

Turning her back to me, she lowers her head as she walks toward the bed. "I told him no."

"No?" I stare at her. A roar becomes a rage. "No to what, Ally?"

She looks back at me. "To marrying him." Tears sparkle in her eyes like diamonds, but I wish they had the same pretty shine. "And to his advances."

My heart stops beating. Images from earlier—makeup smeared and a crooked tiara barely hanging on to messed-up hair—flood my mind. My next question comes slow, the words calculated. "And then what happened?"

"He didn't take no for an answer."

23

Princess Arabelle

QUIET . . .

Pretty and quiet.

Don't make a sound.

"Hutton?" Like every other rule in my life, I manage to break the cardinal palace rule. I never was good at following them. "Wait, Hutton," I shout, holding the railing and reeling around it.

He only had a two-second head start out the door, but he's a lot faster than I am. Running barefoot isn't helping me. The echo of the door slamming against the wall reaches my ears, and I pick up my pace, running down the stairs.

A loud roar rips from Hutton's chest, and I hear the sound of a table breaking before I reach the door. Entering the media room, I come to a rapid halt, covering my mouth in horror.

Hutton yells at the top of his lungs, "You're a fucking dead man," while Bennett pulls him back. Chips have exploded around the room, and a bloody-nosed Dick lies on top of the broken poker table. Jakob stands between the two men with his arms out wide.

Mr. Yamagata leans against the buffet laughing. I move in front of Hutton, pushing my hands against his chest. "Hutton. Please," I plead, "stop."

"Stop?" He turns his ire on me. "He forced himself on you, and you want me to stop?"

"Yes, I do."

Bennett loosens his hold on his brother and tells him, "Let's go. That fucker's not worth your time."

His anger coats every breath. His eyes are locked on Dick as though he's eyeing his prey. Swear words I've never heard before fill the air, but I hold my hands to him, hoping he backs down.

I had hoped my father would have already retired for the night and not been here to witness this, but my eyes close in defeat when I hear him speak. "You're a princess dressed like a whore. You've been nothing but trouble, and you'll never be queen." *What? He's making this about me?*

My hands fall from Hutton's chest as I look at what I'm wearing—boxer shorts and a cutoff concert tee that hangs off one shoulder. No socks. No shoes. No bra. I can't look my father in the eyes. I don't want to see how much I've disappointed him. *Have I finally lost the last of the love he had for me?* "I apologize. I didn't expect to leave my room tonight."

My reason will be seen as an excuse because I was raised that even in private, I should be dressed appropriately. I've failed my family name again, and now I've shamed them.

I look up into Hutton's usually comforting, warm eyes, but even he can't save me from the humiliation coursing through me. Tears sting my cheeks as they topple over my lower lids. Hutton reaches out to wipe them away, but I take a step back, knowing I can't make another wrong move or my father's threat will become a reality. He says, "Don't let them win, Ally."

"They already did."

My father demands, "Get away from daughter, Mr. Everest, and pack your belongings. I want you out of my home immediately."

Hutton hits my father with a harsh glare. "No problem, Prince." Holding out a hand, he whispers, "We can go to New York together just like you wanted. We'll leave tonight."

My father sets his drink down, the Scotch spilling over the lip of the glass. "How dare you proposition a Brudenbourg princess like she's a streetwalker."

"Your words. Not mine."

"Leave before I have you arrested or maybe you've missed your natural habitat."

"Fuck you," Hutton replies, treating my father like he's bothersome gnat. Turning back to me, he changes his demeanor, softening toward me. "Come with me, Ally."

Dick pushes off the broken table and holds his head back. With his eyes on us, he asks, "Why do you keep calling her Ally?"

Jakob steps into the mix. "What are you doing, Hutton? That's my sister."

Bennett comes around and drops his shoulders. "You need to step back, Jakob."

"Or what?" My brother's hand pushes my hip. "Get back, Belle."

I hate the pain I've caused my family. "It's okay, Jakob. He won't hurt me."

Hutton calls my name. When I look at him, he says, "I'll take you anywhere. I'll give you anything you need."

Dick yells, "What the hell is going on?"

As if my wounds weren't deep enough, Margie shows up. I brace myself for the betrayal, but it doesn't come. She walks over with a robe I don't recognize and wordlessly drapes it over my shoulders.

My brother is as confused as my father, and asks again, "Belle, what's going on?"

Glancing at my father, I say, "You can take away what's rightfully mine, but that will only change history. I'll live on."

"Somewhere else," he says, "if you walk out with him."

Jakob touches my arm. "Don't do this, sis."

"I'm not. He is," I say, gesturing to our father. I take Hutton's hand and start to leave. "I just have to pack a few things."

To my back, my father shouts, "Everything you own is Brudenbourg property. You own nothing, so you'll take nothing."

I never look back. It's not an image I want to remember my father by because he wasn't always that mean. Outside the media room, Hutton stops me. "You don't have to do this for me. I love you. I'll love you if you stay. You don't have to give up anything for me."

"I'm not giving up anything. I'll fight. It just won't be tonight. Everyone is too heated to make sense. A few days off and a few days apart will be good for all of us. It will be fine."

"Will you be?"

"Yes. I'm fine. I'm always fine." I exhale, not wanting to be like this with him. I don't have to be strong with Hutton. I get to be me. I squeeze his hand. "I am. Come on. I can help you pack."

I know he doesn't believe me when I say I'm okay, but he lets me breathe anyway, knowing when to push and when to let it lie for the time being.

Bennett joins us. "Damn, girl. You know how to rile the pops up."

As we walk up the stairs, I keep my head down, trying to

keep my father's words out of my head. "It's not the first time. He'll get over it."

"I'm glad Marielle wasn't down here, or we all would be going to hell together."

"New York's not hell," I say. "It's a paradise compared to how the past few years have been here." Hutton's silence reveals his concern, so I poke him, hoping to eke out a smile. "Hey, it's going to be okay. I will be, too."

"I can't believe—"

"This is a long time coming. I'm just sorry you've been mixed up in it."

Bennett says, "The jet will be ready in thirty minutes. How long do you need?"

"Ten minutes tops."

We walk farther down the hall after Bennett enters his room. As soon as we walk into Hutton's quarters, I'm tempted to hide like I used to, to pull the covers over my head and wait for a new day to begin. That's not going to happen this time. "My father called me a whore."

"You're not a whore," Hutton says, setting his suitcase on the bed and opening it. "There's nothing wrong with what you're wearing. You were wearing it to bed, for fuck's sake. What does he want you to wear to bed? A nun's cloak?"

"It's complicated."

"You're telling me."

I sit on the bed next to him and watch as he tosses his stuff inside the case. Shoving my hands into the pockets of the robe, I'm met with something hard. I look into the pocket and find a passport—mine to be precise. *Margie.* After the fight we had, I'm surprised to see this sleight of hand with her helping me out in my time of need. This little gesture gives me hope that we're not too far gone to mend our friendship.

Leaning forward, I ask, "Are you okay? Are you hurt?" I reach for his hands to inspect for damage, but he pulls away.

"I'm fine. I just want the fuck out of here. I'll grab my stuff from the bathroom, and then we're gone."

Returning with a small leather bag, he tosses it in the luggage but then flips through his papers. His eyes flash to mine. "You need your passport."

I pull my passport from my pocket and wiggle it.

He says, "That's convenient."

"Maybe Margie doesn't hate me like I thought."

Stopping to look at me, he asks, "What's going on with Margie?"

"What's going on with Margie?" *How do I explain that without crying? For many years she'd been my best friend. Yet now . . .*

"Let's just say that two years together in Texas were not good for our friendship. Or rather, they weren't good for Margie. Some of that is on me. Long story for another time."

"We have a seven-hour flight ahead of us, and I'm all ears." The suitcase is closed, and while he zips it up, he looks me over. "You look fantastic to me, but do you think they'll let you change clothes?"

I can't go to my room. If I do, I'll break down when I see what has been my whole life for so long. "No." My father doesn't deserve the satisfaction of my tears. I pop my chin in the air, feeling stubborn. "I don't need anything from them."

"I'll have Singer loan you clothes until you can buy what you need."

"With what money?"

He sets the case down on the floor. "What's mine is yours. I can and will buy you anything."

"Anything." I walk to the window and look out over the roundabout where an SUV already waits. "From my parents' daughter to your care."

"Ally?"

"Huh?" I look back at him.

"I didn't mean—"

"I know what you meant. I just . . ." My voice trembles. Taking a deep breath to help stifle the sob lying in wait to break free, I turn around completely. "I have these degrees, but they're basically worthless because I was ultimately trained for one thing."

"To be the queen." I nod, and he adds, "But guess what? You can be anything you want to be."

"Where?" I snap. "In New York? Texas?"

"Anywhere you want to be. You're intelligent and brilliant. From the moment I met you, that drew to you."

"I don't even say what I want to half the time."

"Then imagine how incredible it will be when you do." Crossing the room, he closes the distance between us and stands next to me. "Don't hold back anymore. I'm not your father or your mother. I want nothing else other than your happiness."

"How do you do that?" I reach for his hand, rubbing my thumb over the veins on top of it. "You're offering me anything I need, but don't you see? I have nothing to give in return."

"I want to kick your father's ass for what he called you—"

"Hutton."

"What?"

"You can't say things like that. He's the crowned prince."

"He's not mine," he replies incredulously.

"He is mine, though."

His frustration shows in the way he looks at me—sharp gaze narrowed—so I say, "Don't worry about me. He's mad, but he'll cool down. Anyway, he doesn't have the final say. My mother does, so I'll be fine. But what can I do for you?"

"I'm good." He runs the back of his hand gently down my cheek. "I get time with you. You're all I need, baby."

Leaning my head on his arm, I hug him. "I'm scared."

His arms come around me. "I know, baby. But you'll be okay. I'll be here for you however you need me."

"Promise?"

"Cross my heart."

With the suitcase in tow, we walk down the hall together. Easy. I was crying earlier over the sharpness and stabbing of my father's words, but Hutton's right. He's the easiest decision I've made in years. I reach for his hand, and when he takes mine, I bring it to my lips and kiss it. "Thank you."

"For?"

"For loving me through thick and thin."

"That's easy, Ally. You're easy to love."

We descend the grand staircase—the one where my mother held me when I was introduced to the world, the one where we took our family portrait every year, and the same stairs I'll walk down for my coronation. They're called grand for a reason.

As sure as I am of my love for Hutton, I'm sure that one day I'll still be the queen, no matter what my father said. Those were only words spouted in a heated moment. As for Dick, after tonight, I will never be forced to share his company again, and I most definitely won't be his wife.

New York will be a necessary break for all of us. This trip will give us the time we need to think and to clear our heads. We'll talk later in the week, but for now, I'm going to support my man.

Yep. *My man.*

I don't think I've closed my mouth since the jet landed. "These buildings are bigger than they seem on TV."

"We have some in Houston, but not everywhere you look like here."

"Where do you live?" I ask, sitting back in the car we took from the private airport. It's taken over an hour to get into the city, and I have no idea how much longer it will take, but it's an incredible sight to see for the first time.

Reaching over, he slides his hand under mine and holds on. "Not too much farther. I'm glad you're here."

"Me too."

"Are you scared? You left everything."

"It was nice of Birgit to give me her clogs." I hold up my feet and wiggle them. "Not the sexiest, but they're pretty comfortable."

"You know what I mean. You're wearing a robe."

"Good thing there are no cameras around." I try for humor, but it doesn't reach my heart. "I don't think it's fully set in."

"You sure you don't want something from my suitcase?"

"No. I'm fine."

"Fine," he repeats, looking unsatisfied. Glancing out the window quickly, he then turns back to me. "We're here."

I bend to look out the window and see a mirrored building leading straight to heaven. The car drops us off at the curb. A doorman wearing a suit similar to the duke's opens the shiny brass doors for us. I tighten my robe around me, and whisper, "Okay, now I feel like a crazy lady."

Hutton wraps his arm around me.

The doorman says, "Welcome home, Mr. Everest."

"Thank you, Jimmy." I live in a palace, but this place is amazing. White marble fills the lobby, making it appear pristine with modern seating off to one side and Jimmy's desk on the other. "Jimmy, Ms. Edwards will be staying with me indefinitely. Can I get a key made for her and access to the facilities?"

"I'll take care of it right away, sir, and welcome, Ms. Edwards."

"Thank you," Hutton and I say at the same time.

When we step into the elevator, he pushes the button, and says, "I live on the twenty-sixth floor."

"That's really high up."

"My brother Ethan owns the penthouse. I'll take you up there later."

"Where does Bennett live?"

"Same floor as me." Touching my chin, he says, "Are you tired?"

The overnight flight allowed us to sleep, but I still feel like I'm dragging. "Exhausted."

"I'm going to take a shower unless you'd like to take one first?"

"I really want to sleep, but I think I should shower first."

"You got it."

"Why did Bennett have to go into work right away?"

"He needs to close down the file and check on some of the clients we've not been able to talk to while we were away."

"The communications file for my country?"

He nods. The doors slide open, and we step out. "There are only two doors?"

"Bennett lives down there. I'm on this side." I look down the hall one way and then follow him down the other direction. With a smirk on his face, he opens the door. "Home sweet home."

I walk in with my mouth hanging open again. "That view."

"It's amazing, right?"

"I've never seen anything like it." Moving inside, I hear

the door click behind me and head for the windows. With my hands pressed to the glass, I can see the Statue of Liberty and for miles beyond. Whipping back to him, I say, "You must do very well to afford that view."

Chuckling, he replies, "I do. Let me show you around."

I marvel at the kitchen and how open everything is. "Birgit would love this kitchen." Wobbling my head, I add, "Gerhart would hate it." It's an inside joke, but Hutton's sweet enough to laugh. "Show me the bedroom."

"Happily."

I'm led into the master bedroom and look around. Cool grays and dark navy accent the white sheets and pillows. "That's the largest bed I've ever seen. I can't wait to climb into it."

Scooping me into his arms, he carries me to the bed, and says, "I'm so glad you're here."

I'm dropped with a bounce on the mattress. Being very un-princess-like, I sprawl my arms and legs out. "Now this is heaven."

Jumping on top of me, he shakes his head. "No, heaven is having you here with me."

"I love you, Hutton Everest."

"I love you, Ally Edwards."

"Guess I'm back to my old alias."

"You're in New York. That means you can be whoever you want to be."

Mrs. Everest has a nice ring to it, but so does Queen Arabelle of Brudenbourg. I have no real idea what my future will now be, but whether here or there, I need to see if I can reconcile the two lives together. My life makes sense with Hutton in it, and I will do anything it takes to keep him there.

24

Hutton

I EXPECT to see Ally when I walk in from my errands. When I don't, I set the flowers on the kitchen island and call her name. After sleeping for hours, I got up to grab a pizza and picked up flowers for her along the way.

"Ally?" She was restless when I got up, but now I'm met with silence. I head to the bedroom, hoping my girl was able to get some more sleep.

My steps are quick, but stop altogether when I find her asleep in the bed, curled on her side and hugging a pillow like it's me. It should be. I slip off my shoes and undress as I maneuver to the bed. Climbing under the covers, I move so I can wrap myself around her.

As the sleep wears off, she says, "Jet lag is a bitch."

I laugh. I don't even know if she's trying to be funny, but she speaks the truth. My body is heavy; my mind fuzzy from the craziness during the last week. "We're supposed to stay up and get on East Coast time. We failed."

"Sleeping felt too good, so I'm good with our choice,"

she says, rolling over to face me. "I did get up long enough to call and refill my pills since I left them in Brudenbourg." Stroking my cheek, she smiles. "You packed some extra bags since we've arrived."

"Ha. The bags under my eyes are carry-ons from the lack of sleep. I feel like I could sleep for a week."

"Let's do it. Stay in bed with me all week. We can order in and make love. We can be each other's world for just a little while. Sounds amazing, right?"

I kiss her softly on the lips. "Amazing."

Her arms come around me, and she gets as close as she can, one of her knees wedging between mine. "I missed you."

"I was gone longer than I wanted to be, but I don't want you getting sick of me." I wink and run my hand over her hip.

"Never. I never have enough time with you, so I won't be sick of you anytime soon." She winks right back. *The spitfire.* "Will you be working every day while I'm here?"

"We should talk about your stay here."

That sets off alarms, and she starts to push up. "If it's a burden, I can stay at a hotel."

As I'm holding her too tight to let her escape, she relents and stays put. "You're not a burden. You're . . ." I look at her mouth, her nose, her neck, and her shoulders. I look everywhere, anywhere but in her eyes. We've told each other we love each other, so the rest should come easy, but with her life in transition, hopefully transitioning into mine, I wonder if my confession is too much, too real to say right now.

"What am I?" she whispers.

When I hear my anxiousness reflected in her question, I'm quick to ease her concern. "You're the best thing I've ever come home to. You're the reason I came home. So you're not a burden to me. You're welcome here as long as you want to stay."

She snuggles against me again; her breath warm against my neck, and her heart beating steady against mine. "Good. I have no money, so you're kind of stuck with me for the time being anyway."

"Have you thought about what happened yesterday?"

"It's all I could think about. It's why I finally gave in to the jet lag. I needed to shut off my mind."

"And?"

"I'm okay." Lying on her back, she glances outside the window before staring at the ceiling. Rubbing her eyes, she yawns. "A part of me wonders if my father meant what he said."

I roll onto my back, keeping my arm along the length of hers, liking the contact. She knows her father better than me, but what he said didn't sound like a threat. It sounded like a decree. I've kept my mouth shut since my opinion won't change a thing, but her mind is going to station itself in the worst of outcomes soon enough. When she looks at me for an answer, I take hold of her hand and hold it on my chest. "You said 'for just a little while' and 'for the time being' like this is temporary, like we are. I don't want to push you in any way, but what are you thinking?"

"I never meant—"

"I know you don't want to hurt me—"

"Never. But I also never meant to insinuate we're temporary, Hutton. You're not to me. We've been on the verge of this conversation so many times but have managed to avoid it. Living in the moment. Not wanting to risk the good we were having. Whatever the reason was, the situation has changed, and we need to talk about it. About us."

"Do you want to talk over dinner?"

"I'm starving," she says, climbing out of bed, bare-ass beautiful, "but I'm not getting dressed."

Grabbing the remote from the nightstand, I flick the

button to close the blinds. That sweet little ass is only mine for the lookin'. "I wouldn't want it any other way."

She twirls twice—hands in the air, up on her tiptoes, smile on her face, hair swinging around her shoulders—as she heads for the bathroom. Walking backward, she says, "That goes for you too, sweet cheeks."

"Sweet cheeks?"

She shrugs as she spins again and disappears behind a closed door.

I've never felt luckier in my life than I do right now, but how do I hold on to the magic she brings into my life when it can be so easily ripped away?

I get out of bed, hoping we can find a way to be together because right now, we've lost the sun through the clouds. I'm willing to do whatever she needs from me, to be who she needs, but will that be enough *if* she's not the queen?

With a blanket covering her, Ally's cuddled up on the couch and staring at the screen. "What happens if the quarterback falls?"

"Falls? Quarterbacks don't fall."

Pointing at the large screen, she says, "He falls if the guy in green takes him down."

"You mean if he's tackled? That's a quarterback sack if he's behind the line of scrimmage and can't deliver the ball down the field."

"TMI." She leans her head on the back cushion while I chuckle. "American football is very slow." I recognize the football frustration. I've experienced it many times. She points at the screen, and says, "They've only gone a few feet in the past ten minutes. Why are there so many commercials and delays?" She seems to stop to ponder while wiggling her toes. "Let's get to the action. Come on, Texans."

I reach over and rub her leg. "The game's recorded from earlier this week. We can fast forward."

"What? Why have you been holding out on me? I can't handle any more of those macho men pill commercials that air during every break."

Tempted to make a joke about her handling things, I know I shouldn't. Like she said earlier, we've become masters of avoidance when it comes to certain topics. I click off the TV. "We can watch that later. I'd like to come back to our earlier conversation."

Angling my direction, she keeps her body covered with the blanket as she rearranges. This is the first time I feel like our relationship isn't teetering on the next thing I say, and we have space to air our thoughts without any interruptions. That's a good start.

Sitting forward, I hold her ankles and run my hands up and over her calves and back down. "Let's talk about you being queen. I think decisions can be made based on that answer."

"What's the question?"

"If you have the choice, I can only assume you'll take the throne." I try to be careful on the next part, but I think being direct with her is best. "Whatever you decide, we'll handle it together. You're my future, Ally. I love you." She smiles and nods, but I'm not truly sure what is going on in her mind yet. She hasn't denied *us* for the first time, so, should I feel relief? "What if you don't become queen?"

As if the idea has never occurred to her, her brow furrows. "I don't understand what you mean. It's my born right to claim the crown."

"Unless—"

"Unless nothing, Hutton." She sits up, the blanket slipping down. Gripping it as if she finds security in the fibers, she says, "I will be queen, even if I have to fight for it."

"Your father said—"

"My father called me a whore. They'd have to prove I've broken the law to keep me from the crown."

Feisty has always been one of my favorite qualities of hers, but when it comes to this sensitive topic, I worry that she's hiding behind it instead of dealing with the possible repercussions. "Can they do that?"

"Do what? Prove that I'm a whore? That I'm not a virgin?" Even saying it makes her eyes change, amusement filling them.

"No." I move closer and take her hand between mine. "We both know you're not a whore. What the fuck? Who even thinks like that about women? Says a lot about your dad."

"Father. Anyway," she replies, seeming to shrug it off, "I guess they could if they wanted. One visit to the doctor could confirm their suspicion."

"Would they do that?"

She pulls her hand back. "I doubt it. The throne is mine, Hut. Why are we talking about this? We can watch more of the football game? Or . . ." Getting up, she crooks a finger for me to follow. "We can have fun in the bedroom." She spins on her bare heels and heads down the hall, the blanket trailing like a train behind her.

I follow because yeah, I would go anywhere when it comes to her. The thought makes me pause. In the space between the living room and the master bedroom, I stand and ask myself the question I didn't realize was a real possibility until now. *Would I?*

Would I follow Ally anywhere? Give up my life in the US to live out hers?

I blow out a push of air. Somehow in the past few days,

my life hasn't just flipped upside down, but it has also jumped the rails. I start walking again because these questions seem to come secondary to the ones I'm asking of her.

I open a drawer and pull out a pair of underwear and a shirt, slipping them both on. I hand her a T-shirt as well and then move farther into the room, clicking the blinds open again and standing in front of the windows looking out at the nightscape. Not knowing how much room I should give her, I let her decide by staying put. "It's important for you to take a minute to look at your options."

Turning toward the middle of the room, she pulls on the shirt that hangs mid-thigh, and asks, "What are you talking about?" I have a feeling she knows what I'm talking about, but as usual, she's pushing the fear away instead of facing it.

"I understand this is a tricky *and* touchy subject, but it needs to be discussed. We both need a plan in place."

"There's only one plan for me."

"Then what about me?"

"Are you going somewhere?"

"No, but when your life leaves the station, I don't want to be left on the platform."

Her shoulders fall with her expression. "I wouldn't leave you behind like that. It's confusing. We're making life decisions as if we've dated for years. I shouldn't have hidden who I was from you once we started seeing each other exclusively, but do you understand why I did? Why I had to?"

"I do understand, but I didn't like it. I still don't. That last night we had in Austin, you should have told me. You were leaving. Your heart was already gone, so you could have spared mine."

"That's where you're wrong. It's the reason when I see you, I can't stay away. I don't *just* see you. I feel you inside me." Even now, she struggles to maintain the five feet of distance that divides us, but then she comes to me, winning her own battle. With her hands on my chest, she asks, "Do you feel the heart that beats inside you? That's mine. That's mine because I left it with you in that hotel room."

I cover her hands with mine. "If I would have known, I would have taken better care."

She smiles, but it doesn't reach her eyes. "You've taken the best care. I appreciate everything you've done for me, Hutton, but what if . . . *what if* I'm never crowned queen?"

Reality starts to sink in, and I hate that I was the messenger, even if she did need to consider all possibilities. Bringing one of her hands up, I kiss the tips of her fingers. "Then you'll be the same person. You'll be Ally."

The room seems bigger with her in it. Her frame appears smaller in her sadness as if she's shrinking away. "Ally was only supposed to be temporary."

"I think you're more Ally than you ever were Arabelle."

Backing away, I hate it, but I'll let her go if she needs the space to think. She balls the hem of the shirt in her hands. "Because you don't know that side of me, but that's who I am."

"I only know who you were with me. I like to believe you gave me the real you. Did you?"

"You know I did," she says, sitting on the edge of the bed. "But that's not who I want to be forever. I would choose Arabelle any day over being plain ole Ally."

The insult burns. "How can you hate what I love so much?" I strike back. My words cause her to jerk her neck back in response.

"Hate? I don't hate being Ally. Ally is quite freeing from my daily pressures, but I was born to be—"

"I know what you were born to be. *I get it.* But you were Ally of your own accord. *Choice.* That's the difference here. Deep down, I believe Ally is who you really want to be, but because all your life you've been groomed to be queen, you've never thought any other option was a possibility. And I get that too. But what if you now have a choice?" Her mouth hangs open, but I keep going because it needs to be said. "What's this bad reputation everyone keeps talking about? What did you do that got you exiled the first time?"

Standing in defiance, she gasps. "I've never been exiled. I went to school in England because my horizons needed to be broadened. I went to Texas to further my studies to help my country."

"Help your country or spare your parents the embarrassment?"

She turns toward the bathroom but stops and drops her head. When she looks back at me, conflict is warring in her eyes. "I thought you were different."

"I am. That's why you haven't run away." Coming closer, I say, "I'm team Ally. I'm team Arabelle. I'm team *you*. Whoever you want to be, I'm rooting for you."

"Then why are you arguing with me?"

I like that she's been bold, standing her ground, standing up to me when it's something she believes in. But I also like that she's not running from me or hiding. "I'm not. I'm trying to make you see that no matter what you say to me, I'm still not your enemy. So when you mistakenly think I'm here like every other person in your life, looking to gain from you or to judge you, you'll be wrong. You can trust me."

"I know."

"Don't you see, Ally? I'm the one with everything to lose."

She does trust me, and I can still hear the softness of her tone when she asks, "What do you have to lose, Hutton?"

"You."

25

Ally

ME.

With the mess I've caused him and the loss of a billion-dollar deal, how does Hutton Everest still only care about me? "You mean that?"

"I wouldn't say it if I didn't." In business, I imagine the man before me is a force to be reckoned with, but to me, he's always so endearing. I don't know what it is about this moment—maybe it's the way he's looking at me or because I know I can trust him—but I spill the only other secret I've been keeping from him. "I need to tell you something."

While he sits on a bench under the window, I move to the edge of the bed. "You've heard about the press trying to ruin me in Brudenbourg through bits of conversations that shouldn't have been spoken in front of you."

"But you could've, and I wouldn't have told anyone."

"I know, but I didn't want Jakob or anyone else saying anything because I didn't want you to think less of me, but being with me means certain things won't remain secret. Being with me, you should know what you're getting into—"

"I'm already in too deep to turn back now, princess."

"I love your spunk."

He suddenly looks traumatized. "What?"

"What?" I volley back unsure why he's reacting that way.

"You love my spunk?"

"Yes. What am I missing?"

His handsome features relax, and he starts chuckling. Rubbing his hands over his face, he replies, "I thought . . . Never mind. My thoughts are in the gutter. Sorry."

Why do I feel like I've missed something big here? I make a mental note to research spunk later.

Getting us back on track, he asks, "Why did the press make up lies about you?"

"They didn't. I never said the press was wrong. I said they tried to ruin me. I was so good, always keeping up appearances, but on the inside, I was unsettled. I liked to *challenge* my parents, as they call it. But I wasn't challenging them. I was challenging the world I lived in. No kissing. No dates. No boys. Dress a certain way. Wear my hair pulled back. No jeans. No shorts. Don't show my legs. God, it was a nightmare. And when I say that, I realize I sound spoiled, and that some people have real-world problems. But as a teenager, with my hormones out of whack, everything is emotionally bigger than it really is. So I rebelled."

"Against?"

"The system. The laws. My parents. My country's traditions. I snuck out to go on dates. I kissed boys until my lips were swollen and hickeys had to be hidden by turtlenecks in summer. I would go to the beach and wear a bikini and hang out with my friends. I'd drink and party, but you know what I never did that was thrown into their gossip column without regard to how it might affect me?"

"What?"

"The ex that I caught with Sabine Rosalie finally got his revenge after I broke up with him for cheating on me."

Hutton takes a deep breath and slowly exhales, then he flexes his fingers and stands, bracing his arms to his sides. My injured heart hurts him. That's how much he loves me. With every fiber of his being.

"He told everyone I had sex with him," I say, and then shrug like it didn't affect me when, in reality, it destroyed my reputation . . . and me. "Doesn't seem like a big thing, but in my country, we have a law—"

"The chastity law." Closing the distance between us, he rubs my upper arms. "And then your father called you a name."

"Whore. That was part of the headline. Princess Whorabelle. It's quite clever, don't you think?" I try to lighten the mood, though I feel the same pain as the day I read it.

"No. It's cruel." His eyes don't leave me, and although I want to put on a brave face, when I raise my chin, it quivers, so I lower it again, sucking in a stifling breath.

"They sold the story worldwide, but I was soon forgotten when a European royal stepped out of line, but it still hurt."

Settling between my legs, he stands before me and holds my arms. "They're assholes. Regardless if the attention shifted, they hurt you. If I could fix it, I would. I'm sorry you had to go through that. I take it your father sided with the article."

"And put me on a plane to England for university. You can't throw a stone without hitting a royal over there. Then later to Texas. I was told to blend in, keep my head down, and study." I sighed. "I did. Until I came home. Some wild ways can't be tamed. The name came back as soon as I landed on Brudenbourg soil. Why fight fate?"

"Because that wasn't your fate. That was bullshit made up

about you. Only you determine your destiny." *If only that were true. My country determines my destiny. It always has. And for some reason, I've believed I wasn't really to blame for having to leave, that it was the stupid laws at fault.*

He takes a step back when I stand. "I've been lying to myself."

"About?"

"I tried to pretend I wasn't exiled, but you're right. I was. Even if it was for a short time in the scheme of my life, I was forbidden from returning. I should start using the correct terminology. It's going to be the only way I will heal from that betrayal." I stretch my neck to the side, noticing some of the normal tension is gone. "Acknowledging the truth is kind of freeing. I already feel lighter."

"Share those truths and free your whole being."

"I have one for you."

I like his smile—kind, trustworthy, friendly. "Hit me with it."

"I'm not a whore." I shrug for an entirely different reason this time. "I may act like one when I'm in bed with you, but that doesn't define who I am to the world."

"No, it doesn't." With his head tilted down, he chuckles to himself while rubbing the tip of his tongue over his bottom lip. Peeking up, he says, "I have a secret."

My body stills, having no clue what he's going to say. "What is it?"

"I looked up the chastity law."

"Oh. Okay. This is not where I thought this conversation was going."

"Did you know we've broken not only the chastity law about a hundred times over?" Seriousness belies his expression, then he starts laughing. "But we've violated at least eight other of your laws."

I burst out laughing. "Oh my God," I say with a smile so

big on my face that my cheeks hurt. So much so that tears form in my eyes. I try to catch my breath, but my laughter causes me to bend over. "And here I was only worried about the one." Finally catching my breath, I say, "I needed that."

"Yeah, you did." He comes over and hugs me again. "Let me know what I can do for you, or how I can help, and I will. Anything."

My head is kissed. "Same goes for you." I lift up to kiss this awesome mountain of a man on the chin. "I love you."

"I love you."

"I think I'm going to take a bath. Want to join me?"

"You. Naked. Water. Me. Hell yes, I want to join you."

Moving into the bathroom, he starts the water to fill the tub. We're okay in the silence because we're good. *Team us.* I pour bubble bath in and slip my hand under the water as I sit on the edge of the tub.

When it's more than half full, Hutton takes my hand, helping me to balance so I don't slip while I get in. The heat of the water feels so good to my sore muscles from traveling.

Hutton strips down again and steps in, settling opposite from me, our legs tangling. He asks, "I might be the reason you're not the queen?"

"You're not. It will be all on me. I knowingly broke the law with you."

"When you say that, you make it sound like you were a virgin when we slept together." He laughs, but when I don't, he stops and stares. Understanding sinks into his melty chocolate eyes. Water splashes over the edge when he bolts upright. "Why aren't you laughing?" The question is asked with a serious edge.

I bite my lip, knowing I have to be honest and expose the truth just as we've been doing since we arrived. I should have been honest from the beginning, but it felt so good to be someone else when we first met. We were drawn together as if destiny played a hand in bringing us together that night. The right place at the right time. The short version of us meeting in a bar will never capture the magic of how our great love story started.

Gliding through the water, I sit on his lap and bend to kiss his neck. He grows between my legs. His hardness feels slick beneath the layer of bubble bath and I move enough to let him know what I want. "You taught me everything I know."

His shoulders are tense, so I massage the muscles while I rub other parts of his body with mine. I close my eyes as the sharp points of his five o'clock shadow scrape against my cheek. The pleasure of this pain takes my mind off anything except him. My hips are stopped, held in place, and he says, "Look at me, Ally."

"I am." My gaze goes from his eyes to his mouth, then to his chest and his forehead until my jaw is captured and angled, so I look into his eyes.

"Were you a virgin?"

"Everyone's a virgin before having sex."

"I'm serious."

"What's the big deal anyway?"

When he lowers his eyes to the water, I see the conflict written in his forehead. His hands dip under the water and seem to find my ass on their own accord, holding me still on his lap. After a heavy sigh, he says, "The big deal is that we did things I don't normally do. With you, sex isn't sex. It's an experience—mindful and deeply connective on another level from physical. You push me for more, and because I want to please you, I do whatever you need. But then I become self-ish. I didn't treat you right that first night, for your first time. Had I known, I would have done things differently."

"You did everything right. That's why I loved it so much." He's about to speak, but I place a finger on his lips.

"Please understand what I mean. I've always been treated like a princess. It's amazing in so many ways, but other than my family, I've never felt a strong connection to anyone. I used to sneak read romances and learned about love from books. I wanted that so badly that I tried to find it in the wrong places and in the wrong ways with the wrong guys."

"That's a lot of wrongs."

"Truer words never were spoken. But then I met you. Do you believe in soul mates?"

His hands cover my lower back and slide down over my skin. Slipping me back in place, he causes my breath to stumble from the sexual connection. Focusing becomes harder. "I believe in you and me. As for destiny, I don't think I believed before, but now I do."

Our lips come together as our bodies slide even farther under the water. Then he leans his head back on the side of the tub, and asks, "Why'd you choose me?"

"Because you treated me like me and not who everyone else sees. You had a look in your eye like we were always meant to be. Cinderella and Prince Charming."

A slow roguish grin works its way across his face. "I treated you like Ally."

"You did."

"I only want what's best for you. *You*. Not your country. Not your parents. You. I want you to be happy. As much as I love having you here, I know you might not stay. I think you assumed this was only for a few days. My truth is that I'm worried I'm going to lose you."

"I'll fight for you."

"They're never going to let you be with me and still be the queen."

Skimming water onto his body, I'm not sure what to say. "I only know how I feel. I love you, Hutton. I'll never marry someone out of obligation. I'd rather reign alone than be stuck in a loveless marriage."

"Can a queen really date?"

"It worked for Queen Elizabeth I."

"Did it, though? She died alone." Although it seems to pain him, he says, "You're welcome to stay here as long as you want. But while you're here, I want you to think about what you really want and how you see your life going, because it might not be with me."

"I—"

This time, he presses a finger to my lips. "Think about it. When you're alone, when you're rested, when you're feeling ready. We don't have clear heads right now."

I kiss his finger and suck in the tip. His breathing picks up, and I'm held tighter around the hips. I gyrate on top of him, but I know I won't be able to wait. Like our relationship, I don't need slow or to warm up to this man. I want all of him—fast, hard, and like a whirlwind.

Our bodies connect as he slides inside me. I drag my nails down his chest, not to break the skin, but to see him burn the way I do deep within. The room magically goes dark, the city lights providing all the light we need to see each other. As I move on top of him, I say, "I know why you said when I'm alone."

That smile that wins me over every time it appears, and he says, "Oh yeah?"

"Because when we're together, I don't think clearly at all." I let my head fall back. "God, you feel so good. Will this ever get old?"

"No."

I look up, surprised, but not really by the simplistic answer, because he's right. His hand sneaks around and touches me, making my thoughts blur and my body weak to his attention. Lifting up, I push back down and repeat. Again and again until my body clenches and tremors course from my center.

My shoulders are held, my body pressed down as I embrace his release and it becomes mine again, tearing through the darkness I found behind my eyelids and shining his light inside me.

This is right.

Hutton is right.

But how do *we* play into my role as queen?

In the middle of the night, both sated and Hutton asleep, I slip out and grab a shirt on my way to the living room. I open the blinds but leave off the lights. After making a cup of tea, I stop to smell the roses. Holding the bouquet, I bury my nose in the soft petals of the pink flowers.

I spend a few minutes searching the cabinets for a vase but don't find any. That Hutton doesn't own one makes me smile. I get creative, and when I'm done, I'm the one smiling.

Taking my tea, I move to the windows, raising one panel so I can see out. With this new world at my feet and being alone for the first time in longer than I can remember, I allow myself to think about who I really want to be.

26

Ally

THE DUKE SCRAMBLES *up the stairs after me. "You will not ruin this for me, Belle."*

I run, but I'm unstable on the cobbled terrace. I reach the door and am about to scream for help, but my mouth is covered, and I'm dragged backward.

One hit to his head knocks him sideways, but he takes me with him. Catching his balance, he hides us from sight behind a large column. "I know what you've done." His breath, which is as rancid as his heart, burns my nostrils. "I know how you let him fuck you, soiling your body as well as your reputation."

The fight leaves me in a harsh breath, and my feet come to a stop.

"That got your attention," he says, releasing me.

"I don't know what you're talking about."

He laughs. "If you didn't, you wouldn't still be here." He leans against the column and rubs his ear where I whacked him. "I still made the offer knowing my future Queen, the one I was promised when I was ten years old, laid with another man."

My hands are shaking, my heart thundering in my chest. Oh shit. Surely he can't know.

This man has been a part of my life since before I remember. I may not have known I was promised to him, but some part of me I refused to acknowledge knew he was in the running. When I thought he was being a friend to me, I was only a means to an end.

Look pretty. Be quiet.

My mother's words haunt me, but I obey, fighting against my will to resist. Don't give him anything. He paces just far enough to remain unseen from anyone inside and back again. "The day you were born, my parents made the appropriate arrangements and then told me to see you as my one and only. I did that. I waited for the day you would be—"

"For sale?" *Sometimes, my snarkier side wins.*

Disgust fills in the unremarkable features of his face. A lack of emotion when he looks at me causes me to shrink, my back hitting the stone column. "You joke—"

"No, I don't. I know you don't love me. I actually think you loathe me, but you've stuck around because you want the pot of gold you were promised. At ten, you didn't realize that the gold came with the price of my life, but it does."

"You know the laws. You know how things work, but you chose to defy our traditions, to deny your husband his earned dues."

"I'm not your wife, and I never will be, but you haven't earned my respect, much less any other part of me." *I walk to the door. I don't run or hurry. He can blackmail me or not. Nothing I say will change his mind at this point, so I'll walk away, hoping for the best and expecting the worst.*

What could he possibly believe he'd achieve by outing my impurity? *All I can hope is that he'll not disrespect my family, as that would be unforgivable.*

"Princess!"

I stop and look back. "Whatever you think you know, you don't understand anything behind it. You can ruin me, Duke, if that's what you want to do. But I only ask that you consider my family before you do."

"What are you doing?"

Hutton's voice cloaks me like warm sunshine even though it's well past three in the morning. His body is silhouetted by the light coming in behind him from the bedroom. Seeing him in the reflection of the glass highlights his intimidating size as he prowls toward me, but I've never felt safer. *My protector. My lover.* My heart squeezes because he's so much more already.

I try to keep my eyes on the million little lights outside, but he makes it hard to look away. "Thinking," I reply.

"About?" When his arms wrap around me, I lean my head back on his shoulder, loving the feel of his arms under mine.

"My life."

The spot behind my ear is kissed and then my neck, which makes all those pesky goose bumps return, covering wherever he touches. "That's a heavy topic, considering the hour."

"You were right. I need to figure out what I truly want before I can ask anything of anyone else."

The tip of his tongue tickles the shell of my ear. "Would anyone else happen to be me?"

Our eyes meet in the reflection. I can't read his thoughts, but I can feel how he tightens his hold around me. Angling just enough to reach his neck, I kiss him. "I never had more than the throne to consider before."

"I threw a wrench in your plans?"

"That's a weird phrase," I say with a soft laugh, which evokes one from him.

"It is."

"You did."

My hair is moved over my left shoulder, and then the right side of my neck is kissed. "I won't apologize."

"I don't regret anything when it comes to us."

"What regrets do you have?"

"No regrets. Just disappointed in myself. I don't know if I will ever be what my parents want me to be."

"Your parents should want you happy. Are you happy, Ally?"

Such a simple question. It should have a simpler answer. "I'm happy I met you."

He seems to accept that answer, understanding the layers that corrupt the other aspects of my life. "Can I coax you back to bed?"

Spinning in his arms, I wrap mine around his neck, finally getting the first glimpse of those sleepy eyes that look at me as if I can do no wrong. "You can coax me anytime you want."

"Come to bed." He bends, and I'm lifted into his arms. I'm not sure if we'll sleep or make love, but it doesn't really matter. He is my calm in this storm.

I lean on his shoulder, holding him around the neck as he carries me into the bedroom. Setting me down on what has already become my side of the bed, he tucks me in and then climbs in on the other side. He moves all the way across this huge bed to be near me. It makes me wonder why he bought it if not to take up all the space.

His large frame could justify it. "You're built like a Viking."

"I'm built like a Texan, princess."

I kind of hate that I love hearing him call me that with that note of sarcasm. "You and that Texas pride."

"It's ingrained at conception."

"Ew."

"Not ew. Do you want to have kids?"

"I'm taking it the talk of conception is the connection?" He smiles in the dark. "Not right now, if that's what you're asking, but yes, I want children. I would love to have a boy and a girl."

"We don't get to choose. What if you only have boys?"

"No chance. Bruden's generally breed girls. That's why they outnumber boys."

"You've forgotten one very important detail."

"What's that?"

I'm pulled by my hips right in his arms. He kisses my cheek, and then whispers, "I'm not Bruden, and Everests breed males."

"All male indeed," I whisper, looking into his eyes. One kiss leads to endless kisses and getting lost in his starry eyes until my body is exhausted and my mind too content to worry about anything.

Jeans.

Chemises.

Silky, sleeveless tops.

Cardigans.

Tons of underwear from thongs to full coverage.

Five bras.

Yoga pants.

T-shirts

Shoes of all kinds from flats to a pair of super cute wedges to flip-flops and sneakers.

"How did you know my sizes?" I ask in complete astonishment.

He shrugs. "I didn't. Singer ordered everything."

"And Singer is your brother's . . ."

"Wife."

"Ah.

"I don't have to go shopping at all. She did an amazing job. It's like Christmas in here." I pull on a pair of jeans that fit me perfectly and a white-buttoned top with a pouf at the shoulders. I slip on mustard-yellow shoes that make me smile, reminding me of our sandwiches. "She didn't miss anything. How does my hair look?" The hair straightener and little bag of makeup she sent this morning with the muffins and orange juice are seriously impressive.

"Beautiful."

If I'm not mistaken, I think I just heard him gulp. Touching his cheek, I ask, "Are you doing okay?"

"I'm fine. You just look so pretty and seeing you here in my apartment . . . I don't know. It's a lot to take in."

My fingers begin to fidget with the ends of my hair. "In a good way, I hope?"

"Oh yeah, it's . . . I don't know. Kind of chokes me up, which sounds ridiculous. Fuck." He turns to leave. "I shouldn't have said anything. I sound like an idiot."

Grabbing hold of him, I say, "Hey," when he looks at me. It's the first time I see the gold that centers his eyes, so bright in the sunshine that floods the apartment at this time of the day. We've never had a whole weekend together, so this is the longest period of time we've spent together. Yet it feels so natural to be getting ready together, moving about like this is my home as well.

I don't miss Margie's intrusive eyes assessing my every movement. I miss her, but not the sense of judgment.

There's a calm that resides with him; a peace that he brings me. I love being here in his apartment. His home. Not a hotel. "You're not ridiculous. I feel the same." *Love and loved.*

Taking my hand, he turns it and kisses the inside of my wrist. "I'm glad you're here."

It may be short-lived, but at this moment, he gives me peace in the middle of my chaotic life. "Me too."

"Are you ready?"

"I am. Let me grab the strawberries and cream." I lift up and kiss him before we part. "Hey."

"Hey yourself."

"I love you, Hutton."

Slipping his arms around my middle, he holds me close again. The bags under his eyes are gone after we slept half the night and day away, but that shadow has gone from five to ten o'clock. "We can be late?"

"That little waggle of your eyebrows is cute, but if we get back in that bed, I won't be getting out again tonight." I start laughing.

"Who said anything about the bed?" My happy whimper bubbles up automatically, making him laugh. "There's the table and the kitchen island, the windows and the shower. This apartment has so many places that your naked body would make so much better."

The man makes me swoon, but I hate being late. Pushing out from his hold, I dash to said kitchen island, putting it between us when he comes after me. I point my finger at him, and say, "You are very dirty-minded, Mr. Everest, and though that's one of the twenty million reasons I adore you, you promised we'd be there in"—I take his wrist and turn it so I can see the bold Tag Heuer black and silver face—"two minutes." My shoulders fall. "I don't want to make a bad first impression."

"No chance of that, baby. Come on, but promise me we have more than a few nights."

"We do." I come around and caress his face, and then slide lower to his neck. "I promise. I want so much more with you, but I want you to think about what you want with me, too. It's important for us to hear each other when this conversation is had."

"When is that?"

"I'm thinking sooner than later." He's right. We didn't really discuss alternatives to being queen.

"I agree."

"Good. Now we can go."

He grabs a bottle of wine and the strawberries while I grab the bowl of sweet cream. Waiting for the elevator down the hall, he says, "That's nice you made it."

I glance at the bowl and get an overwhelming sense of homesickness. "Birgit showed me how to make Bavarian cream when I was ten. She would make sweet bread and use this as the filling. We didn't get to that lesson because I was too caught up in my own world as a teen and then off to university after that." I swallow down the lump in my throat, and say, "She was going to show me how to make bread today."

The elevator doors open, and Hutton pushes the button for the lobby. An arm comes around my shoulders, and he says, "I met her."

"You did? When?"

"The other night. She showed me the staff stairs and helped me get to your room undetected."

"There are cameras everywhere."

"Oh," he says, cracking a smile. "Maybe I wasn't so sneaky after all."

I nudge him. "Here's an insider's secret. No one watches the tapes. When I snuck out of the palace, I never got caught. I finally realized why. They film but unless something happens, they don't have a reason to watch the playback."

"So what you're saying is that basically you're not safe at all when you're there?"

"We still have guards out front and security has tightened over the years, but we need someone to come revamp our whole setup. It's one of the things I listed as a priority when I took the throne. In Brudenbourg, though, we have a very low crime rate."

The elevator door opens, and he says, "Singer's probably flipping out. She's a big romantic at heart, so meeting a real princess is going to make her day. So if she freaks out, just know she's harmless."

"And here I was the one freaking out inside."

"Why would you be freaking out?"

"The people you care about most are going to be there tonight. What if they don't like me?"

"You know Bennett likes you. Ethan thought you were great when he met you. Singer will love you, and my parents aren't here, so just relax if you can. I want you to enjoy the night. There's no pressure to be anyone other than yourself. And no matter what, you always have me."

My knight. "I love you." His words really sink in, and my eyes go wide. "Wait a minute. Your parents won't like me?"

Laughing out loud, he wraps his arm around my neck and kisses the top of my head. "Stop worrying. They'll love you, too."

"I hope so. We have enough obstacles in our way."

He stops and bends down to look me right in the eyes. "Do you realize what you just said?"

"Yeah, I hope your parents like me."

A slow, wicked smile slips onto his face, and he says, "You just said we have a future."

Confused to what he's getting at, I continue to stare at him, and then it hits me too. A smile that matches his shapes my lips. "I did, because now that I've had a taste of life with you, I don't want to know what it's like without."

"Should we call my parents?" My side is poked.

"Let's not get ahead of ourselves. Dinner with the brothers first."

Chuckling, he says, "Fair enough."

27

Ally

WE STEP into the lobby and wave at Jimmy. I start for the door, but I'm spun around and guided toward a back exit. He says, "See ya, Jimmy."

"You heading to see Mrs. Everest by chance?"

We stop, and Hutton looks back. "We are."

Jimmy rushes over with a large dish. "Do you mind returning this dish to her? The wife broke her ankle, and Mrs. Everest baked a casserole. I've already given her a thank you from the little missus. The food was delish, but if I don't return this dish, I'll get my ass kicked." His eyes jet to mine, and he tips his hat. "Pardon my language, Ms. Edwards."

"It's fine."

Hutton takes the dish from him. "I'll return it for you, Jimmy. No worries. Hope your wife is recovering."

"She is. Thanks." The front door swings open, letting in a gust of warm air. "Change is in the air."

"It sure is," Hutton replies and looks at me before

directing me in another direction. "There's an elevator to the side we need to take."

I watch as he enters a number code, and the cream metal door unlatches. Just inside the small room is an elevator. "Why are we here?"

"Safety. As you know, my brother is very well off, but he's also well-known. With money comes . . . let's just say there are people who would like to take that money away, and they're not concerned with little things like lives."

"You're freaking me out. I don't have security."

"Margie really wasn't security."

"No, but having someone there looking out for me gave a sense of comfort."

"I look out for you."

The door opens, and we enter the elevator. "You do. I didn't mean to imply—"

"It's okay." He sighs and presses his hand to a black pad. When the pad turns green, he pushes the button for the penthouse floor. "I know what you mean. The only reason I haven't been worried about you is this is the safest building in Manhattan. Top-of-the-line technology has covered every detail. This elevator becomes a locked box if someone breaches the room downstairs. It won't go up, and they can't get out unless they know the code or have the proper clearance. Ethan's security team would leave the intruder on lockdown in this box until the police arrived."

A shiver runs up my spine. "This is more fortified than the palace."

"Yeah, the danger is real for them, so there are three ways to access or exit the penthouse, and every option has different codes associated with it. This elevator. The stairs in case of a fire. And the last . . ." He shakes his head and chuckles. "I don't even know the last way out. Top secret stuff."

"Have they ever needed the last option?"

"Not yet, and let's hope they never do."

The door slides open, and my mouth follows suit. "Oh my God."

A gallery hall painted black with large black and white-framed photographs greets us. "This is amazing," I whisper. I've never seen anything so stunning. My pace slows, and I look at each of the photographs as I pass.

Hutton walks slightly ahead and nods toward one of the women with a smile that feels so personal as if a spy caught it on film without her knowledge. "This one is of Singer."

"She's beautiful."

And then I hear a woman's voice—full of bubble and life. "Hi. You're early."

Oh my. I guess everyone runs late around here. Hutton's demeanor changes when he sees her; their affection for one another is obvious. There's no tension in his shoulders, and he appears completely at ease. "Hi, we thought we were late." He kisses her cheek, and they give a side hug.

Glancing back at me, he says, "I want to introduce you to someone."

With her hair pulled back in a high ponytail, it swings when she moves around the corner. Wearing fitted jeans that hit right above the ankles and a pretty blue top that flows over what seems to be a tiny midsection, Singer Everest has such an ease in her beauty.

Staying close to Hutton's side, she tugs at the hem of her shirt, and says, "I'm sorry, I guess it's us running late. I didn't have time to put on shoes. I thought it was Bennett. Now I'm a little embarrassed." It's not the first time I've made someone uncomfortable. The royal title tends to do that. One of the downsides of being a princess.

"No, please, it's your home. You should be comfortable."

Hutton switches and stands by me, one hand rubbing my lower back. "This is . . ." He pauses to look at me.

The question lingers, and the silence grows, so I shift the bowl to one arm, and say, "Ally," and hold my hand out.

"Ally Edwards," he follows. "Ally, this is my sister-in-law, Singer Everest."

"It's so nice to meet you," she replies, taking my hand between hers. "Welcome. I'm so happy you and Hutton could join us for dinner tonight."

"It's great to be here and to finally meet you. Hutton has told me so many wonderful things about you."

The rosy of her cheeks deepen, and she hits his arm, laughing. "How much did you pay her to say that, Hut?"

"Spoken of her own free will."

I hold the bowl out. "I made Bavarian cream, and we brought strawberries to dip."

"Wow, this is great. Looks delicious. I have a sweet tooth, so I might have to dig in now."

"I won't tell, but I will join you," I say.

"I like her, Hutton."

He winks at me, then asks, "Where's Ethan?"

She turns and heads into a huge open concept living space, and says, "We were . . . ummm, working out. I took over the bathroom to get ready, so he had to wait. He'll be out in a minute."

We follow her into the kitchen. It's similar to ours but probably three times the size. I catch myself as soon as I think it.

Ours.

I referenced *his* kitchen as *ours*. What is happening? I love Hutton, but am I willing to give up my life for his?

It's only been twenty-four hours, but I really like this life. I clearly need more time to think, but now is not that time. "I met your husband in Austin in the spring."

"He mentioned that. Oh!" Her hand covers her mouth,

and her ponytail whips around. "I'm sorry. I don't know the custom. Do I curtsy or bow to you?"

Hutton cracks up but forces me to answer. "This is not a formal event. This is Hutton's family. I'm the same as everyone else."

"I bow to my wife every night. That's normal, right?" Ethan comes in with eyes only for Singer. Kissing her temple, he laughs. "You snuck out."

Nodding her head toward us, she clears her throat. "We have guests, babe."

Ethan, like Bennett, is shockingly handsome, but I glance at Hutton who takes hold of my hand. My heart begins to race, because I was once more focused on Hutton's looks, but I see how his heart beats only for me. He's still the best-looking man I've ever seen. That will never change.

Bumping against him, I lean on his arm and smile. Something about Ethan and Singer makes me feel like one of them. They don't hold back or hide their affection for each other. They're really captivating to watch, and I can't help but wonder if this will be Hutton and me one day.

"Hey, where is everyone?" Bennett calls out when he arrives.

"In here," Ethan says, coming over to me. "It's good to see you again, Ally."

And then I do what I never do. Without thinking, I hug him, and he kisses my cheek, breaking the protocol of greeting a royal in my country. "You too. Thank you for having me over."

"Of course. It's our pleasure. Wine?"

"I'd love a glass." Bennett comes around the corner with beers in hand. Opening his arms wide, he says, "The fun has arrived. Oh shit, is this a double date thing?"

Hutton hits his brother's chest. "You always made a good third wheel. Tonight you get to try on fifth."

"Dude, that's harsh," he jokes as the men embrace with pats on the back. When Bennett sees me, he leans down and hugs me. "How are you, Princess?"

"I'm good, Bennett. How are you? How's the jet lag?"

"I'm right as rain. Good as gold. I rise to the occasion. Beer?" His charisma gets your attention, but his good nature keeps it. I understand Marielle's conflict. If he put as much effort into kissing her as he did the deal, she never stood a chance against the youngest Everest.

My stomach twists, thinking about my sister and my brother . . . and even my mother. *What are they thinking? Why haven't they contacted me? Sent someone to get me? Do they care? Do they worry what I might be going through?*

Am I being erased from their lives like my father says they'll remove me from the history of our country? *As if I never existed . . .*

"Ethan's pouring wine," I reply quickly so I can sink back into my concerns again. Does anyone even miss me? My mother has a cold side, but I'm still her daughter. My stomach twists as my heart squeezes.

"Of course, he is." Bennett rolls his eyes. "Hut?"

"I'm drinking bourbon."

The reunion carries on around me, and with family on my mind, I watch the interactions, the teasing, the brotherly love and hard time they dole out to each other. I watch how they are teddy bears to Singer, and even though she's around my height, she's ten feet tall in their eyes.

They love and respect her without a crown reminding them it's necessary. It's real. I've never seen my father look at my mother how Ethan looks at his wife. I've never seen a true interest shown in my mother when my father speaks to her. Hutton always speaks to me as if my answer matters.

This is what family is—the playful jibes, the celebration

of little and big victories, the meaning of being a tribe displayed so openly.

The difference is stark.

Laughter and conversation go on around me as the group helps with the preparation of some part of dinner. The closest I ever had to this was with Birgit and Gerhart, two people who may not share the same bloodline, but share a piece of my heart all the same. Birgit was the only person to check on me each week when I was away for my studies. She's the one who dried my tears when I caught my ex with Sabine Rosalie. She's the one who made me clean up after I made a mess during a cooking lesson, claiming it was as important to the glory of the cooking.

Does she miss me? Does she even know I'm gone, exiled for the time being? Again. I miss her.

All the thinking I did last night hasn't gotten me any closer to an answer. I know I want this camaraderie in my life. I want my children to experience closeness to me, their father, their family, and their friends. That's what I was missing growing up. Stuck in the Stone Age of laws and formalities, I missed out on what family truly means.

Seeing me get lost in my thoughts, Hutton hooks a finger around the top of my jeans, and says, "Hey, come help me make the salad."

I'm pulled to his side, pulled right into the middle of the chaos and into his family as if I always belonged.

Bennett picks up Singer and carries her to the end of the kitchen, setting her on a barstool. "Have a seat. You've done enough already. We'll take over from here. What can I get ya, little lady?"

Singer's laughing, but her eyes find me on the other side of Hutton. "See what you have to look forward to?"

I know it's in jest, but I do see. I see how the brothers tease, but the love is constant and unfiltered. I see how Singer cares for them, anchoring them in one way and letting them soar to greater heights in another. But most of all, they don't see me as a pot at the end of a rainbow. They treat me like I'm part of the family. And I love it . . . and never want to lose it. This. *Them.*

28

Ally

"To the outside world, they have egos bigger than the Empire State Building, but to the people they love, there's no one sweeter." Singer props her feet on the coffee table and crosses her ankles. We've been chatting for the past hour as if we're old friends. Leaning back, she whispers, "I'm sure you've found that Hutton, like Ethan, tends to keep his worries hidden. Bennett's the same. Just like their father I'm told."

"They hide things on purpose?"

"Yes, but to protect us, not to hurt us. Ethan never wants to worry me, but how can I not? Not knowing anything makes it worse. No secrets. Stand your ground, Ally. Hutton will respect that just like Ethan does."

"Can I ask you something?"

"Anything."

Maybe it's the wine, or maybe I'm simply tired of holding my worries inside, concerns I can't necessarily share with Hutton for fear of hurting him, but she's put me at ease, and my guard is down. I tuck my legs under me and sink into the back cushion. Angling toward her, I say, "I had a fight with my father, and he kicked me out."

Her eyebrows rise just a little, and then she reaches over and touches my arm. "How are you doing?"

"I'm fine, but like you said, Hutton is worried about what I'll decide to do." I look down at my glass of wine and swirl it around.

She sits back. "Decide?"

"My father said he'll keep me from becoming queen."

"Can he do that?"

"My mother may be the queen, but my father has equal rights when it comes to me." I take a deep breath and exhale before sipping my wine. "That night, I was sure he was just mad, and he'd get over it, but it's been two days, and I haven't heard a word from anyone. I'm starting to worry that I made a mistake by leaving."

"He told you to go, so what are you going to do?"

It's been so long since I had girl time, really since Austin, that I'm savoring every second. It helps that Singer is an open book and makes it easy to relax and talk openly. "I don't know. I was born to be the queen. I was raised knowing I would be. It didn't matter what I'd done or how far I pushed my father's buttons, I never thought I could have my birthright taken from me."

Thinking about what has happened in the past forty-eight hours, it starts to sink in. I might not have the choice I thought I did.

She asks, "Do you mind me asking what caused the fight?"

I smile, not because of the fight, but because of the reason. Anytime I think of Hutton, I feel happy, even when I'm down. "I embarrassed him. I wasn't dressed appropriately, so he called me a whore."

"Oh wow. That's harsh. That must have really hurt."

"It didn't at first. I've made him mad before, and I've been yelled at plenty of times. But as time has passed, I see the difference in his words and how he treated me, especially because he said it in front of company. This isn't going to be me being grounded for a night or under lock and key for a week." His expression comes to mind and more hate than anger filled his words. "I think this time he meant everything he said."

"I'm sorry. He's wrong. I don't even have to know what you were wearing to know the clothes don't matter. It sounds like he was looking for a fight, and he found one."

I set my glass on the table. My emotions are growing heavy, and I don't want to be drunk under the weight of them. "He figured out there's more to Hutton and me than meets the eyes."

"Ohhh. That changes things but really surprises me. He doesn't like Hutton? Everyone loves Hutton."

"He liked him when it came to business. When it came to his daughter, yeah, not so much." The duke comes to mind. "My father is very old-fashioned and follows Brudenbourg tradition."

"Regarding you?"

"Yes. Love isn't a factor that's considered when deciding which proposal to accept."

"He decides who you'll marry?"

"My parents have the first and final say." I sit up as my anxiety grows deep inside. "Offers are submitted, negotiations are had, and a deal is struck." *I've never thought of myself as a pawn before. I never knew love would be so important to me either.*

Singer sits up too, setting her glass down. "Has a deal been struck?" Her own concern whispers through her words.

"An offer was accepted. One that's been on the table since

my birth. It's a suitor I was aware of and he's always been in my life, but he's . . ." I've never been one to share every feeling the moment I feel it. I'm much better at burying my emotions and acting out. "He's always felt more like an older brother to me, a bully at times. He scares me, but he's not my prince and certainly not a lover."

"That's horrible. And Hutton?"

"He's everything the other man is not." The response comes so naturally that I surprise myself. As her smile brightens, I look back at Hutton over my shoulder. The guys are laughing while Bennett tells a story.

"You love Hutton."

"Yes."

She glances at them as well but then turns back to me. Her smile sets, and worry rises in her expression. "He's in love with you, so what happens if you go back?

"To him or me?"

"Both of you."

"I'm not sure."

A gentle nod of her head makes me feel bad when our time has been so good. Wanting her approval, her friendship back intact again, I say, "Am I supposed to give up something I was born to do?"

"It's a difficult situation. I worry about Hutton, but now that we're friends, I'm worried about you too. I don't know the answers or what you're going to do, but all I ask is whatever you choose, be gentle."

"To Hutton?"

"And to yourself." Standing up, she says, "That cream is calling my name. Come on. Let's go eat it." She holds out a hand, and I take it.

She's given me a new way to think about things, and although I knew the impact of my initial decision, I never thought about the long-term effects of it. She may push me away, call me a weirdo, or feel the same. I don't know, but when I stand, I hug her. And she hugs me. "I'm always here to lend an ear if you need to talk, Ally. The guys are great, but sometimes we need a female friend's company." *How did she know I needed to hear those words? Feel this support?*

Camaraderie.

Friendship.

Family.

"Thank you."

Just after two in the morning, Hutton and I walk back into his apartment. Walk might be an overstatement regarding him, but we make it back. He heads to the kitchen and pours a glass of water. I set the bowl that held the cream in the sink and fill it with water to soak, feeling very domestic and loving every second. This feels like us—our place, our bowl. What a regular night together would be like. I turn around, leaning on the sink, and say, "I like the penthouse, but I love your apartment."

"Why is that?"

"It's cozy." When I look at the island between us, there are two glasses. Even drunk, he thinks of my needs.

He chuckles. "It's forty-one-hundred square feet. It's bigger than my parents' house."

"I know it sounds crazy, but the palace is so big that I used to get lost. Here, with you, I feel like I've found myself."

"Come over here."

I push off and walk around the island. There's always been an electric current that draws us together, but this time, it's our heartstrings. I walk right into his arms and am embraced in his love. Closing my eyes, I listen to his heart, memorizing the sound, the steady beat, and the rhythm that plays for me. "I want to tell you to stay." The top of my head is kissed. "But you have a country to rule. All I ask is that while you're here, you're mine."

"That's not all you can ask of me."

"We both know that once you leave, this is all there will ever be."

My arms tighten around him as his do me. "I'm not leaving."

"*Yet*. And with that yet, all I ask is that I get a little warning this time." He exhales and releases me. Finishing off his water, he says, "I like the way you arranged the flowers."

I look at the table and the three mugs full of pretty roses. "Why did you buy pink roses?"

"I bought them for you, but you were asleep. I'm sorry I didn't give them to you."

Running my hand over his chest, I look into his tired eyes. "Don't feel bad. When I woke up and found them, I thought they were so pretty. I couldn't find a vase, so I got creative."

"I like them like that. It's very girly, like you."

I know what he means. In an apartment that feels modern with clean lines and grays and navy blues, the soft pink adds such a light and pretty feel. "Did you buy pink for a reason?"

"Love. Gratitude. Appreciation." A slight embarrassment comes over him. "I cheated and looked up the meaning. I feel all those things for you, so pink seemed to be a fitting color."

My heart tightens. I don't want to lose this man. Holding him tight again, I close my eyes. "I feel the same for you."

He rubs my back, and after a few seconds, he says, "Are you ready to go to bed?"

"I am." We hold hands, and I take a glass of water in the other. We're both tired, but I've had a few glasses of wine, so I need the water.

"You talked with Singer for a long time. How'd that go?"

"I adore her." We head for the bedroom. "I felt so

comfortable around her. It was as if we'd known each other forever."

"She has a way about her that makes everyone feel at home, but I could tell she really likes you."

"She's very fond of you, protective." He nods as we part in the bedroom. I slip off my shoes. "I told her I didn't need to shop because she sent me a whole wardrobe."

"Like my brother, Singer has gone through a lot in the past year. It's good to see her coming out of her shell with others again."

"Ethan's very enamored by her."

Just as I slip off my jeans, Hutton's warm hands heat my waist. "I'm very enamored by you." Leaning down, he kisses me—not to lead to more, just sweet and shared affection. "Want the bathroom first?"

It's a simple gesture, but it means the world to me. "How about we brush our teeth together?"

"I'll get them ready."

"I'm not using the bathroom in front of you, though." I laugh because I've never done it before, and I'm not starting now.

"Good. You don't need to see behind the curtain. We'll just keep things clean."

"And here I thought you preferred me dirty."

"Ahhh," he groans as if I've hit a weak spot. Sucking a breath between his teeth, he then releases it. "I might be talked into getting dirty if you're up for it."

"It's not me I worry about being up." I glance at his pants.

"Oh, cheap shot. What'd my dick do to you for such a mean comment?" I love seeing this playful side of him.

"It's what he's not doing that warranted the comment." I fling my bra at him and walk by, teasing him with every step I take.

"Why'd you let me drink so much?" he asks, trailing me into the bathroom.

"You were having too good of a time to stop you."

Stepping behind me, he presses his body to mine, and his hands slide up my middle until he cups my breasts. The pulse in my core begins to throb, but I know we need to sleep. Tomorrow, we'll face our problems and start making decisions. Tonight, we need to turn off our minds.

He kisses my neck. "Bed?"

"Sleep?"

"Yes to both."

The shower is started, rousing me from a deep sleep. The blinds are still pulled, but the daylight is trying to sneak in. I turn and glance at the clock. It's 8:14 as Hutton comes in.

Unaware I'm awake, a sober and sexy Hutton walks out of the bathroom wearing gym shorts and sneakers. With his back to me, he slips off his shoes and socks. I sit up to take in the full view. His muscles are tight and on display. His body glistens from sweat, his hair wet from a workout.

The shorts and briefs come down and his buttocks contract and tense with the motion, highlighting the indents on the side of his cheeks. I admire the body, but I admire the man more. He takes care of himself physically, but how is he holding up mentally? I'm sure he's just as confused as I am.

He tosses the clothes in the laundry basket and returns to the bathroom. We've shared a thousand emotions and our fears, worries, and laughs. With so much light shining back into my life, I decide now's the time to make my move.

29

Hutton

WORKING out is always a surefire way for me to sweat out the toxins after a hard night of drinking. I wasn't drunk, but I was past the stage of being useful. I was having fun, and seeing Ally and Singer bond made the night even better.

When all she wants is to be the queen, is it possible for her to see herself in this life, in my life, permanently?

And what do I want?

I want Ally.

What does that mean when her father will never let her marry me? Will she marry the duke?

Makeup smeared. Crooked tiara. Messed-up hair.

Fuck.

She'll be with him over my dead body.

I won't lose her. Not again. *Not ever.*

Having her here with me has made my apartment feel like a home for the first time since I moved to New York.

I want her laughter echoing in the kitchen and to see her standing at the window. I want to leave the office at a decent time because I have someone to come home to. I want her middle-of-the-night kisses and to hear that soft snore she doesn't even realize she does. I'll eat Bavarian cream every night if that's all she ever learns to make. I can order the rest. I can learn to cook more than a few bachelor meals. She can rule my kingdom, make any decisions she wants, and I'll be her loyal subject. Ally's the queen of my heart.

But can I be the king she needs?

Will I have a choice?

Guess that remains to be seen. I hope she got a good night's sleep because we have a lot to discuss today. I step under the hot water, letting it roll over my sore shoulders. It wasn't arms day, but I did a full body workout anyway, needing to burn energy and take my mind off things. It only worked temporarily, so I jogged four miles on the treadmill at a higher than usual incline. Even after all that work, the freed mind space was flooded with the same concerns I've had for days the moment I walked in and saw her in my bed again.

While I soap up, the door to the bathroom opens, and I catch sight of my beauty before she sees me. We both can see everything through the glass shower surround. Our eyes meet through the steam as she walks toward me. Opening the door, she says, "Good morning."

"Good morning. Sorry I woke you."

"It's okay. I got a nice view." She asks, "Can I join you?"

"Please do." I have showerheads all around, so I spin her to keep her warm under the few I've turned on while I activate the others. She rubs soap all over her body, stealing my job.

Silently, we both wash our hair, the act of watching each other intimate. It's impossible to not react as her hands slip between her legs, causing her lids to waver. When she looks back up at me, she releases a long breath and then licks her lips. As the other rain showerhead covers me in water, I watch as she rinses her hair, tilting her head back. Her eyes close, and her moan goes straight to my dick, waking my whole body up.

She doesn't fail to notice. Coming closer, Ally slides her hand along my length and then grips me firmly and comes back up. "Kiss me, Hutton."

It's not a desperate plea but comes from a place of love. I cup her face as she continues to work me and kiss her, evoking a deep sigh of contentment. She brings the same out in me.

Every stroke fans the fire inside until I'm a raging blaze of desire. "Turn around." I'm not asking, my own need taking over.

Her hand stops, and she puts space between us. "No." A challenge is thrown down with a look of lust in her eyes. The water rains over our shoulders, and this time, I ask, "What do you want, Princess?"

I reach out and run two fingers between her legs, feeling her need. She says, "I want to please you."

"You do."

"I want to serve you." Her breath is rough around the edges when she sucks in, and I caress her cheek to help steady it. I'm about to ask what she means by serving me when she kneels in front of me.

Weaving my hands into her hair, I hold her by the back of her head. As if waiting for me, I give her the permission she's seeking. "Don't stop until you've swallowed every last drop. Do you understand me?"

She nods. "Yes."

"Yes, what?"

"Yes, *my* king."

And here I am, finally playing the role she wants. I nod, and she takes me, her hot mouth hardening me more than I thought possible. I ache for relief as she sucks me deep and glides back with a tease of her teeth. Guiding her head, I set the pace, and she bends to my needs.

There's no complaint as she takes every thrust as though she can't get enough. When I grip her hair, I pull enough for her to look up. Her usually clear blue eyes are gray with brewing rainstorms. Her hands slide around, holding me, and I give up control to let her have her way. "Take what you need, baby."

Long hair slick down her back, shoulders straight, weighted teardrop tits bare with begging nipples. Her body squirms as she sends me to the edge. I press my hand flat against the glass behind me but struggle to stop her. I should but—"Fuck. Get up."

The command startles her, but she's on her feet, her breath heavy, lips swollen. Fuck me. I touch her mouth, dragging my thumb harsher than I intend. "These lips will never touch another man. Do you understand me?" I levy my thumb right in the middle of her bottom lip. "They will only kiss my mouth. They will only suck my dick. They will only ever say my name in ecstasy. Do you understand, Princess Arabelle?" Her name is a growling curse on my sharp tongue. "Do you?"

"Yes . . . *my king*," she says without prompting.

"Turn around and brace yourself." She starts to turn, but I say, "Wait." When she looks at me, I hold her face and kiss her, treating her like the woman I love before I treat her how she really craves.

When I pull back, I keep my eyes steady on her as she turns. She spreads her hands, and without asking, her legs go wide. I put gentle pressure on her head until she bends forward. Moving her hair to the side, I kiss down her spine until I reach the top of her round ass. Her ribs expand with her deep breaths, and her head lowers. Her body becomes mine once again as she gives in. I lick from one lower back dimple to the next and then run my thumb down the center of her crack.

A whimper escapes her when I pull my hand back. I could do a million things to her, and she'd let me because she trusts me. One of the many reasons I will never hurt her. *One of the many reasons I know I'm the luckiest bastard.*

Running my dick through her sweet little pussy lips, I stop when the tip dips into her. I want to fuck, be the selfish bastard I thought I was going to be. But her need is mine, and if I rush, I'll leave her empty.

I hold her around the waist and push in slowly. Reaching around her hips, I find her clit and mimic the pace of my thrust. Once I'm seated deep inside her, I can't keep steady. I move on instinct, being the animal she brings out in me.

I know she's close because her clit swells enough to show off for me. I can read her body well. I fuck my princess until she falls apart in my arms, sending me into my own release.

The water is still warm, but we've been in here a long time. I still take a minute to rest against the glass while staring at her. Her arms must be tired, but she stays bent forward. I watch carefully for another few seconds before I help her. Slowly taking one arm down and then the other, I turn her and bring her into my arms.

A sob rushes through her, and though she's quiet, too quiet, her body rattles. I sit on the bench and hold my sweet girl in my arms, letting her cry. She's curled on my lap, her falling tears blending with the water from above. "Hey, look at me."

She struggles to lift her gaze to mine, but when our eyes meet, I say, "I love you."

That brings another sob bursting from her chest. Her hands roam my chest and neck, and she lifts up to kiss my neck. "I love you, and my heart is full, but my body feels depleted. Empty without you." Her fingers tap across my jaw as if I'm the breakable one between us.

"Souls," I say so quietly as I feel the meaning for the first time. All the questions lingering in the back of my mind while I gave her time to think are answered.

"What?"

"I feel the same because we're soul mates." I catch her hand and bring it up. "Do know what that means?" She stares into my eyes with such innocence. "It means we fight for this. We fight to be together." Kissing her wrist, I keep my eyes locked on hers. "You can be the queen, and we will be together. I'll give everything here up for you. I'll give up everything . . . *except* you."

Her staggered sob is caught in her throat, then she gets to her feet. "What are you saying?"

"We can go back."

Determination tightens her focus. "With you by my side, I'll reclaim what's mine."

"How? Your parents—"

"Once I'm the queen, it's all up to me. I don't have to marry before I take the throne."

"So how can I help you?"

We both stop when we hear the doorbell. "What was that?" she asks, looking through the glass enclosure.

"The doorbell." She looks shocked. I am too, but possibly for a different reason. "That's weird."

"It sounds just like in the movies."

I shut off the water and grab a towel from the shelf for her and then one for me. "You haven't heard a doorbell before?"

"No. The palace doesn't have one, and no one ever came to our place in Texas since no one knew we were there."

Stepping out, I dry off just enough to walk out and pull on work-out shorts. "Not even to solicit?"

"No. They couldn't get past security downstairs."

The sound of a doorbell has never elicited so many thoughts before, but as she said, someone would have to get through *my* security to get to my apartment. Before I exit the bedroom, she comes out of the bathroom wrapped in a towel, and says, "Be careful."

"Stay here." I wish I had time to tell her about the panic room, but the doorbell rings again. Hurrying into the living room, I activate the security system monitor and go to the camera covering my front door. "Oh shit."

30

Ally

HUTTON'S T-SHIRT swallows me whole, but I love the feel of it, so I pull it on over my yoga pants when I hear a ruckus in the living room. I stand still, trying to decipher if I should run and hide, call for help, or . . . *is that Jakob's voice?*

Bennett's laughter reaches the bedroom, and although my heart is racing, I begin breathing again. "Oh my God!" I dash out of the bedroom to find my brother, my sister, Margie, and Bennett in the living room. I'm not sure who to hug first, but my brother opens his arms to me, so I go there. "I can't believe you're here."

"We can't either," he says. "It took a lot of convincing to let us come to visit."

The word "visit" doesn't sit right with me, but I'm not going to ruin the reunion. I embrace my little sister. "Hi."

Her hug is tighter than usual, and when she leans back, she rolls her eyes. "I know you won't believe me, but I missed you."

I give her hand a little squeeze. "I missed you, too."

Although I've been conflicted about Margie recently, I very clearly remember what she did for me a few nights ago. I wouldn't have been able to leave with Hutton if she hadn't snuck me my passport. "Hello." I start slowly, testing the water that flows between us.

"Hello," she replies and then curtsies.

When she's up again, I say, "You're here."

"I'm not just your secretary, Belle. I'm your friend, and I was worried about you."

It isn't an apology, but that needs to be done in a private setting. Taking into account the passport and the fact that she traveled to check on me, I hug her. It could be that I just missed my friend. Or all three. Either way, she's here. "I missed you."

Peeking over to Bennett, he sticks out his bottom lip. "No hug? Wow, you act like we just saw each other or something."

Hutton's not wearing his watch, but it can't be much past nine. "Yeah, maybe like, oh I don't know, seven hours ago." I go and hug him anyway.

He points at my head when I hug him, and he says, "See, Hut, old man, the women love me."

"Yeah, yeah," he replies. "Why didn't anybody call me?"

I push off him and lean against Hutton, and whisper, "Your phone is still by the bed."

Jakob says, "I called Hutton, and when he didn't answer, I bothered Bennett."

Bennett says, "I sent you three messages that they were here. We finally decided to barge in. Well, we knocked just in case—"

"Okay," Hutton says, "we get it."

His arm comes around me, and I hold on to it until Jakob, Marielle, and Margie's eyes all go wide. I realize too late what

I've done. Fighting my instinct of propriety and everything I was raised to believe, I stay, then I take Hutton's hand and hold it. Right. In. Front. Of. Them. With Hutton in Austin, I never felt the need for propriety. Never kept physical distance in front of people. *That's because I was only ever Ally in America.* But now as my two worlds collide? Now I'm Princess Arabelle *and Ally.*

"Guess you've done more than kiss," Marielle deadpans.

"Wow. This escalated quickly," Jakob says, "You've renounced the throne and already look at home. With Hutton."

Hutton holds me and says, "She hasn't renounced the throne. Tell them, Ally."

I catch the flash of annoyance on Margie's face when she hears the name. I let it go and lead them to sit down. "I'm not giving up my birthright. Why would I? Because I fell in love? Because I shamed the monarchy? No," I say, shaking my head. "They're trying to teach me a lesson. They want me to marry the duke—"

"Ew," my sister says, scrunching her face. "He's like a brother." Patting Jakob on the arm, she smiles sweetly. "No offense to you."

With his hands up, he replies, "Offense taken. The guy is a dick."

"Literally. And I agree. That's why I told him it will never happen."

Margie says, "Never say never."

"Never." But that wasn't from me, though I was about to say it. Hutton crosses his arms over his chest, and says, "She'll never marry him."

Margie seems surprised but doesn't say anything more when she sits back.

The doorbell rings again, and Hutton says, "What the fuck is with the surprise visits today?"

Bennett heads for the security monitor. "It's Singer. I'll let her in."

I smile at the thought of my new friend meeting the people I care about. "Great timing. I can't wait for you to meet her. She's pure loveliness."

Jakob asks, "Is she hot?"

Hutton taps his shoulder when he gets up and walks into the kitchen. "She's off limits."

"Says who?"

"My brother."

"Ah. Yes, that puts her firmly in the off-limits category," he jokes.

I've never seen this side of him, but when I think about it, we've really not spent a lot of time in the same place since we turned twenty-one.

"Coffee or juice?" Hutton asks, taking orders.

I hear Singer chatting away like a bluebird when she enters the living room with Bennett. Stopping in her tracks, she holds her hands out in front of her. "I didn't know you had company. I can come back later."

"No," I say, standing up. "Come in. I want you to meet my family and friend."

She blushes and giggles. "Sorry. I'm sort of freaking out inside right now."

Bennett gives her a side hug. "Not just on the inside."

"Stop teasing me. It's like a royal trifecta in here."

That earns her a rousing round of laughter. I introduce her to my family, and Jakob kisses the top of her hand, and then says, "I hear you're married?"

Singer laughs. "Happily." When she meets Marielle, she says, "You're even more beautiful than you are on TV." That instantly wins my sister over. Singer's smile momentarily slips when she meets Margie. Her tone changes, but her etiquette is still intact. "It's nice to meet you."

I still don't get Margie, especially when she replies, "And you, Mrs. Everest." It's not the words but her tone that comes across as rude.

No more. We will talk today.

Hutton turns on the coffee machine, and asks, "It's nine fifteen in the morning. How did you guys know we'd be up?"

"Ethan told me you were working out earlier," she replies matter-of-factly.

"How'd he know?"

"He knows everything." She narrows her eyes and points a finger at her brothers-in-law. "Don't tell him I said that, though."

Bennett laughs. "Your secret's safe with us."

She gets up and heads for the kitchen. "I stopped by to see if Ally—"

"Princess Arabelle," Margie grits, correcting her while she stands in opposition.

"Margitte," I snap.

My sister asks, "Who's Ally?"

Bennett squeezes between her and Jakob and drapes his arms along the back of the couch. "I was going back to bed, but maybe I'll stay and watch the fireworks."

From the kitchen, Hutton yells, "Go home, Ben."

Popping right back up, he says, "I'm out." But then he turns back. "Want to hang out at my place, Marielle?"

"Oh, um," she stutters, and her cheeks turn pink.

"No," Jakob snaps, "she doesn't."

I've been stewing in my anger for minutes. So I finally stand. "Singer, I hate to be rude, but can I call you in a little while? My family and I have business to discuss."

"No problem at all. Just call me if you have time."

I walk her to the door and say goodbye before marching back to the living room, realizing I've not explored the apartment since I arrived. "Hutton, do you have a room where Margie and I can talk privately?"

"Down the hall past the front door. Take your pick of rooms, or there's another living room you can use." He comes to me with a cup of coffee and also hands one to Margie.

"Thank you." I lift up on my bare toes and kiss him. I don't even care if the whole world sees me. Screw stupid, outdated laws. We're in America anyway. Let the Bruden police come get me.

Margie and I carry our coffees with us as we walk past a row of guestrooms and into the sunshine of another smaller sitting room. Like how I see Margie these days, I see this apartment with a new perspective. Hutton feels like home, but could this place be the one *we* call home?

"Please sit," I direct and sit across from her.

"Are we talking as friends or you as my princess?"

"I want you to speak freely as my friend." I turn my mug around in my hand, and ask, "What are you doing, Margie?"

"What are *you* doing, Belle?" She lowers her voice. "Did you take a shower with him?"

Thinking about my wet hair, I volley back a question, because I don't owe her answers, "Why did you come to New York?"

"I'm your last saving grace, Princess. Your father has reviewed the security tapes that date back to your teens. He knows I was with you half the time. That I was an accomplice."

"To what? To having a good time. Jeez," I say, rolling my eyes. "You'd think the man never partied before he was a prince."

"He was allowed to. You were not, and you knew that."

"I know it, but that doesn't make it fair or right."

"Fair?" she scoffs. "You're spoiled." She stands as I sit in shock. "You've been given everything, and you're tossing it away like it means nothing. My mother worked her ass off, and here I am, trying to do what's best for you instead of me, and you don't even care."

Standing, I walk to the window, allowing a moment for her words to sink in. *She thinks I'm spoiled. Selfish.* "I do care. About you. About my family. About my country and the people of Bruden."

"*Your* country because you basically own it. I'm just a simple servant to the monarch."

"You've been given a life of luxury and still have the right to quit any time you like. What really keeps you there if you hate it so much?"

"You, but you're too blind to see that everyone is trying to help *you* succeed. That passport was a peace offering to help you out."

"I appreciate you doing that, but what happened to us?" I turn away from her and look out over Manhattan. It's easy to feel like queen of the world from up here, but do I need the world or just the little country of Brudenbourg anymore? "When did we become enemies?"

"When you put your own needs in front of your country's."

"I can't win with you. I love my country, but when does loving my country mean I'm not allowed to live a life I love too?"

"It's never been this way before—"

"I know. Isn't it time we catch up with the times? You and I both know I've had sex and that alone could knock me out of the line of succession. But why? Why does that mean I'm not fit to be queen? My mother is the queen, and news alert, she's had sex."

"I didn't make the rules, the laws, nor have a say in the matter. But you knowingly broke them, and if there are no consequences, then what keeps everyone else from cherry-picking their way through our laws?"

"I didn't murder anybody. I had sex with somebody I love. Heaven forbid." Shoving my wrists in front of me, I add, "Lock me up and throw away the key."

"That's just it, Belle. You didn't love Hutton when you had sex. You simply gave him the best part of you for free."

Her lack of tact in delivery hurts. Yet I try to overlook the bluntness and take in her words. Sitting, I lean my head back and cover my face with my hands. This is where we are —we will never see eye to eye. It makes me sad to lose this friendship. It makes me mad that she won't see my side. It's so frustrating, but most of all, it's hurtful. I sit up and look at my friend, the one I used to play dolls with, dream of what our Prince Charmings would look like one day, and keep each other's secrets under a vow through a pinky promise that meant something. With no energy to continue a losing battle, I say, "That you think my body is the best part of me, that it's the best I have to offer, says it all. I have so much more to offer than being a pretty talking head for Bruden-bourg. If that's all that is expected of me, maybe I don't want to be the queen."

Standing back up, I take my coffee and sip, savoring its taste. What *I* see as the best part of me is the man who loves me selflessly. He made sure this coffee was exactly how I like it . . . with a little dash of cinnamon. I won't take that lightly, and I will never take Hutton for granted.

"That's ridiculous."

I'm about to leave, knowing this conversation is as over as our friendship, but add, "If you can't support me and my relationship with Hutton, then we're done here."

"I can't and won't." Her words are like daggers. "Your parents know you've had sex."

"What?"

I thought I was only stabbed in the heart, but no. I've been stabbed in the back. I'm almost too angry to cry, but this stings. "You're my friend. My best friend since we were eight. How can you do this to me?"

"I'm a servant of the monarchy. I was raised to fulfill my role, and I intend to. By doing this, I am being your friend."

"No, you're not. You're a traitor."

"To you. To your country, I'll be a hero."

"If that's what helps you sleep at night . . ." She's not even worth the fight. I leave her standing there mentally armored to battle me. Fighting this battle isn't worth losing the war. Things have changed, so I have to prepare for the onslaught.

31

Ally

HUTTON'S SITTING with my siblings when I return. By everyone's ease, it solidifies my decision. Like Singer said, everyone loves Hutton. If my parents truly want me happy, they will have to make the choice to get to know Hutton. To see the incredibly loyal, intelligent, and wonderful man he is. And . . . most importantly, accept him as a part of me.

He stands when I cross the room. Catching his eyes, I say, "I need to speak with you privately please." I head for the hall that leads to our bedroom. *Our* bedroom. Exhaling when I enter our sanctuary, I turn with my hands behind my head. What am I going to do? "Can I really do it?"

"Do what?" Hutton asks, closing the door behind him.

I lower my hands back to my sides. Not wanting to hide anything from him anymore, I say, "Abdicate."

"What? Why would you do that?"

"I'm not. I . . . *we* need to talk about everything. I thought we had more time."

"We don't?"

"No. Margie said my parents know I've had sex."

"How?" he asks, coming to sit on the bench under the window.

"I assume she told them. She's the only one who knew. Well, other than the duke's wild accusations."

"They're not wild if they're accurate. Did you tell him?"

"I didn't have to. He could tell."

"How?"

I shrug. "Maybe I'm not good at hiding how I feel about you."

And there's that roguish grin reflecting his mood, or maybe a sense of pride. Either way, I can't let it distract me like it usually does. I say, "I need to talk to my siblings."

I wait for him while he gets up, my heartstrings pulling him closer. His arms come around me, and he kisses my temple. "You're not in this alone, Ally."

"I know," I whisper.

"Whatever you need."

"I know." I take his hand and lower my lips to the inside of his wrist and kiss him. I taste him and the salty mix of his skin, the soap from the shower, and me. My gaze goes up to look at this man, who came into my life so unexpectedly but is willing to fight to stay forever. "I love you."

"I know." He squeezes my ass, and says, "I'll always be wherever you need me, so go do what you need to do."

I kiss him on the mouth because it's Hutton, after all, and those amazing lips should be kissed regularly. I return to the living room, and Jakob and Marielle are standing at the windows, pointing at different buildings while Margie sits at the table. Her eyes go from the flowers to mine when I walk into the room. She stands as if she still respects me. I walk to my sister and brother, stepping between them. With my eyes on the vast view, I say, "What have you heard?"

I don't need to go into the backstory. They're both well aware of the hot topic of me back in Brudenbourg.

My sister says, "It's wrong if you don't become queen."

"You understand what you're saying, right?"

She turns to me and nods. "You deserve the throne; not just because it's your birthright, but because you'll bring life to our queendom. We haven't always been close. I used to see you as someone I didn't understand." Touching her lips, she pauses. "But now I've come to admire you. You didn't wait for life to happen. You created your own. You're so brave, Belle. One day, I hope to find the same courage to live the life I want."

Taking her left hand in my right, I say, "I hope you do, too." I start getting choked up.

Jakob says, "What are you going to do, Belle?"

"I love Hutton." We all glance back at him.

Sitting on the couch, he says, "That's me."

Jakob's face twists. "And how do you feel about my sister?"

Hutton, my Texas gentleman with his easygoing smile, replies, "I'm in love with Arabelle, *my Ally.*"

"That's settled then, but when did this happen? It seems sudden."

"I've loved him since we were together in Texas."

Marielle asks, "You dated before?"

Jakob is rubbing his left temple. "So you weren't strangers when he came to Brudenbourg? When his company came to . . . Okay, that's a lot to take in right now. Let's focus on the here and now." Unlike how he usually acts, he takes my hand, and says, "What do we need to do?"

The three of us hold hands as a united front, giving me the strength to know I have an army of my own willing to fight alongside me. "I need to return to Brudenbourg and talk to our parents."

"When?" Hutton asks as if he's been waiting for this shoe to drop. I look back and see him approaching with concern etched in his forehead.

"I guess as soon as possible."

"I can have the jet ready within a few hours." Nodding, Hutton touches my shoulder.

Jakob releases my hand and crosses his arms over his chest. The stance is defensive, but hearing the tone of his words, he's calm. "We have our plane here. We'll leave tomorrow. We just arrived. Anyway, we're supposed to be talking some 'sense' into you. If you hop on a plane today, you'll make me look good but yourself bad for folding."

Hutton says, "I think he's right. If we wait, we'll have more time to prepare."

I'm not sure how to say it without hurting his feelings, so I turn to him, and whisper, "I think I should go alone."

"Not alone. No way."

"I meant, I'll go with my siblings."

His head tilts, and he rubs a temple. "You mean without me?"

Holding his hand between mine, I plead, "You'll upset them."

"They're already upset. What you're asking me to do is watch you fly halfway around the world and trust that you'll not only be safe but allowed to return to me. Anything could happen to you, and if I'm kept out from the beginning, I may never be allowed back in."

Jakob steps in. "I'll take care of her. I'll make sure she's safe, but I have to agree with her on this. You'll upset my parents more than they already are. My mother may be the queen, but she's sat idly at my father's side for decades. She never had an interest in ruling; she only took the position because of expectations."

The sound of Hutton's heavy breath fills the space. "So whatever your father says goes?"

"Even when it came to us." Marielle's voice is soft when she speaks, but we all stop to listen. "I was kept at a distance from Belle since birth. Do you know why that is, Mr. Everest?"

I know, but it's something we've never spoken about; a darkness that has never had the light shined on to expose it. I fought against it, but I never had success until now. My sister and brother are here. They're by my side. We're winning the war.

"No, I don't."

It's a lot to have all of us speaking at him, so I move and wrap my arms around his middle. When his arm comes around me, I start to say, "If—"

"In case Belle wasn't deemed capable," Margie says, coming into the living room. I'd almost forgotten she was there, witnessing the plotting of our revolt. I hoped she would finally see my side, but she probably believes I'm not capable now. "If deemed incapable, the officials and the monarchy would remove her from the line of succession, and Marielle would become the queen."

"What does that have to do with them getting along as sisters?" Hutton asks.

Marielle replies, "Because if she was capable but they wanted to remove her, they would need my compliance. How could I stab a beloved sister in the back?"

"They bred antipathy?" Hutton sits on the arm of the couch. "Royals are really fucked up, you know that?"

All of us nod this time. Jakob says, "It's not a new thing. Sadly, it's a matter of tradition. It was bred into them."

Marielle goes back to the window and looks out. "We've never met our aunt. I didn't even know we had one until I was twelve and the staff let it slip. I assumed she didn't want to know us. Now I know, she wasn't allowed to. She was dismissed from the palace on the day of the coronation."

"I was raised to do everything right and good and proper. Where has that gotten me? Forgotten, that's where. As long as Belle is alive, capable, and deserving, which she clearly is, everything I have done, been, and every rule followed has been for naught." Looking back at us, she adds, "I'm the same as our aunt. I don't even know her name. But as soon as Belle is crowned, I'll be dismissed to the countryside somewhere in Brudenbourg. Nameless. Penniless? I have no idea what will become of me."

Jakob puts his arm around her as tears bubble up. "We'll take care of you. I promise."

She wipes away an errant tear, and says, "I refuse to betray my sister because betraying her is betraying the crown and Brudenbourg. But more so, I care about you, Belle. I love you. I may not have shown it over the years, but I do. You are owed the crown. Whatever you need me to do to help you, I will."

I release Hutton and go to my little sister. She's someone I didn't know I could rely on until now. The lack of familial love was never encouraged or nourished the way I now can see between the Everest brothers. I own my part in the roles we played and live with regret.

I had Margie, but who did she have? She'll have me from now on.

Taking her by the shoulders, I say, "You're strong and clever. You wrap everyone you meet around your little finger with your charm. You have a soft heart and a brave soul." My heart squeezes, so I embrace her like I've never done before—like a beloved sister.

She starts to cry, and this time, the tears flow. Trying to catch her eyes when she looks at me, I ask, "Why are you crying?"

"Because I've only ever been called pretty."

"You are pretty."

"I'd rather be strong, brave, and clever."

I hug her again because she's all those things and more, but most importantly, she's my sister. *She will not be ostracized under my reign. She shall have an important place in our land. And in my heart.*

When I release her, I look at Margie. "Tell me where we stand. I don't want to fight with you. I need to understand how you feel so I know how to move on from here."

"I don't think I've ever seen the three of you together and so close. Hearing how you speak to one another . . . I fell for the lies, the façade, the belief that a country is more important than its people." Coming closer to me, she lowers her voice, shame seeming to shape her face. "I don't know how to undo the damage I've done."

"That you want to is what matters."

"I'm sorry, Belle."

"Tell me where your allegiance lies because it can't be on both sides."

"With you, *my* queen."

Jakob says, "Those are treasonous words."

I hold my hand up. Margie comes to me, and says, "That's how you know whose side I'm on."

Studying her for a long moment, I finally step forward and hug my old friend. "Thank you."

Everyone's eyes are suddenly on me. Glancing at Hutton, I take a deep breath and then exhale, feeling some of the pressure lifted from my shoulders. That's what he is to me—freedom. Life. *Forever.*

"As for your question of how to undo the damage done . . ." I finally see my future laid out for me. "I know how."

32

Hutton

"I NEED TO GET LAID."

My hand goes up. When the waitress sees us, I move my finger to order another round. I'm going to need ten rounds to talk sex with Ally's brother, and even then, I'm not sure I want to get that deep with the dude.

Thank God for Bennett. "You're a fucking prince. If you can't get laid, the rest of us bastards don't stand a chance. Oh, wait. Correction. I get laid all the time." He pats me on the back. "I can't speak for this guy, though."

"Let's not make me speak at all since I'm dating his sister."

Jakob says, "Is that all it is? Dating? Looked like more when we were there."

I can keep my relationship private, or I can start sharing it with the world. Family seems like a good start. "I want to marry her."

Beer is spewed on my face and shirt. Fortunately, I jump

off the barstool fast enough not to be dripping. "Fuck, dude. Really?"

"Shit," Jakob says.

A waitress walks by and drops a stack of bar napkins on the table. "Here you go, cutie."

"Sorry about that," Jakob says with a slightly drunken slur. "But you can't talk about my sisters like that and not expect a reaction."

"Reaction." I wipe my face with a napkin. "Yes. A beer bath. No. Also, sister. Singular. One. The one. The one for me. Ally."

"Whoa. That's a lot of deep stuff right there to process."

Just as Jakob takes another drink, finishing off his beer, Bennett says, "I made out with Marielle."

Bennett's faster than I am. That spew just covers the table. Jakob swears up and down the bar at a quick pace, then says, "I should hit you."

"One. You don't tell a guy that you're considering hitting them. You just do it. Two. You realize I'm bigger than you, right?"

I step between them. "You only have like an inch or two on him. Your arrogance is what gets you into these messes, bro."

"I'm drunker, though," Jakob proclaims like he's ready to duel. "Liquid courage, man."

"Okay, settle the fuck down."

The waitress brings three more drinks. "Thank you."

Jakob perks up. "She's hot. Think she'll want to hook up with a royal?"

"Sit the fuck down," I say, pointing at his stool. "You're a drunk-ass lunatic. You're not hooking up with anyone on my watch. We were told to go watch the game while the ladies went shopping. I'm not looking to get arrested, and I definitely can't let you get arrested."

"Arrested again you mean."

"Save the snark or I won't bail your ass out."

Nails drag down my back, making me arch forward. "What the fuck?" I whip around.

"Hutton Everest . . . and Bennett. Mmm. Where have my favorite brothers been hiding the past month? I've missed you." Starla's catlike eyes land hard on her next victim— Jakob. "And whom do we have here?"

"Technically," Bennett says, raising a finger in the air. "It's *who* do we have here because the most common usage wins and since whom has all but disappeared from our spoken language, the rule bends, and now it's who."

"Your mind works in scary ways," I say.

"I know."

Nothing is going to grab her attention from the prince. I think I'll keep that tidbit under wraps to protect the innocent, namely, Jakob.

Bennett's almost offended when he doesn't land a laugh. "Tough crowd."

I ask, "What are you doing here, Starla?"

"Is that how to greet an old friend?" She bats her eyelashes my way. It never worked on me before, so I'm not sure why she thinks it will now.

Friend is a big stretch of the imagination. I'm not sure what to say to her, and I sure as shit don't want her hanging out with us. Firstly, Ally would kill me. Secondly, Singer would kill both Bennett and me. Thirdly, I have a horny prince and a woman who would do anything to sink her claws into someone with money. Yeah, not gonna happen. "We're having a guys' night."

"It's four o'clock in the afternoon."

"What brought you here?" I counter.

"You, silly. I still have the tracking on your phone turned on. How else would I know where you are?" That psychotic behavior right there is why I'm glad I never hooked up with her. Jakob has sobered, and Bennett is shaking his head.

"You've been tracking me?"

"We did go on two dates. It's like the lead-up to commitment. You left your phone on the table, and I switched it on. Don't worry. We're even. You've been able to track me the whole time, too. Why did your location disappear from Manhattan this past week? Were you traveling?"

I grab my phone and find the app on the sixth screen, shutting it off immediately. She protests, "How am I supposed to find you now?"

Standing, I reply, "I think we're done here."

"What? But we almost kissed."

"No, we didn't. I bent down to tie my shoe. I wasn't making a move."

"Details."

Bennett holds his glass, swirling the ice around with the amber liquid. "Details matter, sweetheart. You ate my eyelash after plucking it and telling me to make a wish." His bottom lip goes wonky. "That's creepy as fuck."

She turns to Jakob, who says, "Before you even say anything, I'm out."

With a huff, she says, "Thanks a lot, Hutton, for scaring him."

"Yeah, I'm not the one who scared him."

Gnawing on her thumbnail cuticle, she looks around the bar. "Whatever. You're just snobs. It's like you want a perfect little princess."

"Actually—"

"Don't even say anything," Jakob says when she storms away, heading straight toward another group of guys she seems to recognize.

When she holds her phone up like she did to us, Bennett chuckles. "I think that's the first time in my life I've been called a snob." He sips his drink and then adds, "Ethan maybe, but me, I'm innocent."

"Sure you are, Ben. A perfect fucking angel."

––––––––––

Three hours later, the women walk into the apartment to find Ally's brother passed out and Bennett scrounging through the fridge looking for snacks. Ally holds up a bag. "I brought dinner."

The bag is confiscated by my brother before she can even tell me what's inside. Fuck, I'm starving, but seeing her there makes me wonder if it's for food or for her. "Well, I did bring dinner," she adds, laughing.

Something's different about her, and it's not just because I'm drunk-ish. She seems almost carefree, like how she used to be in Austin before the end came to that dream. I get up from the chair and greet her properly. Taking her by the waist, I dip her. A cross between happy and worried moves through her eyes. "I love you so fucking much."

Happiness wins, and she touches my cheek. "Why do you love me?"

"I love you because every day with you feels like I'm living for the first time. I love you for your strong will and determination. I love you, Ally, for being you and for the man you believe I am. I'll live up to it. I swear to you."

"You can't say things like that, Hutton, and not expect me to cry––"

"I just did." I kiss her before she tries to take control, insisting she gets to run this show. It's my dedication, so I kiss her again after we catch our breath. When I swing her to her feet, I say, "No great love affair comes without its obstacles. No matter what happens with the crown, I promise to give you the fairy-tale ending."

"Is that a promise for a promise?"

We're way past beating around the bush. "That's a promise of marriage, princess." I kiss her again and leave her leaning on the edge of the couch with bones of jelly.

Singer wraps her arm around Marielle's shoulders, and says, "I'm telling you those Everest brothers are trouble."

"Of the best kind," she replies.

I say, "Be careful. Jakob was not happy hearing about you and my brother."

"And you?"

"Whatever makes you happy. How serious are you?"

"Not serious." Her reply comes fast. "I'm not the woman for him, and he's not my Prince Charming. But he's a lot of fun in the meantime."

Bennett has definitely rubbed off on her. *Maybe she's changing too.*

We walk into the dining area, and I sit down, asking, "So it's all good with Marielle?"

"Yeah, she's hot, but that situation is more complicated than I like to get when it comes to women right now." He takes another large bite of the noodles. "Good Chinese food, by the way."

Now that I know he won't be heartbroken over Marielle, I make my way back to my princess. They turn up the volume to the TV, the college game we were watching now blaring. With their eyes glued to the screen, I'm about to whisper something in Ally's ear, when she stands. "Open your eyes, ref!" she shouts at the TV. "That was a clean quarterback sack."

My pride in her knowledge is crazy. That she not only learned about something I love but can get into it? *So fucking hot.* "Can I make you something to eat?"

"I'd love it. Thank you."

Singer follows me into the kitchen. "I'm heading out, but

I wanted to come tell you privately that Ally is wonderful, Hut. What an amazing woman."

"She is."

She hugs me. "I worry about you, but I'm worried about her as well. Is it safe for her to go back?"

"I don't think so, which is why I'm going."

"I think that's best," she says, "but be careful and keep in constant contact."

"I will."

"Where's Margie?"

"Jakob got her a room at the Westin across the street. He thought it best to give Ally a little space today to have fun."

"Did she have fun?"

"She did. You might even have a little fun later once you see what she bought."

Eyeing her, I ask, "Oh yeah? What is it?"

Singer zips her lips but then laughs. "I should get going. Ethan called me looking for his car keys."

"Did he lose them?"

"Nope." She pulls them from her pocket and dangles them. "I took the girls for a spin. It's not every day someone gets to ride in a Lamborghini, even if they are royalty."

"So Ethan doesn't know you took his baby?"

"Eh, it's not his baby." With her hands on her hips, she wiggles. "I am. Gotta run. Later, Hut."

She says goodbye to everyone and then slips out.

Checking to see if there's anything left of the food Ally brought home, I grab a container from the table in front of Bennett. "I saved some," he says.

"Not enough. I'm ordering pizza." I place the order, but I notice the girls are getting louder and louder as they yell at the TV. I can relate . . . every Sunday.

Ally looks back at me, and says, "Football is so fucking frustrating."

As if she wasn't already a dream come true, now she's cussing over football too. While we wait for the pizza to arrive, I take Ally and Marielle glasses of wine, and I'm rewarded with a kiss from my favorite girl.

I ask, "Have a minute to talk?"

She pushes up. "Yes, this game is too frustrating to watch anyway."

I chuckle as we walk down the hall into the bedroom. She closes it and asks, "What's up?"

"I'm going with you. I know what you said, and I'd like to honor that request—"

"It wasn't a request, Hutton. You'll upset my father the moment he lays eyes on you. I don't want him operating from a defensive position."

"I don't want you to go either. So how do we reconcile the two sides?"

She comes to me, and her hands slip under my shirt. "So what you're saying is you're coming even though I believe you shouldn't?"

Cocking an eyebrow, I take the bait and give her what she's aiming for. "I will be if luck is on my side."

"You don't need luck."

"What do I need?"

"What you've given me in telling me you're coming to Brudenbourg. We don't act as team Hutton or team Ally. We are team *us*." She finally gets it.

I smile with a goofy pride that whether or not I ever sit on that throne, I'll always be by her side. "Exactly."

She bites her lip. I pluck it out from under her teeth and rub the pad of my thumb over it twice before kissing her. When we part and her eyes open, she says, "I missed you today."

I push her hair behind her ear, admiring her. "Show me how much, baby."

"Luck is definitely on your side."

Thirty minutes later, we return to the living room. Bennett's dumped Jakob in a spare bedroom down the other hall and made sure Marielle had everything she needed before going back to his place.

While I eat pizza with Ally, I take the time to enjoy this moment between us, because tomorrow could bring more than unforeseen trouble.

***

We buckle our seatbelts and prepare for takeoff. "In eight hours, we'll come face-to-face with your parents again. Are you ready?"

"I am," she says with confidence. "It's not going to be easy emotionally, but it needs to happen."

There's an endless sky of beautiful clouds outside the window. While she settles in with a good book, I lean back and watch her, discovering her unfolding story much more fascinating than any pretty scenery.

I'm not sure of the role I'll play when we return to Brudenbourg, but I know who I am to her and who she is to me. It's not always been the easiest relationship to define, but it's been interesting. *And worth it.*

I'm pragmatic in my everyday life. My routine had become predictable. *Stifled.* Ally has breathed life into my days and love into my nights. There's nothing rational about what we've become so fast, but it doesn't scare me. Time is a number. I'm good with numbers and facts.

I love her.

I love her spontaneity.

I love her thoughtfulness.

I love the anger that drives her.

Determination.

Passion.

Whiplash moods.

I love everything about her.

And because of that, I will be there for my girl however she needs me.

33

Ally

WE'RE ALLOWED TO LAND, and an SUV is waiting for us. I'm not sure if my parents know I'm here with Margie, Jakob, and Marielle or not. But no doubt security will advise them shortly.

Among the quiet chatter of the group, Hutton takes my hand on the seat between us and brings it to his lap. "Don't be nervous," he says.

"They don't know I'm here, and they definitely don't know you're here. But the worst part is that they know what I've done."

"What have you done, Princess? Fallen in love. Yes, it's not as headline-making as they'd like for an excuse to kick you out of succession, but that's all they have on you. Your case would be a PR nightmare for them in the court of public opinion. So don't stress. You're holding the cards. All you have to do is play your hand."

"Which is?"

Shaking his head at himself, he chuckles as he looks down at our hands. "A royal flush."

I want to roll my eyes, but his cheesy reply has me giggling with him. "That was really terrible."

"I know." He's still laughing. "Just awful."

Sliding across the seat, I bump up against him, and say, "Promise you'll always tell me terribly unfunny jokes."

He kisses my head. "Don't worry. I have a lifetime full of them."

The palace comes into view, situated in the middle of rolling green hills with a blanket of hovering fog. The midday sun will burn it off soon enough, and I can't help but want it to melt my father's cold heart. I don't know if I'm walking into anger or hate or if we can talk and get past this and back on track. I'm still hurt that he called me a whore. Is that what he really thinks of me, or were they heated words shouted in the moment?

My hand tightens around Hutton's. I sincerely hope whatever I'm threatened with or how I'm treated never touches him.

His love is pure, obvious, and not hidden. It's simple. He's a man who fell in love with a woman. We might have been physical at first, but the bond was there, the emotions tied in from the moment we met. I wish I would have seen the possibility sooner, to know he'd want to be a part of this crazy life . . . maybe things could have been different.

I still have those awful, antiquated bylaws to deal with, even if I do convince my father to let me keep the crown I was born to wear. With my mother's lack of action, I'm determined to help women get out from under some of these laws. We're a progressive country until you dig deeper. And even though no one technically holds anyone to some of them, the threat remains.

The SUV comes to a stop, and the group looks around at

each other. It's the quiet before the storm. Margie and I haven't talked much since yesterday, but we've laid down our weapons. For now. Ultimately, the next few hours will determine where our friendship finally lands.

Jakob says, "I should talk to him first. I have the least to lose."

I look at Hutton who gives him a simple nod. No words. What can we say anyway?

Everyone files out, and I walk hand in hand with Hutton right to the center of the palace steps. Most of the staff has lined up to welcome us home, including Birgit and Gerhart. Birgit smiles so joyfully and then curtsies. She's the most stubborn woman ever. Privately, I've told her never to curtsy for me again. I should be bowing down to her. Warm souls are a rare find. She made me feel as though I belonged when I was floundering. But she insists on respecting my royal title and does it to make sure everyone else does too.

The large blue and gold doors open, and we enter the grand hall. A gilded coffered ceiling and crystal chandelier larger than Hutton hangs in the center. The architecture and murals never cease to take my breath away. It's one of my favorite places in the palace. "When I was a young girl, I used to lie in the center of the floor and stare at the little murals in each box of the ceiling." Hutton looks up. I add, "They're each a story."

"A fable."

"Yes. Each represents a different fable."

His eyes find the last square protected by the golden beams. "Why is that one blank?"

"That one is for me and my story."

His soothing browns come back to me, and he says, "You're not fiction."

"I will be one day." I glance at my sister, her words of despair about the people the monarchy sees as irrelevant coming to mind. "We'll all just be a fable told to the young one day."

"That's the saddest fucking thing I've ever heard. Why would you choose that life?"

"I'm not." My smile returns. "That's why we're here."

"Damn fucking straight."

Two soldiers enter from behind us and stand at the base of the stairs. "Really?" Jakob mumbles under his breath.

My parents appear at the top of the stairs. Jakob is about to step forward, but I feel it's my duty. I place a hand on his arm, and say, "I'll take care of it."

When I glance at Hutton, he whispers, "You were born for this." He brings my hand up and kisses the inside of my wrist, and says, "Show them who's the queen."

Marielle and Margie part, allowing me to walk through. Marielle says, "Strong. Brave. Clever. I'm just like my big sister."

My soft heart wins, so I look at my friend, who says, "Take back what's yours."

Smiling, I reach out and wrap my pinky around hers. "I intend to." When hers holds mine in return, I know we'll be okay.

Heavy history fills my shoulders with tension when I watch as my parents descend the staircase. I compose myself, holding my weaker emotions in and putting the others on display. Walking toward them, I straighten my shoulders and raise my chin, but this time, I won't be quiet. "Are the guards necessary? We're your children."

"My mistake," my father replies. "I took this as a coup."

"Revolt maybe, but not a coup."

"Semantics, Arabelle." They stop on the bottom step, I'm sure wanting the height advantage.

"*Princess* Arabelle."

"Not anymore."

"You can strip the title, but I'm still your daughter."

"Are you? he snaps. "My daughter would obey. Your actions speak as a libertine, a commoner, and then you expect to be treated like royalty. You were named after one of our greatest queens, but you've brought dishonor not only to Arabelle but also to the Sutcliffe name and to Brudenbourg. You're no longer welcome here. Your title and your names will remain in these palace walls. You can retain Allyson and Edwards. The rest are no longer yours to use."

"You can't do that. I know my rights by birth and law. You can exile me but can't take away my names or my trust funds. Those are mine because I'm of legal age." Stepping forward, I add, "And don't think you'll get away with ghosting me in our country's history. I will do everything in my power to make sure everyone knows why I'm not the queen."

My mother sighs. "I went terribly wrong, Arabelle."

"With?" I ask, taking another step closer.

The guards punch their staffs against the marble floor before crossing them in protection of the queen and prince. They might as well have stabbed me because the pain's the same.

I don't have to turn around to know Hutton's at my back. I feel his presence inside me as well as surrounding me, helping me hold on to my remaining strength. What I didn't expect was to hear my brother take my right, and whisper, "You're strong, sister."

That's when I realize I don't have to fight this alone, but I also have more strength than I knew. I have theirs too. "Is this what we've come to? You fear me?"

"Move." My mother steps down after the staffs are brought back vertically in front of each guard. She comes to me despite my father's protest. Standing in front of me with her hands clasped between us, she says, "I failed in so many ways, my daughter. I failed to lead my country into modern times, to teach my daughters the way of our land, and to be there as the mother you deserved."

She looks at my father. "I gave *you* too much power." When she turns back to me, she adds, "I didn't give you enough credit. I never wanted this station in life. I actually loved someone else."

"Aemilia!"

Her hand pops up. "Silence, Werner."

She may have given him too much power, but he's wise enough to know who's the queen. I want to say I'm surprised, but I'm not. They've never been a couple who made public displays of affection. I assumed they cared for each other in private, but they were still a match made by my grandparents. She's just lucky she fell for him. She says, "I think we should talk. Will you join me in the living room?"

That's a room we used to get in trouble for entering when we were little. Full of antiques dating back more than five hundred years, we were always told to touch with our eyes and not our hands. Margie and I would sneak in after tea and before supper and touch everything. I smile from the memory. The carpet gave us away, small footprints dented from our Mary Janes. We'd get grounded, but it was worth it.

She holds out her elbow, and I take it. But I stop and look back at Hutton. My mother says, "He may join us. Everyone may."

I don't know what she plans on saying once we're there, but that she's allowing Hutton to come with us feels like progress has already been made. We walk in silence, our shoes the only sound until we reach that pale pink carpet. I stop and smile, looking back to connect with Margie, who's also grinning.

My mother takes a seat, and we file around. I sit closest at one end of the settee. Hutton next to Marielle and me. Jakob stands behind Margie as she sits on the other side and my father walks to the fireplace, leaning against the mantle. "Be careful, Aemilia," he warns.

"I've spent my whole life being careful. Where did that get me?"

"Queen," he responds angrily.

She blows him off with a swish of her wrist. "I already had that in the bag." Appearing amused by her comment, she follows with a soft laugh. "Let me get to the point, Arabelle. The prince is not your father."

My mind spins, and my body reels back. All composure, gone in an instant. "What are you talking about?"

"You left too soon for me to stop you. I didn't get word until you were gone." Glancing at her husband, she scowls. "Somebody didn't tell me. I know why, and I'm going against his wishes. You need to know the truth, and I need to release it, finally." I can see the burden gone from her body as she uncrosses her ankles and sits back, looking more relaxed than I've ever seen her. "The prince married me knowing I was with child. I married him as long as he agreed to raise you as his own, and if you were a girl that you would become queen. He agreed."

I'm not sure what to say, too stunned to ask the questions racing through my head. Hutton does instead. "Where is her father?"

"Before I say more, let me preface this by making it clear that I love Prince Werner. Werner had held up his end of the deal . . . until the other night. Unlike what you've been led to believe, he has no true say when it comes to you or your titles. So I don't know why he felt he could take anything away."

"I was protecting you, Aemilia. I was protecting our traditions and Brudenbourg, and now it's being used against me."

"Don't be dramatic," she replies, reminding me of when I say that to Marielle.

Marielle . . . their daughter together . . . who trumps my *biological* father, who I presume was a commoner.

Marielle is the true queen.

My shoulders fall, and my strength crumbles. I look up and repeat Hutton's question with tears in my eyes, "Where's my birth father?"

"He passed away when you were only one." Her tone has shifted, sadness punctuating the words.

"How?"

She is visibly shaken, her voice matching. "I was told it was a hunting accident." *I was told . . .*

"And you believe that to be true?" My hands are trembling, so Hutton wraps them in his warmth.

The prince has taken a seat in the far corner, seeming to give in to the implied accusation. When my mother turns to him, she seems surprised. "Werner?"

"It's true. He died during a hunt."

I ask what my mother and everyone else is too afraid to. "Was he the one hunted?"

"You're out of line, Arabelle."

The answer is obvious in the non-answer. I feel sick, my arms wrapping around my middle. "When I came back, I didn't expect this. Everything I was so sure of has now fallen like sand through an hourglass." I stand, my knees weak under the revelation that I have no claim to the throne much less my name.

My mother stands. "It's a lot to take in. I should have told you sooner—"

"You shouldn't have told her at all," my fath—the man who treated me like a hurdle he had to overcome, says. "That man was a commoner. She's been raised as a princess when I could have sent her away."

"Sent away?" I repeat, quiet like a mouse. "That's why nothing was truly expected of me. That's why I could be exiled without a second thought." My gaze darts to the man I once thought loved me. "*He* had different plans for me all along."

My mother says, "You would have never been sent away. Sutcliffe runs in your veins. You're a princess because you're my daughter, not because of your father."

"I'm not sure what to say. I . . . um." Hutton stands, and Marielle and Margie follow suit. Hutton's hand becomes something that helps me remain upright as my world implodes. I turn to him, craving the safety of his arms, and say, "I never once asked you if you wanted this life, if you wanted to sit by my side, but you came anyway. You came because you love me and you put your needs aside for mine. I don't know how to thank you for that other than to love you the best I can."

"That's enough. That's all I ever needed from you. As for my needs, you never had to ask. Whether we're in New York or your country, I will follow you to the ends of the earth to sit by your side."

The broken pieces of my spirit are collected in his embracing love, and my soul feels right again. *Whole.* The back of my head is stroked, but not by Hutton. My mother says, "Look at me, daughter."

When I do, her gaze shifts to Marielle, and a slight but proud smile graces her lips. It's the same pride she exudes when she sees me. Pinching my chin lightly, her light laughter reaches me. "Quiet is something you were never meant to be." She takes my hand and leads me to the edge of the room. There she takes my other. "You will be the queen. As my daughter, the claim is yours, your birthright."

"Really?"

"Yes. You've shown me that you're more than capable.

Your courage will lead our tiny nation into the future. Screw the bylaws. Love matters more."

My father rushes forward. "No. It's not hers—"

The guards standing at the entrance rush between him and us, then stamp their staffs in warning. He stops, shocked. "This is outrageous."

"Weapons down. Werner deserves respect. He's still the crowned prince of Brudenbourg." Still holding my hand, she says to me, "I love him. I've loved him for many years. However, I wasn't cut out for this job. I look forward to handing over the reins to you to reign." Amused again, she chuckles. I love this lighter side to my mother. "How do you feel about becoming Queen Arabelle?"

34

Hutton

ONE WEEK LATER . . .

I lean back in my chair, kick my feet up on my desk, and stare out the large windows with the incredible city view of my corner office. Balloons are floating around the ceiling and streamers are strewn across the floor.

The door opens, and Ethan comes in with Bennett. I note the click of the latch as the door closes while they sit across from me. "It was a good party," Ethan says.

Putting my feet back down, I reply, "It was."

Bennett says, "So this is it." Not a question. An understanding.

"Seems so."

Ethan stands and walks to the window, shoving his hands in his pockets. "Are you ready for the next step?"

"Definitely."

"No fears?"

"None," I reply, pushing up and grabbing my phone. "What do I have to be afraid of?"

That earns me a laugh. Bennett stands and holds out his hand, not in a handshake but a team huddle. Ethan and I put our hands in. Looking at my brothers, I say, "I wouldn't be here without you."

"That's what we're here for," Ethan adds.

"This would never have been possible without you, Ben."

He's usually the jokester between us, but he struggles to take credit for the important stuff. Like today. Ethan says, "No matter what happens after today, we're Everests. Always."

"Everests," Ben and I repeat. "Always."

Six months later

This flight is too long.

I'm anxious to see Ally. Two weeks . . . I know that's the real problem. Her responsibilities have her living thousands of miles away from me while plans are put in place. No more, though.

Living a night without her next to me is rough, but fourteen has been torture. Singer, Ethan, and Bennett look perfectly content chatting and reading magazines, working, and passing the time as if my whole world isn't about to change.

I'm a fucking palms-sweating mess. It's not every day you attend a coronation or play a part in one.

Our plane lands and parks in an airfield of private jets that have traveled from around the world for this grand event. It's not every day a queen is crowned.

I carry my worries for Ally with me as we travel to the palace. Our conversations have been short and sweet when I've wanted long and on the sexual side. Even with the lonely nights, it's her I miss—her light, her enthusiasm for this life she's chosen, her love. My bed's too big without her in it. Hell, I'd take a twin with her over a king-sized and being alone.

The door is opened, and my beauty, my Ally, comes running down the steps and straight into my arms. Legs wrap around my middle. Arms around my neck. My face—eyes, nose, lips, and cheeks—are smothered in her kisses. "I guess you missed me."

"I did." She leans back and looks me in the eyes. There's a lightness inside those clear blues that was missing for a time. It's good to see the clouds have gone away. "I'm so happy you're here. Want to have sex?"

"Shameless and so fucking hot."

She shrugs. "What can I say? I missed you."

I carry her up the steps because I'm pretty shameless too when it comes to showing off my woman and staking my claim to her. I set her down in the entry hall.

Singer oohs, ahhs, and then says, "This place is spectacular. It easily rivals Versailles."

With a little flash of bitterness, Ally says, "Well, they did steal a few of our architectural designs."

Feisty.

It's good to have her back.

Up ahead, I spy the library. "I'll be right back." I have to make it quick, but it's time to make this wrong right. I round the corner and start pulling the classic tomes. Even if these aren't of his time, the collection is old enough to not be shelved in modern prose. I mean, what the fuck is up with that? I carry five of Shakespeare's books across the room and climb the ladder. Shuffling some of the other old editions of authors I've never heard of, I make room for the small but important collection.

"Feel better?"

Busted. A book flies from my hands and lands with a thud on the floor. Looking over my shoulder at Ally, I nod. "Yes, I do."

She picks up the book and climbs the ladder beneath me to hand it up. I shelve it, and we climb down. She says, "I've wanted to do that my whole life."

"Why didn't you?"

Shrugging, she says, "I never thought I could."

"I find that hard to believe."

"Bad choice of words. I didn't think I could without getting in trouble. Nothing here ever felt like mine, except my room."

"And now?"

"Now it doesn't matter."

Good girl. I kiss her head, and then we return to the others.

As Bennett looks between Ethan, Singer, Ally and me, he says, "I feel like a fifth wheel."

"Gear is here," I offer.

"Yay . . . not. Any hot singles around here, Al?"

Ally replies, "Actually quite a few. And don't forget, there's always Sabine Rosalie."

"She's perfect for Gear."

Ally laughs. "I can introduce them."

"My girl's got jokes," I say. "And when you see him, tell him he owes me a round of drinks. I'm ready to collect on a bet he once made." With a lot on the line business-wise, I should really be the responsible one for a minute. "Don't fuck this up, Ben. This is a working trip for you."

In protest, he says, "First, you get the party at work in your fucking office like I didn't help make the deal happen."

"You got credit, bro, and a lot of money you earned."

"I didn't get balloons or a cake. I want balloons, and I

want some fucking cake. But now you get the girl and to kick back on this trip? This sucks."

"Pretty much." I pat his back. "But that five-hundred-million-dollar bonus doesn't, so have fun running the show. And if anything goes wrong, call Ethan." I wink at Ally. "I'll be a little busy."

Ethan adds, "Take the money. If we go public, you won't be getting money like that. Now go earn it."

Bennett and I squeaked into the billionaire's club when we closed the Brudenbourg media deal. Twenty-five years for twenty billion dollars with first right of refusal after that. Needless to say, we're sitting pretty for generations to come. Speaking of future generations . . . "Have you thought about my proposal yet?"

While the others are shown to their rooms, I'm dragged to hers on the third floor. "It's all I've thought about."

"Any decision yet?"

We enter her room and close the door. She leans against it and then lunges toward me. I catch her again. "You have a lot of energy—"

"To burn. I want you. I want you so badly."

"God, I want you too." I'd tell her how much I burn for her, but she can feel it . . . just as she's currently doing.

She pushes my chest, and commands, "On the bed."

"So bossy," I tease her.

"I thought you said I was your queen."

Picking her up, I toss her on the mattress instead. "My queen. My heart. My lover." Climbing onto the bed, I work my body between her legs. "My life."

"Your soon-to-be wife." She wraps her arms around my neck and smiles so sweetly that I almost feel guilty for doing what I'm about to do to her.

Almost.

"My soon-to-be wife." I kiss her. "Why are you still wearing clothes?"

"My apologies to his grace. Maybe I should be punished." An eyebrow quirks to match her smirk.

"You enjoy me punishing you too much for it to be an effective form of discipline."

"Oh, is that what it was for?" she challenges and then laughs. "It feels too good to be bad."

"You feel too good to be bad."

She steals a kiss. "I tried to turn a new leaf, but you make being bad feel so good."

"Don't ever change, okay?"

"Why would I ever change when I have everything I could ever need right here?" Tightening her arms, she adds, "Now kiss me and show me how much you missed me."

I kiss her mouth and then slide lower, taking her jeans with me. "So much." When her pretty pussy is revealed, I cock an eyebrow. "No underwear, Ally?" I keep my voice firm, just how she likes it.

"Nope."

All teasing is done when a growl erupts from my chest, one of need and desire. I strip her bare and then take what I want, savoring every wet morsel of her body until she's tremoring beneath me.

As I lie there, my cock royally aches, and I wonder if there's time to satisfy the hunger. She doesn't let things like coronations hold her back from what she wants. I'm just fortunate I'm the thing she's craving.

We roll so I'm on the bottom, and as she slides down my thick cock, I sit up, taking one nipple into my mouth and biting just enough to elicit a moan and a rush of desire through her. Her pace picks up as she rocks on top, and soon we're both falling apart, my mouth kissing hers and her tongue making love to mine.

Lying in the beautiful aftermath, I hold her close, knowing we only have a short time left before she has to go. Duty calls.

Stealing a few moments, I appreciate every second I have with her because my life has forever changed, but I wouldn't change it back for anything. Every day, this woman makes life worth living, so I guess it's only fair if she's also the death of me.

***

The pomp and circumstance of the coronation is mind-boggling. I listen to what I'm told and be where I'm supposed to be at the right time. It seems to be working so far.

The doors open wide, and I hold my elbow out. Princess Arabelle's delicately gloved hand wraps around my arm, and as the refrain of the choir hits a high hum, we begin our journey down the long aisle of the church. Her white dress is covered in stones that sparkle like diamonds in the setting sun's rays that peek in from the stained glass windows. Her tiara is anchored top and center, tempting me to crook it to the side. I like her a little messy, a little wild for the church crowd. For her ears alone, I say, "You look beautiful."

With her eyes on the crowd, giving subtle nods of recognition as we pass by, she finally looks my way. "You look very dapper, Mr. Everest," she replies with a sly smile. Tradition can only hold her down for so long, after all.

Wanting to check on her one last time before it's too late, I ask, "Are you okay? Are you sure this is what you want?"

"I am. I'm ready to start this new life."

At the end of the aisle, we stop. "I love you," I say not whispering, not hiding how I feel about her for anybody.

"I love you so much and am so thankful my future has you by my side. That means everything to me."

The trumpets begin to play, and the crowd remains standing as the doors at the other end of the aisle open. We take our seats next to the queen mother and the crowned prince and watch as Marielle ascends to her throne, beginning her reign. With a quick glance at a man in a shadowed doorway nearby, she smiles, turns back, and then bows her head.

She'll never be forgotten, or hidden from the world. Marielle Astrid Edwards Sutcliffe became queen that day.

35

Hutton

ON THE BACK lawn of Sutcliffe Palace, the sun is high, spring is in the air, and Ally and I exchange our wedding vows. It isn't the huge ceremony of the coronation, but it's intimate with our family, a few friends, and the new crowned Queen of Brudenbourg in attendance.

It's cool to tell people that, but what's just as cool is our old friends, The Crow Brothers. Not only had they hit record gold, but they were now one of the biggest bands in the world. They also made the time to attend.

Just like mine, their hearts are on lockdown. I can't seem to get over how much has changed in a year, but I've never been happier.

Under an arch of pink roses, the blue eyes of my bride rival any above my head, and I slip a ring befitting a queen on her finger. No princess cut for her.

A three-carat Royal Asscher cut diamond that blinds me —almost as much as the price tag did—sparkles on her left hand. *Almost.* True love has no price though. She's worth it and more to me. And I'm the proud new owner of a platinum band that I'll wear with pride.

Ally looks up at me with all the love I'll ever need, and says, "I wasn't born to rule. I was born to love you."

I kiss her under an arch of love, gratitude, and appreciation. Something I intend to do every day for as long as I shall live.

"What the fuck? I'm coming." Searching every room I pass, I keep walking until I reach the door. With Ally, Singer, Margie, and Marielle in a bread-baking lesson with Birgit, I've been exploring the place. I'm not sure if I'm allowed to answer a knock at the palace, but no one else seems to be around.

We've been here for over a week, and I'm ready to jet home with my lovely bride, but she wanted to spend a few extra days, telling me she doesn't need a fancy honeymoon because every day with me is a dream come true.

She's got some good lines.

I turn the large brass knob in the center of the blue ten-foot door and pull open the right door. Standing there as if he has a fucking right to is Duke Dick himself. I fucking level him. I'm bad with all the royal terms, so I assume his footmen or whatever they're called running up the steps are here to help him.

Maybe Ally's father was right. There's some bad still inside me. That's what makes me so right for her, though, so I make no apologies for my behavior or for punching him.

While he rubs his chin, he's propped back on his feet by his dudes. I'm about to take him down again when he waves a white hanky. "Is that supposed to be a surrender flag?"

"Yes. Don't hit me again. I'm surrendering."

I stare at him in disgust. "You're weak and pathetic, you know that?"

"Yes, I do, but I don't know why you hit me."

My mind tracks back to a few days prior when Ally found the footage from the night she and the duke were on the terrace. Although I'd heard the gist a long time ago, seeing him grab her and touch her in ways that make me want to kill him doesn't keep me from throttling him against the palace doors now.

I am a Texas gentleman, though, so I let go of him and watch as he slides to the tiled platform. This time, his guys don't rush to help. In fact, they give a slight grin. They can't say it, but I can. "Yeah, he's an asshole."

Ally rushes out the door and skids to a stop. "Oh my God!" As her eyes narrow on him, and she can see he's going to be fine, she hugs me. "My hero."

"You bet your fine ass I am."

When Marielle arrives with her hands fisting at her sides, she says, "I summoned you six hours ago."

On his hands and knees still gasping for air, he says, "I was busy."

"Too busy for your queen?"

"My apologies."

"My apologies, *Your* Majesty," Marielle corrects.

"My apologies, Your Majesty."

She shakes her head and looks at her sister. "This should have been done a long time ago." With her guards flanking her side, she walks until her feet are under his panting head. "Look at me." When he does, she strips the epaulet from one shoulder and then the other. "You, sir, are no longer a duke of anything. You should vacate the premises of your home, the duke's home, immediately. If you don't, you'll be removed by force and will be considered an enemy of our country. Do you understand, Mr. Vaughn?"

"I do," he spits at her feet.

"Good. Go about your day and leave my grounds."

Crossing my arms over my chest, I nod. For the quiet mouse Marielle used to be, she's grown into her stripes and fights like a tiger. He pushes up and heads for the vehicle. The two men remain on the platform. "That's the duke's SUV. You'll need to find another way to wherever you're going."

I say, "That royal thing puts the fear of hell in people."

"So does beheading," Marielle says as she turns and walks inside.

Singer says, "I thought Brudenbourg never beheaded anyone?"

Casual and jovial, Marielle heads back toward the kitchen, the conversation flowing back to us. "We don't talk about it. It's rare, but it's happened." She stops and turns back. "Hey, sis?" she adds. "How'd I do?"

Ally grins. "Spoken like a true queen."

EPILOGUE

Hutton

"Mustard."

Ally giggles.

"Mustard," she calls again. "Mustard. Mustard. Mustard."

When that doesn't work, she weasels out of my hold and dives under the covers. Peeking out, she looks incredibly adorable. "What's the point of having a safe word if it never works?"

High in the sky of Manhattan, as newlyweds, we've settled into the life we've chosen to live—together. My brilliant and tenderhearted wife started The Everest Foundation six months ago. She remains an advisor to the queen of Brudenbourg, but through the foundation she provides women in need with educational support, training, counseling, and job placement. She's also passionate about helping children. From meals to emotional support, she has a team of social workers who are helping to make a difference in their young lives.

I'm still just a numbers guy.

We also bought two thousand acres in the hill country of Texas. I can't have a queen with no land to rule. She says it's a perfect place to raise our Everest clan one day.

One day can't come soon enough.

I climb over her and lie down, putting my weight on her like she makes me do all the time. Well, I don't put it all on her. I'm six foot four to her five foot four. I'm not trying to crush her. I bring the covers down far enough for me to see her face and then rest on my elbows. "Because a safe word is used during sexual acts. I'm just tickling you."

"Oh, is that when I'm supposed to yell spider?"

"What? No. Not spider. Aunt." Now she has my mind muddled.

"What's the difference? They're both insects."

I start laughing. "Not aunt. Ant. Ant is an insect." I can't even continue to torture her with tickles right now. Stitches from laughter are forming in my sides.

"They sound the same."

I fall to the side of her, and say, "You're actually supposed to call out uncle. Not aunt or ant."

"Why?"

Grabbing my side, I sit up. "I have no idea, but that makes me wonder what else you missed out on living in the palace. Did you ever play Marco Polo as a kid?"

"There's a children's game named after the Italian explorer?"

I shake my head. "We have a lot to catch you up on."

She stretches to reach the remote and clicks on the TV. "Another time. It's Monday. You know what that means?"

"Do I need to worry about your football addiction?"

"No. *Shhh.* We missed the first quarter."

Standing totally naked next to the bed, I ask, "What is it that you love about football so much?"

"What's not to love? Tight pants. Big men."

"How do you feel about no pants? I'm working that angle hard right now."

She glances and then does a double take. Clicking the TV off, she says, "No pants on you should totally be a thing, a regular thing. Like always. We can make it a bylaw." She comes crawling right across the top of the bed, and when she reaches me, she looks up. "What do you want to do?"

"You. Are you up for a little role play?"

"Let me get the tiara." When she scrambles to the end of the bed, she lifts her grandmother's crown from the post and sets it on her head. My wife is stunning with her bare breasts, full hips, and the confidence to wear a tiara valued over one million dollars to bed.

It's crooked. *As it should be.*

When she lies back down, she asks, "Want to make a baby?"

"Absolutely."

"Now about that mustard . . ."

"I love you, my queen."

She pulls me to her and kisses me hard. "I love you, too, my king."

You met Ethan Everest in Bad Reputation, but now is the time to get to know him and what obstacles he has to overcome in his romantic suspense story. This bestselling novel will charm you as well as keep you on your toes as the story unfolds. Turn the page for a sneak peek into his book.

The Crow Brothers have a fantastic bestselling series that is NOW AVAILABLE. Rise to fame with these charismatic and incredible rock stars that will have you swooning and falling in love.

EVEREST

Prologue

Ethan Everest

Every female here has eyed me up and down, even the ones with boyfriends. They don't even try to hide it. They *want* me to see. They *want* me to know I can have them if I want them.

Except *her*. Blue dress. Red lips. Hair the color of a golden sunset in winter.

Several girls made themselves more than available. I was offered a fast fuck in the bathroom within fifteen minutes of arriving. Fantasies may be taking over, but there's only one woman who catches my eyes—the demure beauty sitting on the couch.

I want to stare at her.

She'll see me though.

I want to sit next to her.

There are no more spots on the small futon.

I want to talk to her.

What do I say when she makes all the blood rush from my brain and shoot straight to my dick? *Damn, I want her.*

She's given me no reason to think of her naked beneath me. No indication that I should have dirty thoughts about those delectable lips. Absolutely no sign that I could have the pleasure of stroking her bare back while I take her from behind.

Fuck. Me.

While images of her cloud my thoughts, I'm not sure I have a shot in hell of even taking up a minute of her time, much less a night. Nope, not one clue if I have a chance with this beauty.

I'll take the risk, something I'm adept at doing. More often than not I win in the end. She won't be an easy target, but nothing worth having ever is. I'm determined to find out if her tongue is as seductive as her eyes.

Although she brings out my instinctive side, this is not about sex and passing time. It's about spending time with someone who challenges my mind while turning on my body.

Nudging the guy who lives here, I signal across the room and ask, "What's her name?"

"Who?" He follows my gaze. "The hottie on the couch?"

Heart-shaped face, flawless skin, ample tits, hourglass shape at her waist. She's not built like a girl who doesn't eat. She's shaped like a woman I want to meet. "Yeah."

"Dariya Rostavik. She's fucking hot." He pats my shoulder. "And single. If my girlfriend wasn't here, I'd be all over that."

"Cuz you're an asshole." Her name, Dariya, rolls around my mouth, spikey instead of rolling off the tongue naturally. The name doesn't fit her.

"Pretty much." He laughs. "You gonna hit it, Everest?"

"I don't know." I feign interest to him, lying to get his eyes off her. "Fuck, they scored again." My diversion works, and his attention is back on the big screen.

The truth is, I don't know if I'm going to hookup with her. I've caught her looking at me when she thinks I don't notice. *But is she looking at me the way I'm looking at her?*

Was I busted moving closer when she was talking to her friend? Did she see me eavesdropping to hear her voice? Did she notice when I joined a conversation behind her to be closer? Or that I stepped out of the way of the fridge when she wanted a bottle of water?

I never get shot down by women. I've lived on easy street when it comes to my looks and, from what I'm told, my personality, attracting the most attractive. Something tells me I might be rejected by her.

She's not like the other girls here. Nothing about her fits in this environment—a party with a bunch of guys getting drunk while watching sports and yelling at the TV and girls dragged here by their boyfriends or convinced by their friends to stop by.

She's an innocent among sycophants. Everyone wants something from me, except her. Sexy and smart—speaks right to my heart.

I catch her eyes on me again. This time I stare back until she looks away with a pretty pink coloring her cheeks.

This game with her is much more interesting than the one on TV. I follow her with my eyes as she gets up and joins a group by the window. She seems to know the other girl, but not so much the two guys.

Good, I inwardly growl.

Keith hits me in the chest. "Who do you have your eyes on?"

"The woman by the window."

My best friend shakes his head. "No. Check out eleven o'clock. She's a model from Romania. Hot as fuck."

"Not interested. I want more than a fuck."

"I'm sorry. Have we met?" His sarcasm is as annoying as he's been lately at the office.

"I'm for real."

"So am I."

I exhale and shoot him a glare. "I really am. I can fuck anyone. I want to spend time with someone who interests me."

"You're working too much. You're so caught up in your head lately you're missing what life is really about."

Crossing my arms over my chest, I indulge him. "And what is life really about?"

"Doing everything in your power to get it while the gettin's good."

"Are we talking about business or women?"

"Both."

The model is hot, but I feel like I've been there done that. I don't care what he wants. He can have shallow, meaningless relationships. They're more hassle than they're worth.

Glancing toward the woman outside, an ease comes over me, releasing some of the pent-up pressure that's been expanding lately. "You go for the model. I'll go for Dariya."

"Dariya?" I'm knocked on the arm, and he points toward the couch. "That's Dariya, man."

"The model?"

"Yeah," he says, laughing.

Thank fuck I didn't go outside and call the beauty by the wrong name. "I'll be back." I grab two cans and head toward the window. I stop briefly by the group she was talking to prior, but they're buried deep into a conversation about American consumerism. I'm not interested in their philo-sophical views on finances. The only thing I'm interested in is the pretty woman sitting alone outside. The woman excuses herself and I ask, "Hey, you guys know her name?"

They look outside. "Singer."

"She's a singer?"

"No," he says, chuckling. "Her name is Singer. Singer Davis. She came here with her friend, Melanie, who just left."

I don't hear most of what he says because I'm stuck on the woman with the red lips. *Singer.* Singer Davis. "Thanks."

Singer's been sitting on that fire escape by herself long enough to not feel like I'm invading her space, like she's taken over my thoughts. I seize the moment and climb out.

This is where our story begins . . .

From New York Times Bestselling Author, S.L. Scott, comes a ROMANTIC SUSPENSE STANDALONE that will have you on the edge of your seat and swooning over this new ALPHA BILLIONAIRE. Now Available.

ON A PERSONAL NOTE

What an amazing experience it was to write this book and create a new world where women rule and the men who love them. And the reverse because Hutton is awesome and his steady love and patience gave Ally the strength to be who she was really meant to be.

I owe so much to the team that helps me through all the stages of my publishing journey with their insight and friendship. Each person adds so much to make this story shine. Thank you: Adriana Locke, Andrea Johnston, Kristen Johnson, Lynsey Johnson, Marion A., Marla Esposito, and Devyn Jensen.

My family is my everything. I'm so grateful to not only have their support, but their love <3

XOXO,

Suzie

ABOUT THE AUTHOR

To keep up to date with her writing and more, her website is
www.slscottauthor.com to receive her newsletter with all of
her publishing adventures and giveaways, sign up for her
newsletter: http://bit.ly/2TheScoop

Instagram: S.L.Scott

To receive a free book now, TEXT "slscott" to 77948

For more information, please visit
www.slscottauthor.com

ALSO BY S.L. SCOTT

To keep up to date with her writing and more, her website is
www.slscottauthor.com

To receive the Scott Scoop about all of her publishing adventures,
free books, giveaways, steals and more, sign up here:
http://bit.ly/2TheScoop

Join S.L.'s Facebook group here: S.L. Scott Books

Audiobooks on major retailers

The Crow Brothers

Spark

Tulsa

Rivers

Ridge

Hard to Resist Series

The Resistance

The Reckoning

The Redemption

The Revolution

The Rebellion

The Kingwood Duet

SAVAGE

SAVIOR

SACRED

SOLACE

Talk to Me Duet

Sweet Talk

Dirty Talk

Welcome to Paradise Series

Good Vibrations

Good Intentions

Good Sensations

Happy Endings

Welcome to Paradise Series

From the Inside Out Series

Scorned

Jealousy

Dylan

Austin

From the Inside Out Compilation

Stand Alone Books

Bad Reputation

Everest

Missing Grace

Until I Met You

Drunk on Love

Naturally, Charlie

A Prior Engagement